7½

Christos Tsiolkas is the author of one collection of short stories and seven novels, including the international bestseller *The Slap*. His work has won, among other awards, the Commonwealth Writers' Prize, the ALS Gold Medal and the Victorian Premier's Literary Award for Fiction, and has been listed for the Booker Prize and the Miles Franklin Literary Award. He is also a playwright, essayist and screen writer. He lives in Melbourne.

Also by Christos Tsiolkas

CHRISTOS TSIOLKAS

7½

atlantic·*fiction*

First published in Australia in 2021 by Allen & Unwin.

Published in hardback in Great Britain in 2022 by Atlantic Books,
an imprint of Atlantic Books Ltd.

This paperback edition published in 2023.

10 9 8 7 6 5 4 3 2 1

A CIP catalogue record for this book is available from the British Library.

Paperback ISBN: 9781838955670
E-book ISBN: 9781838955663

Printed in Great Britain by Clays Ltd, Elcograf S.p.A.

Atlantic Books
An Imprint of Atlantic Books Ltd
Ormond House
26–27 Boswell Street
London
WC1N 3JZ

www.atlantic-books.co.uk

For Wayne van der Stelt

Novels are not humanitarian reports. Indeed, let us be thankful that there remains sufficient cruelty, without which beauty could not be.

JEAN GENET, *MIRACLE OF THE ROSE*

The burst of birdsong is set in motion by their flight. An arc of white rises into the sky, a family of cockatoos swooping and then descending onto the eucalypts. Abruptly and in unison their squawking ceases, replaced by the calls of lorikeets. I turn away from the forest canopy, half close my eyes, and I can hear the melodic warble of the honeyeater, its song as tender and consoling as the purring of bees. It is an hour till sunset and the sky is aglow with magnificent slants of light. The inlet waters shimmer and beyond is the defiant blue of the ocean. This is an eastern sea. It fades slowly into night and awakens magnificent and overpowering in the morning.

I pour a wine. I light a cigarette. The computer sits on the long hardwood table of the deck. I walk over to it, finger the pad and turn it off. I am in no mood for writing this evening.

There is no silence, even after night's descent. Darkness spreads across water and mountain, the bird cries subside to be replaced by the mechanical scrape and beat of cicadas. Their stridency is muted this night; it doesn't rise and crash in deafening waves, it does not last long. The dark captures the world. Only out in the far reaches of the ocean is there a waning line of light.

So, it isn't that I sit in silence, but near enough. The electronic sensor is activated and if I were to move suddenly, the outside deck would be flooded with artificial light. It is only when the black night dazzles with stars that I realise I have been still for an age. The globe has turned, and I have been lost in this fixity. The ignored cigarette in the ashtray has burnt to the filter. With that recognition I move and abrasive yellow light fills my vision.

This house I have rented for the fortnight is comfortable, with a large wooden deck that stretches over the well-manicured English-styled garden below. There is a narrow galley kitchen, expertly constructed so that there is a surprising amount of storage space, and the stove is only a few years old. The main bedroom is of a good size and off the deck with a sliding glass door that opens the room to the breeze and to the ocean's roar. A mesh screen offers protection for the sleeper and the dreamer. The house itself is built from the ubiquitous industrial red brick that dominated the architecture of Australia's twentieth century. It is not an ostentatious house. There is a further bedroom, and also a study.

Two short flights of stairs descend from the deck to the garden. There is an annexe built there below, and the owners have made a granny flat out of this cellar space. I have deliberately left my phone down there. That way I only need to check it at most twice a day. Also, it means that I am less tempted to use the internet connection on the phone to pair with my laptop. I can control the ubiquity of digital information that flows into my consciousness.

I light another cigarette, and this time I concentrate on the rough hit of the smoke as it fills my lungs. I am approaching fifty-five this year and I have decided to limit myself to five cigarettes a day. This is only my third and I won't have any more tonight.

No, I might have one more. Straight after dinner.

I have brought a cluster of DVDs with me, and a small stash of books. I may not watch anything at all. I might lie in bed and read. In the fridge is a kingfish fillet from the fishmonger below the bridge and a slice of blueberry tart that I bought with some sourdough from the bakery in Cann River, where I stopped for lunch. Clearly, I am not roughing it. Yet there is an almost mischievous defiance in not having the phone nearby, to have already begun my disappearing from the world.

The birds have fallen quiet. There are the croaking burps of frogs. I stub out my cigarette and go into the kitchen to make dinner.

*

3

I have come here to write a book. I don't know yet exactly what it will be. I do know this: I don't want it to be about politics; I don't want it to be about sexuality; I don't want it to be about race; I don't want it to be about gender. Not history, nor morality and not about the future. All of those matters—politics, sexuality, race, history, gender, morality, the future—all of them now bore me.

Of course, they haven't always bored me. And I may one day find myself once again animated and agitated by such things. I still read history and will always love to imagine the currents and sentiments that connect us to past worlds and peoples, as well as trying to fathom the chasms in consciousness and belief that separate us irrevocably from that past. But I doubt very much that I will ever again be engaged or captivated by capital-H History or capital-P Politics. I no longer have faith in the elementary forward thrust of culture and humanity. I have become deeply suspicious of capital-P Progress.

It is treacherous being a writer; it would be so much more simple and desirable to be a musician or even a painter. The abstract is essential to the former and liberating for the latter. With writing, with words, one is always bound to language, and to the imperative for language in the Western and European consciousness to extol progress and to endorse teleology and to revere reason. Even now I feel an imperative for declaration and revelation: before I can begin my work, I must confess my apostasy.

So, here goes.

I am suspicious of the homogenising effect of globalisation and cosmopolitanism and I suspect that ingrained in every manifestation of those worldviews is a rapacious greed for the material over the spiritual. I wish to be—and try to be— a universalist in every human exchange; yet what I truly long for is the specific and the local. In essence, I am egalitarian in my hopes and conservative when it comes to the immutability of human nature. I think the right wing's cataclysmic failure has been its entanglement with the vilest of racist dogma and the equally cataclysmic failure of the left has been its derision of the notions of individual freedom and of independent thought. A pox on both their fucking houses.

Will that do?

I hope that the exploration I undertake while writing this book will stumble towards some kind of doubt. I have abandoned my belief in certainty. The only answers I desire now are those cast in doubt.

These choices—to abandon the city for a fortnight and drive up the coast road and keep a distance from the snares of digital technology—are part of a retreat I feel I must make in order to divine what I wish to do with this vocation called writing. I have a friend who I can imagine now staring over my shoulder as I type and crossing her arms and snorting, 'Just tell a fucking good story.' It is good advice for a novel, but I am not sure whether it is a novel that I want to write. I admire my friend's challenge: you are a writer and therefore a storyteller; write a fucking good story. Yet I can imagine other equally good friends peering at the computer screen, already feeling dismay or contempt for what I have written. But their opprobrium is neither unsettling nor challenging.

I do want to write a good story. But I no longer trust the judgements of my age. The critic now assesses the writer's life as much as her work. The judges award prizes according to a checklist of criteria created by corporations and bureaucrats. And we writers and artists acquiesce, fearful of a word that might be misconstrued or an image that might cause offence. I read many of the books nominated for the globalised book prizes; so many of them priggish and scolding, or contrite and chastened. I feel the same way about those films feted at global festivals and award ceremonies. It's not even that it is dead art: it's worse, it's safe art. Most of them don't even have the dignity of real decay and desiccation: like the puritan elect, they want to take their piety into the next world. Their books and their films don't even have the power to raise a good stench. The safe is always antiseptic.

Is there God in that sky? Instead of looking up at the darkening sky above me, I close my eyes.

•

I am in the Church of the Holy Trinity in Burnley Street, Richmond, in downtown Melbourne. I am not yet five years of age. I am dressed in a light-grey boy's suit, a three-buttoned jacket and knee-length shorts. My shirt is white and I am wearing the clip-on black bow tie my father attached to the collar as he helped me dress that morning. Am I holding my younger brother's hand as we push through the crowd? In my memory it is so.

The clearest impression is of the crowd. There are so many bodies climbing the steps to enter the church, ready to toss coins into the collection box, to grab and light the yellow wax candles and place them carefully and proudly in the sandbox. All I can see are the backs of the men, in their white or pale blue shirts, the outline of their singlets visible beneath, or the sombre palettes of their suit jackets. The women are dressed in a blaze of colours, and I stare up at the strange bouffant sculpting of their hair. The jumble of long skirts and shirts and trousers and jackets and shawls. I am comforted by my father's presence behind me; he has one hand on my shoulder and is guiding me deftly through the crowd. My mother's face is clear and genial, her dark sweep of hair falls around her shoulders as she turns back, looks down, finds us and smiles. Then she drops coins into the slot of the collection box, takes four candles and hands one each to my brother and me, and one to my father. Then my father lifts me as my mother cradles my brother, and with my father's hands holding me high, I proudly bring my candle to the flame of another, watch its wick catch fire, then plant it firmly in the sandbox. Will my candle remain alight or will it burn out? And what malevolence or misery will be augured if the flame is not sustained? But the candle burns and my father twirls me around and now I am at the shoulder-height of the crowd and I can see the thin black and grey ties of the men; their unshaven faces, their dark olive skins; and the powdered faces of the women, the carefully applied beauty spots and the faint hint of scandalous lipstick. I am high above the old grandmothers, stooped and tiny, so high above them that I can see the thinning scalps of those whose heads are not covered with thick black cloth. There are balding old men with sparse coils of white hair on their napes or temples. The bald spots terrify me because they are ugly; bruises, spots and blue veins are visible, and awful puckered skin.

And then I am swung across to where the icons are placed and my father holds my face over the silver leaf-embossed visage of the Holy Mother and the Holy Child. The glass frame is dirty and smudged with the imprints of countless lips and kisses, and there are droplets of moisture—I know it is spit—and I don't want to kiss it because I think it dirty, and if it were only my father with us I know he would let me blow air onto the smeared glass surface so my lips wouldn't have to touch it, but my mother is there as well and she demands loyalty to our faith and to our God, so my father gently, reluctantly—I can sense his aversion—pushes my face towards the icon and I kiss it quickly, and as quickly I turn away. My father settles me back on the ground.

And now, the crowd separates into two. There are the men to one side of me, which I call my writing hand side, for I am not yet confident to claim left or right, and the women go to the other side. It isn't cloth and fabric, hair and height that I notice now. It is the intensity of smell. The smoky odour of the burning candles; the sharp spice-waft of the incense. The hair oil, the perfume, the cologne, the sweat. The aromas have taken on a physical force and I can feel them all around me, sense them settling on my skin. The church is now as much liquid as it is air. I am swimming among the smells.

I look up to see God in the sky. God is aged, the oldest of old men, and his countenance is stern but not frightening. His beard and hair are a sea of white. On the walls the saints are depicted in dark and sober colours. They are strangely elongated, so they appear as emaciated giants. My first impression of the saints is that they are famished, and I am concerned for their health. But these grim and forbidding women and men can't hold my attention for long. Surrounding them are depictions from the Bible, and I have already been told some of these stories: I know the Flood, I know the Garden and about our expulsion from it—and these tableaux have been painted in vibrant and glorious colour. The shade of the sea engulfing Noah's Ark is a shimmering amethyst and Eve's skin is a luminous auburn. These colours do not exist in the world around me and so I think of them as ancient. The mesmerising scenes and the people depicted on the ceiling—they are all gone. Except for God. He is real.

9

At the centre of the church's dome, God's face is incandescent. He is watching it all. He is watching me.

Is it possible that even at this tender young age I had a premonition of sin? I knew shame. I saw that God was watching me and knew that I was tempted by the shaved skin of the men I had looked down on when I was hoisted in my father's arms. I stared across to where a young man, bored, yawning, was scratching his forehead and in doing so he half turns, catches me looking at him and he winks, and as it is summer he has his suit jacket draped over his arm and the white sleeves are folded up to his forearms and the skin is dark and I want to kiss it. I knew that I wanted to kiss it. I wanted to know what it would feel like to rub my lips across the fine black hairs on that arm.

The priest's resounding chanting makes me look away. I don't look up but I know that God is looking down at me. My brother is swinging his feet, banging them against the wood of the pew in front—until a man swings around and orders, 'Stop!' Terrified, my brother freezes.

My father's hands immediately land on each of our shoulders. We look up at him. He points to the back of the sullen man who rebuked my brother, then, wickedly, our father pokes out his tongue. My brother and I are laughing.

This is one of my earliest memories. It is infused with smell and sensation, with touch and the nascent stirring of the erotic.

•

Everything begins with the erotic.

The next morning, waiting for my coffee to brew, I go out to the deck. I sit there with my eyes closed, enjoying the warm touch of the sun, my hands behind my head and my body stretched out in the wooden chair. There is the beginning quiver of an itch at the base of my left nostril. My body still half-asleep, I lower my face to the top of my arm and scratch the itch, at the same time inhaling the strong and pungent smell of my armpit. My eyes open, the blinding flash of the sun shuts them tight again. My arm drops and I no longer have any awareness of the odour. It is the strangest thing, as if my scent does not belong to me. As if it is another's perfume. I look down at the three cigarette butts in the ashtray from the night before, recoil from the stale stink. At that moment the coffee pot begins to wheeze, and I rush to the kitchen.

I have a routine most mornings consisting of a series of push-ups and sit-ups, stretches and exertions, to counter the inevitable sag of my ageing body. I stretch out on the living room floor and I begin.

With the first gasp as I lunge forward, the whiff of my night sweat returns, the scent now commingling with the acrid perfume of the coffee and that lingering hint of cigarette ash. I lie on the floor and again bring my face to my perspiring armpit. I inhale deeply. My nostrils flare and I allow myself to sink into the smell. Of sweat, of coffee, and of cigarettes. In Greek, I hear the words, 'Tell me all about your day, my child.'

•

Until I went to school, we shared our home with a couple, George and Irene, and a young bachelor called Stavros. They were all immigrants from Greece. My family—my parents, myself and my brother—shared the first bedroom, the middle one was rented by Stavros, and the third bedroom belonged to George and Irene. My mother and Irene worked at a biscuit factory by the river in Richmond, the working-class neigh-bourhood in which I was born and spent my childhood. A twenty-minute stroll from our home would bring you to the very centre of the city.

Many years later, I asked my father whether he and Stavros worked together, and he shook his head. Neither he nor my mother told me that he and Stavros had met gambling, but something in my mother's sardonic smile when talking of him has always made me think this must have been the case. Richmond was full of Greek cafes and gambling dens, and it was to these places that my father would retire for relaxation after work. Pubs back then had to adhere to Protestant hours, and, in any case, my father was not much of a drinker. The women, of course, had to stay at home.

I close my eyes and I can smell Stavros. The sharp sweetness of the cigarettes he smoked. The rank, almost shockingly potent smack of his sweat, especially when he'd just got back from work, starting to strip out of his dirty blue overalls as soon as he was in the door. The sting of the apple-scented cologne he used. Each of those intoxications can return to me effortlessly through the decades that have passed since I last saw him. I can see a tumbler of red wine in his hand; over lunch or on one of those late Saturday night dinners when our kitchen was full of people: the women bustling and gossiping and singing while they were preparing the food, the men also lost in gossip, and very soon the ashtrays would be spilling over with ash and butts, and the discarded shells of cracked pistachio nuts. At some point, my father or George or Stavros would rise, put a 45 rpm single on the turntable in the lounge room—I can still see the scarlet insignia of the Attikon label and the black lettering of the Odeon song company; I haven't forgotten any of them—and at the first strum of a familiar chord my mother would call out, 'Turn it up! Turn it up!', and there at the basin, alongside Irene and my aunt Diamanda and our neighbours Stella and Maria—the adults were all aunts and uncles to me; in this new country we were all kin—my mother would start singing and the men would clap along. No one would clap harder and longer than Stavros.

His thumb and finger would expertly crack open the pistachios and flick the kernel to his mouth. I tried to imitate him, but I could never master his insouciance, no matter how much I practised while sitting on the black-and-white-checked lino floor as the women cooked and my mother scolded me for wasting precious nuts. I will never forget him coming home, me rushing to the hallway when I heard his step on the front porch, him in half-shadow, shrugging off his overalls, the front flaps falling to his waist. Me running into his arms and him holding me high, so high that sometimes it seemed impossible that my head would not slam that ceiling, but it never did, it never did, and I was not frightened because I trusted Stavros, and him hugging me close and rubbing his face in mine and saying, 'Boy! Boy! Let me wash—how can you bear this stink?' But I did not care. That emanation from his body, its wetness and its sourness, it was the most delicious marvel of my child's life. He'd put me down and I'd follow him to the outhouse, a clumsy lean-to built from rusting corrugated-iron sheets that was both toilet and bathroom, always cold in winter and always sweltering in summer, and I'd watch him fill the basin with water, the bib of his overalls still falling, his singlet damp and tight against his hard torso, as he bent to wash his face and his neck and his arms and his hands and underneath his armpits, and the shock of thick, black, wet hair there always gave me a jolt. Then, when he was finished, I'd faithfully trail after him back into the house.

I'd have followed him anywhere. There was a joke among the adults: 'Christo would follow Stavros to the bog and watch him take a shit if he didn't block the door with his foot.' And though the joke was meant to be good-humoured, it would always make Stavros frown, and he would respond—only to me, kneeling or squatting so we were eye to eye—'Don't listen to them, boy, they are jealous.' And any disquiet I had felt from the hint of meanness in the teasing vanished; of course they were jealous. He had taught me an early and vital lesson: that the world is jealous of love.

So I'd follow him back to his room and I would sit on the bed and watch him strip off his singlet and finally remove his overalls, and the curls on his chest and belly were dark and his skin was the colour of honey and the underwear he wore was thick, ill-fitting and unattractive; and it is only now, years later, that I understand it was handwoven and homemade, spun and stitched together by his mother or his sisters in the Balkan mountain village he had come from. Standing in front of the small shaving mirror on the dresser, he would carefully measure out a few drops from a bottle of cologne—always so careful in his use of that treasured bottle—and he would slap a few drops on his neck, on his chest and underneath his arms. Then he'd open a drawer, select a fresh singlet that my mother had washed and ironed for him, and put it on. Then, and only then, he'd reach for his cigarettes, sit down next to me on the bed, pull me affectionately onto his lap and say, quietly and with gravity, 'Tell me all about your day, my child.'

My face in his chest hairs, so soft on my cheeks. My nose slowly, daringly, even then intuiting that this was a transgression, searching and wanting to inhale the odour under his arms, the perspiration only subtly veiled by the soap and dabs of cologne; and the strength and swooning safety of his arm around me.

He'd smoke, listening to my prattle, then kiss me on the top of my head. He'd hoist me off his lap, sniffing the air and patting his stomach, winking while giving the ultimate Greek compliment: 'Your mother cooks as well as mine does!'

From the moment of his shadow in the corridor to the final butting out of his cigarette in his room, no one else existed: not my parents or my brother, not my aunt Irene or my uncle George. The world consisted only of Stavros and me.

•

I finish my sit-ups. The coffee has cooled and I sip the last of it with distaste. Two lorikeets screech, swoop and dive as I walk down the narrow stairs to the room below. There is the stinging clout of the sun on the back of my neck—it will be a very warm day. My phone is sitting on the small square coffee table. I glance at it and smile. A text, loving and brief, from Simon, my lover. I will call him tonight. And a missed call from Andrea, who has left a message.

I make sure not to look at anything else, not to enter the world. No news, I want nothing of news.

The world is not just myself, nor just me and Simon. The world is not just a memory of Stavros. The world is greater than all that. And I don't want it.

I wipe Andrea's message. As if I am deleting the world.

I have to force myself to ignore the lure of the phone, force myself to follow the sun. Nothing better exemplifies the perversity of our present age than the fact that I have to will myself to shun it. The digital intrusion wrought by the phone has shattered my equilibrium. There was no urgent demand in the message; Andrea had simply rung to say that she had heard I was there and, given that she was only an hour or so down the road, should we catch up? But as I delete the message, my action inadvertently opens a browser window and the news of the world floods in. A race riot in America. And possibly a responding one in Australia? Some sexual scandal and impropriety involving a media financier. Is he Brazilian or French? An opinion piece on the misunderstood subversion of 1990s bling culture. Without even noticing, I'm scrolling through the feed of headlines. Realising the idiocy of what I am doing, I switch off the phone.

I am out of breath. The poison of white noise has entered my head. Surely I need to read more about the race riot? Surely. Yet I don't. I know what will be said about it and, even if I agree with the righteousness of the sentiments, I will be nauseated by the smugness and the puritanical zeal with which they are pronounced.

I will force myself to follow the sun. I drop the phone back onto the table.

I had said to Simon that I wanted to leave my phone behind when I came on this retreat. He responded that I would kick myself if I then found myself in trouble—say, the car didn't start one morning, or I slipped and sprained an ankle on a walk and was unable to get help or contact him. In the end, I brought it along. But I have resolved to keep it at a far remove: to make it a physical effort to retrieve it.

I lock the back door, slap some sunscreen over my face and neck and arms, stride up the drive to the street and begin my walk. I head down the hill that leads to the inlet. Andrea's message is forgotten. The image of an enraged face at a protest; that too is gone.

The surface of the water is alive, all dazzling play and wavering light flashing silver and sapphire, producing an almost absurd rush of joy in me.

The tide is low and a brinish scent rises from the mangroves. The graceful slope of the mountain in the distance is a deep lavender in the play of light, a fragile cirrus shrouding its twin peaks. Apart from those wisps of white, the heavens are one vast blue stratum.

I cross the path under the bridge and walk the length of the boardwalk. Stepping onto the sodden planks that lead to the beach I take off my sandals and carry them to the water's edge. Now the skies have a rival for my attention: the tumble and roar of the waves, the chant from the ocean.

There are a few solitary figures at the far end of the beach; their dogs leap and bark and retreat from the waves. In the bobbing swell, four surfers are lying patiently on their boards, waiting for the next set: they are stabs of black oil paint on the overexposed whiteness and cyan of sky and water. There is a young woman lying on a scarlet towel, her skin glistening from tanning oil, large sunglasses shading her eyes. Her left hand lies straight and palm up beside her body; the other clutches her phone.

Had I been anxious, resentful, such a short time ago up at the house? Resentful of that other world coming in, that world of capitalised demands: Politics and Meaning and Justice? Now I feel foolish that I had let it bother me; in the sensual beat of sun on my eyes and cheeks, from the splendid, bracing chill as the waves run across my feet, a chill that only lasts a minuscule bite of a second before I am immersed to my waist and my body adjusts to the water and it is no longer cold but as refreshing to my flesh as spring water is to thirst. I look out to the horizon, and I have to raise my hand to shield my eyes; it's not yet mid-morning and the sun is already blazing. A dog barks, as if indeed animals are blessed with a connection to the natural world lost to us trapped in self-consciousness; in that glint of time between me raising my hand and the dog's bark, a significant change has taken place on the water: a swell is building, rushing in from the far depths. The barks are joined by faint cries from the surfers. They are alert on their boards now, and are paddling further out. One of the surfers turns and is on a wave, and before I can blink she is standing, as exquisite and simple a figure as those painted on walls by archaic man, and she rides the wall of wave with confidence and with awe, and though again this beauty only lasts a few seconds—the wave rolls and roars and the surfer is heaved into the sky and then as quickly dumped by the ocean god—in those few seconds her nobility and prowess are such that my hand rises to my chest and I offer a thanksgiving. I have seen something exquisite, something elemental.

Is it any wonder that those who live outside cities, on mountains or on plains or in valleys or on naked stretches of coast, is it any wonder that they are by nature conservative? Not that revolutions and annihilations can't be wrought by famished or humiliated and betrayed farmers and peasants. But they won't seek to change the Eternal.

I realise I have betrayed my peace, and I am lost in my own head.

I concentrate on the line of surfers, all now chasing the waves. To shake the wearisome thoughts that have entered my head, I turn my back to the surfers and start walking along the beach.

The damp sand shifts beneath my feet. I walk as far as the rock cliffs at the northern edge of the beach, then climb the weathered stairs to the hill overlooking the ocean. As I begin the slight climb away from the beach, the heat intensifies and I start to sweat. My odours mingle with the sweet smell of the sunscreen, the tang of brine all around me. I rub the sand off my feet along the grass, flicking it off my heels and calves with my towel, and put on my sandals. All I can feel is thirst. I find a water fountain and I drink uncouthly, the water dripping and drenching my chin and the front of my shirt. I keep drinking, hungrily and greedily, till I am sated.

I look up. At beauty. There is the beauty that is the Eternal, cognate to the natural world. And then there is the beauty that is discrete and exists only in the gaze bestowed on the one who possesses it. A son is helping his father prepare a boat for the water. The youth is sublime. The father is also good-looking, a little extra flesh on the jowls, a plumpness at his midriff. His hair is unkempt and falls messily over his ears to his shoulders, but his lack of concern about his appearance gives the father the most attractive of qualities: an easy masculine confidence. It is clear, even at a stolen glance, that the son will grow into the father: the same sun-touched blond hair, long limbs, and strong and elegant neck.

My glance has to be furtive. To let my stare linger for too long will betray the wantonness of my desire. This is the reality of homosexuality that all the rhetoric of liberation and the assertion of equality can never undo: that when confronted with the magnificence of heterosexual masculinity and beauty, the homosexual must submit. Even raging against the desire, perverting it, mocking it and wanting to destroy it, what traverses the rage or the perversion, the mockery or the resistance, is the indubitable power of the desired male.

In a breath, I once more take in the beauty of the son and the father, and then keep walking along the boardwalk back into town. The blare of sun mellows into dappled dashes; the placid water flowing beneath the boards is a startling jade green. For a moment a stingray, its flesh mottled black and grey, glides alongside me, slapping its wings on the surface before plunging into the depths. Though I am aware of the water and the bridge and town in the distance, of the creaking hardwood boards and the cool air along this stretch of board-walk in the shade of the towering gums, and though I take note of the tiny silver-bellied fish darting through the water and the cormorant that dives after them, and also register further out a pod of pelicans gliding serenely on the glassy water, though I see all of this, it is the flush of desire that animates me most of all.

It is this urge to make beauty the focus of my work that has precipitated my retreat from the world and brought me here. Yet to do so I must be as a neophyte. I have been too well trained in the notion of the novel as it is celebrated in the Western world: that which is deciphered, analysed and dissected—there supposedly lies truth. The natural, sensual world lies outside the reach of arbitration and condemnation, and therefore all of it is deemed ephemera. It is the great scandal of contemporary fiction that novelists think beauty unworthy of their efforts.

I must extol that father and son whom I have just passed, who are as beautiful and fine as anything wrought by nature. I am jealously guarding the brief images I have of them; I will make of them a memory.

It is in this precise sense that beauty has a connection with the erotic; it is in resurrecting them as memory that we focus and perfect them both.

•

I am twenty-seven, I have had my heart broken, and in the misery of loss I have returned to the places of my adolescence. I want to rewrite the timidity of my youth, and in doing so reclaim the potency that has been stolen from me by being rejected in love as an adult man. So I have returned to the parks and ovals, the public swimming pool and its change rooms and toilets, where I spent my early adolescent years yearning to touch the bodies of the men and boys showering with me, pissing at the urinals beside me. I want to act on the longings that I was too frightened to pursue as a boy, to be desired again and, in the reflection of that desire, soothe the agony of a betrayed heart.

I am twenty-seven years old, and I am at the Elgar Park swimming pool. I have swum my laps, I have showered and changed, and as I leave the sports centre I do not head straight to my car but walk assuredly to the toilet block. I stand at the urinal and pretend to piss, and as I am standing there, my heart drumming with anticipation and fear, my desire more urgent because of the fear, I hear the scrape of a lock being undone and I look over my shoulder and there he is, an angel; and if that word seems hyperbolic and risible then please forgive me for that is what he is. In his paleness and his fairness, in the physical grace of his athletic body, he is what I believed in my teenage years to be the antithesis of my swarthiness and darkness, the very opposite of my flawed, repellent self. I thought myself to be the very negation of such sublime beauty. Of course I cast him in the form of purity.

And this youth, his black denim jeans fallen in a crumple around his feet, his white shirt collar unbuttoned, his eyes looking at me with both terror and anticipation, even in fear his cock erect in his fist—he was an angel, I assure you of that. And it was also clear, in the hunger of his gaze, that he wanted me. And not bothering to zip myself up, I stepped off the urinal platform and walked over to him and I grabbed the back of his head and I kissed him hard and the kiss was returned, and I was lost in him. What was remarkable was the relief I experienced as his mouth ground onto mine, as our tongues lashed together, our spit passed between us. The astounding confidence of such a kiss from someone so young; and then my hand reaching under his shirt and touching his skin and him trembling from the touch and kissing me harder and I had never touched such pale skin before, like touching light. The skin I touched was cool with his sweat, and hence the perfume of his fear and his desire, but it also boasted a union of hardness and softness that only ever belongs to the young. The hardness was the nipple and the softness was the gentle concave of his belly; the hardness of his abdomen and the softness of his buttocks. When my finger touched the soft down between his balls and his anus, he moaned; still kissing me, he moaned inside my mouth. My other hand reached lower and stroked the coils of hair at the base of his cock. I released his mouth and looked down: the hair there was fair and gold. The youth touched one finger to my cheek, and I looked up at him. His smile was tender and sad and yearning, and he whispered then, 'Kiss me again,' and I rose to my feet and again I grabbed the back of his head and brought his face closer to mine and it was then, looking at those pleading eyes, that I knew he was going to ask me to fuck him, and instead of waiting for that entreaty, I asked, 'How old are you?'

'Sixteen.'

The jeans still around his ankles. The unbuttoned white shirt: it was a school shirt.

I allowed fear to conquer desire. I hoisted my own pants, fumbled for and buckled my belt, and I pulled away from him. Or did I throw him off me? I was fearful of the world and I acted in that calamity of shame, of what the world would think, which now, so long later, I realise was a pitiful and unworthy fear: for what did I renege on in panicking and rejecting this boy? I made him ashamed of his beauty and infected him with my shame. I said something like, 'I'm sorry, you're too young,' which was pathetic moralism and therefore complete falseness and he must have known it too for he looked away—I had failed him—and I slinked out of the toilet: unproud.

•

The boy assisting his father with the boat, that boy's fairness recalls that shame to me.

The boardwalk curves and the shadows of the gums are scattered by sunlight and I pass an elderly woman walking her dog and I say, 'Good morning,' and her reply is a surprisingly firm and welcoming, 'G'day,' and the sun on my face is the kiss from the schoolboy in the toilet block and I realise that people readily confuse evil with sin. But evil is inhuman, and sin is human. It would have been a sin to fuck the boy.

Soon after that incident I stopped haunting the places of my adolescence. My wounded heart began to mend and maybe the gift of being desired by such an angel was what healed me. I owe him gratitude and an apology. I had wronged him in fleeing from him so spinelessly. Before running away I should have told him that he was beautiful.

'How long are you here for?'
         'A fortnight.'
   'And you are up here to write?'
   'Yes.'
   'A new book?'

I hesitate. Is it a new book? And if I answer that it is
a book, then do I have to explain whether it is or is not a
novel? When does a book lose its contingency and become
not merely possible but probable? When there is a first draft?
When it is printed? Or is it when it is spoken about?

   'Yes,' I answer. 'A new book.'

There is an uncomfortable pause. My friendship with
Andrea extends from our immaturity and eagerness and
ruthlessness as youth, and it has been sustained in age. We
know when we can laugh at each other. She wants to see me

27

but I will not offend her if I tell her the truth. I am birthing a book. I can't see you. Nothing else matters.

But our friendship goes back decades and I am both resentful and sincere when I suggest, 'Why don't I come up and stay a night?'

It is a wise compromise. My assuming the right to invite myself acknowledges the love and affection of friendship while at the same time confirming that this house I am renting is a sanctum that cannot be breached.

'Good,' she says. There is no longer any anxiety in her voice. 'The beginning of this week is better for me.'

'Tuesday?'

'Perfect.'

And we make the arrangements.

The phone is heavy in my hand; before returning it to the room downstairs I call Simon at work. He answers immediately, his voice cheerful.

'Hey, babe. How is it up there?'

'It's beautiful.'

As I say it, I glance out over the garden. The lawn has only very recently been mowed, probably in preparation for my booking. There is a studied order to the three rosebushes planted just below the deck, each a metre apart; in between, there are tufts of geraniums. Summer is passing and neither plant is in flower but the green of their leaves is still luxuriant. Yet amid this European simplicity, the gardener has also placed indigenous shrubs and ferns, their colours sandy and sun-bleached and ancient, their foliage jousting spikes and lances that break forth out of the earth; such energy makes inviolate claim to this land. And then my eyes lift towards the horizon and the two planes of water, the silver shimmer of inlet and the turquoise gleam of ocean, restore calm.

Simon answers my delight. 'It always is. Next time we'll be there together.'

I speak my love to him, and he speaks his love to me.

I quickly take the phone back downstairs.

It is not yet eleven o'clock. I brew another coffee and take the mug and my laptop out to the deck. The dark screen lights up and there is the screensaver, an old black-and-white photograph of a young, blond boxer sitting on a bench, a group of equally youthful sailors on the benches behind him, their occupations clear from the sharp V-neck of their black naval uniforms. The boxer has his legs spread; he is smiling amusedly and pointing to what looks like a ticket stub. The smile is knowing and innocent at once, revealing both his manhood and his youth, and though the uniforms of the sailors seem to denote they are North American, it is this carefree, phlegmatic grin that makes me think of the boxer as Australian. One of the sailors is looking over his shoulder at the same ticket stub, and this sailor's face is inscrutable: neither curious nor uninterested. It's possible that this only arises from the angle of the photograph, that the boys might have been further apart in the real physical space, but the way the photographer has composed the shot it looks as though the cheek of the sailor and the boxer's cheek are touching. Their closeness separates them from the crowd. Except that over the boxer's right shoulder, keeping a clear distance, is another sailor whose gaze is firmly on the slip of paper the boxer holds in his hands. There is an identical plane to the broad foreheads of both sailors, and an identical shape to their eyes and their noses. So, are they twins? The more closely one examines them, the less confident we can be about making such an assumption. They are surely brothers, though. The brother's interest is more circumspect. He is curious about the slip of paper in the boxer's hand; yet as I gaze at the photograph, I can't help but muse if that curiosity is not also about the intimacy between his brother and the young fighter. But that is mere conjecture.

Isn't it from such questioning and interpretation that stories begin?

If I am not going to begin with Morality or Politics or Race or Class or Gender or Sexuality, if I am going to resist the authority of Purpose, then how should I begin? The world of nature is all around me, breathing and stirring and pulsating. Light and colour, sound and movement. And then there is this photograph from a now-distant black-and-white twentieth century, and the fighter's clear-eyed and democratic grin, his strong legs and golden hair, connect him to the boy helping his father this morning, to the boy in the toilet whom I failed; and through the wondrous alchemy that is synchrony—synchrony being the one essential condition for all artists, regardless of their craft—the gentle voice of my lover is also connected to those legs and to that grin.

What connects the sensuality of the natural world and the sensuality of this image? Just that: sensuality. All writing, all true writing, begins from the erotic—this is true for poetry and the novel, at least. The direct sensual nature and danger of poetry has been recognised from its primeval roots in the exaltation, the singing and the dancing, the trances and transfigurations of ritual, the daring of pain and the urging of ecstasy; all are found within the sacraments and ceremonies: the chant and the ululation and the dance.

Less so with the novel. That may be because the novel emerges from splendid isolation. Though there is *The Tales of the Genii* and the grandiloquent carnival of *The Thousand and One Nights*, stories of bodies in splendid communion, as is so with the fragments of the ancient Greek novels we can read—I am not counting Homer, for Homer is poetry; it is ritual and sacrifice and rebirth spun into song—the novel's great forging was initiated from labours of solitude and introspection. The novel was birthed by the individual. Or, if you prefer—and I think I do prefer it, as I have the wicked ego of a novelist—the individual was birthed by the novel. If poetry emerged from bodies in unity and exaltation, the novel emerged from the body quarantined from others. Thus, the novel is masturbation. Defoe daring to touch himself, to grip his hard cock on his lonely island, finally liberated from puritan eyes, and so free to conjure that most dangerous of temptations, the body of a virile African. Dostoevsky also wanks, the spasms violent and shocking on every page, in a furious Eastern concord of bliss and shame, ecstasy and self-subjugation. Genet and Proust and Joyce and Stein made onanism their revolution, and George Eliot concealed her subtle, constant massaging of cunt and clit by hiding it in plain sight. What is *Middlemarch* if not the most sustained and languid reverie in the English-language novel? She is God the Creator, breathing into being a whole world; and a sensual world at that. Like a youth daring to challenge the authority of first the parent and then, inevitably, their god, Rushdie thrilled to the explosive charge of blasphemy. Is there a greater transgression than incest? Yes: to usurp God.

I begin to write.

Or I begin to write three times. For me, a child of Christians, and a child of peasants who believed their mountain world was populated by spirits, both benevolent and malicious, the number three is auspicious. Three is the Trinity. Three is also possibility and risk. This was taught to me very early on in my apprenticeship as a writer by my friend Andrew, one of the people who instructed me on theatre and the stage, and he said, 'Chris, you are always writing scenes that are dialogues. Introduce a third person, a third element: introduce risk.' Maybe this would have been taught in Drama, if I had studied it, but I use the term 'apprenticeship' deliberately. I learned and failed and, in failing, learned that writing is work and not study. (The observant reader will have noticed that I capitalised Drama. I am running away from that creed, that *purpose*, as well.)

I have three stories I wish to tell. The simple nature of our craft is how to vomit these stories out on a page. It is an ugly analogy but I think it apt. And again, I envy the poet as I envy the musician not caught in the bind of language, of words. They can sing their stories. By defining the novelist's art as a hurling, a spewing, I am being deliberately crude, because I am writing at a time when the novel is unbearably timid. It doesn't think itself so. It often mistakes itself as being Revolutionary or Progressive or Subversive. But it is none of these things. It is the novelist looking over her shoulder, seeking the approval of her peers, her colleagues, her friends, her social media feed. This is the worst failing of the intellectual, to be simultaneously sanctimonious and cowardly. (And allow me to interject here and state that, unlike my Revolutionary or Progressive or Subversive fellow writers, I bear no animus towards the privileged; or no more than I do towards any class. I was born to peasants and raised as working class, and then gambolled with, and was seduced by, the middle class. I have fucked with the lumpen, and have stood over a European duke who pleaded with me to come and piss all over his face. Each class has its foibles, and each has its cruelties. Cowardice is the worst sin of the bourgeoisie. And the vast majority of artists of the moment in which I am writing—I am trying to evade History, but history grins and taunts, for it runs faster than any of us—are bourgeois.

They hide behind the capitals of Gender and Race and Sex, but they are faint-hearted, they can't evade their nature.) I use the word vomit because it makes us cringe. It returns us to our bodies, the shock and humiliation of an urge or an impulse that cannot be resisted.

I have three stories. Which to tell?

The first story I have already intimated to you, and I may already have begun. It begins with the scent, the smell of Stavros, the first man I adored. To continue with this story is to pursue fragrances that will lead into the past. It begins in the first memories of childhood, when I understood that a man's arm wrapped around me and a man's scent could arouse me, and so it begins in the shared migrant houses in which I grew up. It's a world that I need to reinvent, for it is an inner-city world that has disappeared, and it is a migrant wave that no longer excites, a community of young migrant men and women, mostly Greek but not only Greek, who for a while walked and jostled and laboured and loved in my city and were the most beautiful people on earth. The child's voice and perceptions must guide such a novel and its momentum, and its narrative must be sequential and oral for that is the world of a child. And this happened and this happened and then this happened. That is how a child tells their story and, if I am to write about the child, I must begin just before this child's world was bound to words and sentences. Even as I write it, I must speak it: it needs to be oral. I must speak my memories.

Watching the moon landing on a black-and-white television: we were one of the first families on the street to have a television and so the neighbourhood crowded into our small lounge room and I remember clearly the scratchy and shaking image of Neil Armstrong taking his first step; and I remember the pink fluted glass of the ashtray in the middle of the coffee table spilling over with discarded butts and ash. I am so young that it is not the momentousness of space and human hubris that overwhelms my remembrance: it is the joy of being cocooned among adults, and the wondrous safety of that love.

Another scene must be set at the circus grounds at the edge of the park in Burnley, the carnies setting up their campsite and their towering tent on the stretch of grass between the oval and the railway tracks. Every year without fail the circus would arrive, and it seemed to us children that its covenant was with us: it came for us. My brother and my cousins and I would skip between the caravans to find the elephant that gazed down at us with its sad, round eyes as we overcame our nervousness and patted its hard, wrinkled grey trunk. The circus people let us children roam and play between their tents and cages, only yelling out if we were coming too close to a horse. 'Watch out, kid, she can kick!' An exquisite freedom was experienced in that blurring of worlds; and when our parents took us to watch the circus, I am convinced that our cheers were louder, our applause more deafening and our laughter more ringing because we had shared a small communion. The carnival people were not sentimental towards us children. They never asked our names. But they were, in their brusque way, indulgent of these dark-faced excited children, jabbering away in a patois of English and Greek. All of it reeked of shit: of the animals, and also of the precarious latrines that the circus folk set up near the tents.

The smell of shit returns another memory. And another. Returning from Greece at ten years of age, I proudly took my slingshot to the park. The slingshot had been whittled and carved and strung by my cousin Manolis back in my mother's village. Manolis, or Mani, was a few years older, and the tough working life of a shepherd had hardened him and aged him: my brother and I were soft and childish in comparison. I followed Mani everywhere, including scrambling up a cliff face—only a few metres high, when I think of it now, but for the chubby young boy from Melbourne it seemed impossible to scale. Mani would not let me surrender. 'You will climb it.' There was nothing of the bully about him; it was not said with contempt or spite, just cold certainty. The other boys were already at the summit of the rock, looking down at my graceless climbing—my knees bleeding from being scraped against the hard stone—and jeering, calling me names in a Greek slang I did not understand. And below was Manolis, arms crossed, shouting up at me. 'You will do it.' That unre-lenting encouragement forced me to the top. I knew that a small discharge of shit, a leaking of urine, had occurred in the terror of the climb. As soon as I was on the clifftop, I ran into some bushes, dropped my trousers and shat. The other boys were no longer scornful. One of them must have pointed out which leaves to use to wipe my arse. I would have had no idea; I was from the West, from a city. Mani's head suddenly appeared as I was shitting. He had hoisted himself onto the clifftop. He was smiling at me.

I do not remember the love I had for Manolis as sexual. I had already begun to experiment with wanking by then, only fitfully and clumsily of course, but I never admitted him into my fantasies. From him, I first gained respect for diligence and discipline. As a youth, he wore his denim or corduroy work shirt in the Balkan style, with the collar buttoned. Even to this day, four decades afterwards, I often wear my collar in this style. I have just realised it is in homage to him.

When we were leaving Greece, he gave me the sling-shot that he had crafted himself. He had instructed me on its use, hitting empty Pepsi cola cans. Back in the park in Melbourne, I saw a crow sitting on the lowest branch of a gum tree. I remembered Mani's instructions. I took aim and fired. The bird spun rapidly as it dropped to the ground. I ran over to it, but when I saw the vacant stare of its yellow eyes, the weeping of silvery shit on its black tail feathers, I began to cry. I never used that slingshot again.

And not long after my killing of the crow, going to the toilet block at this same oval, two men at the urinal immediately spring apart, but not before I saw the shock of steely pubic hair on the older man, the plump and shiny pink head of his cock. Did the men run out as soon as they had zipped up? Had they entered a cubicle? I already knew the arousing temptation of the words and drawings scratched and scrawled on those cubicle doors and toilet walls. I looked down as I stood at the urinal. My own little dick was fattening. The sting of urine was everywhere, in my nostrils, in my lungs. My dick was hard.

I want to re-create a world that has disappeared through the sensual experiences of the child I was. Is this novel permissible? Is it even possible? I swear, for me, it is truth.

The second novel I am thinking of writing has a title. It is called *Sweet Thing*, which is the name of a song by Van Morrison, from his album *Astral Weeks*. The album is sacred music—there can be no other way to describe it—and it is a euphoria that is both Christian and pagan. Bear with me, accept this paradox: I know it is so, for I have been raised in this contradiction. Morrison, from the far west of Europe, from an island that was a gateway to the monsters and spirits and changelings and leviathans of the western ocean, sings odes and oratorios to the one God and to the transvestite Madame George.

I was born into the Orthodox Eastern world, cradled between the Balkans and the Levant, where veneration of the Trinity and also of the Panayia was not inconsistent with the worship of spirits and daemons. One of my grandmothers was a witch in her village. She was also a Christian. Religious awe is the reverence for all that is incomprehensible to human consciousness and reason, and so to respect the demonic is not necessarily to grant it allegiance. This is an understanding that is lost to the puritan of any faith or creed. I only met my grandmother twice in my life: once as a child of ten and once as a young man. She knew the names for every rock and stone, every flower and tree, every crag and brook and boulder on her mountain. She had lost the ability to walk when I last saw her, but she recalled the taste of chewing tobacco, of running her hand in clear spring water; of listening to the varied tones of the winds, and how delightful it felt to raise her heavy widow's skirts and have those winds swirl past her naked legs. From her I comprehended that the world of magic also belonged to the erotic. That is the awe that suffuses Van Morrison's *Astral Weeks*. It is a knowledge at the outposts of continents and nations. Morrison from the far west and my grandmother, my *yiayia*, from the far east. The sacred and the erotic border each other. That is a truth I wish to avow as a writer.

To me, 'Sweet Thing' is the most beautiful track on the album. It is one of those works of art in which there are innumerable doors opening into secret chambers. The song is, I often say—and not out of morbidness—one that I wish to be played as a funeral march. There is nothing gloomy about it. It is exultant. I suspect the first time I heard it I was on drugs, and it is a piece of music that returns me to that drug rhapsody even when I listen to it sober. When I listen to the song I don't hear the lyrics; they might as well be in Gaelic, and often I prefer to think of them as so. It is the release and surprise in Morrison's voice, and it is the rapture of the music, rising and twirling and seducing—was this the song the Pied Piper played to the children of Hamelin?—that I hear.

The story I want to tell in *Sweet Thing* is one I have carried with me for over a decade now. Very recently I asked a fellow writer whether one must abandon an idea if, after ten years, it still hasn't come to fruition, if it has refused to be birthed. He replied, 'Yes. After so long, the story has decided it isn't yours to tell.' Yet this story will not fade; its call has never weakened. There are stories that come to you in lucid detail: you can see your character and you hear her voice, and you know what she has done and what she might do. Then, with time, you realise that her voice is not as clear as it once was, you have trouble imagining her face; you find that you no longer care what will happen to her. These stories you cannot write—physically, I mean. You feel depleted with every stroke of the pen and every tap of the keyboard and know that the story is leaving, is disappearing for good. Yet *Sweet Thing* remains vivid. I still work at it, persist in its emerging—never successfully thus far—first as a screenplay and then a short story. I have tried to write it as a play and now, possibly, it is a novel. But it is as a film that it first came to me, and the final scene of the film I was directing in my head gave origin to the title.

Paul, the main character, has flown home from the United States. Weary, jet-lagged, he is picked up at the airport in Brisbane by his wife, Jenna, and his son Neal. They drive south, crossing the border into New South Wales, and the unrelenting vista of sun-blasted concrete apartments disappears and they are in the verdant Eden of the temperate Pacific. That ocean—the same one that I can see now as I peer over the laptop to the horizon—is a glorious seam of blue. The surrounding forests are a revelation of green. Neal is driving with Paul beside him, and Jenna is in the back seat. Van Morrison's 'Sweet Thing' starts playing and Neal, who knows that his father loves this song, turns it up. (In the imaginary film all sound is diegetic.) As Paul listens to the song, he remembers the miserable failure that is his family in America, then he looks across to his son, and turns his head to see his wife smiling at him. Recognising how fortunate he is to have his life blessed by both of them—and also, of course, being enraptured by the song—Paul starts to weep. The song plays, the son touches his father's hand and the wife places her hand on her husband's shoulder, lets it rest there, reaffirming their bond. And the man weeps, in both sorrow and gratitude.

That is the final scene.

But I should tell you the story from the beginning so you can judge its effectiveness. And it begins with a porn actor

named Paul Carrigan. (I have warned you: all stories orig-
inate in the erotic.)

I am not sure of the exact date that I first saw him in a
video, but it must have been some time in the early 1990s.
I had bought a VHS porno from a sex shop in Bridge
Road. I am alone in the house in Richmond that I am renting
with two friends. They are both at work. I slip the video into
the console, and he is in the first scene, kissing another man
in front of an open fire. Paul Carrigan is white and the other
actor is black, and the only artfulness I recall in the whole
of the video is the play of shadow and light on those two
bodies, one pale and one dark, as they kiss and start to fuck.

It is important to emphasise how transfixed I was by that
first sight of Carrigan. It was the same rapture, the realisation
that dream can indeed become reality, which first made me
fall in love with cinema, and I have no hesitation or embarrassment in including Carrigan in that pantheon of gods
whose illuminated arms reached from the screen, grabbed
me by the hand and led me into that netherworld. The young
boy in *Kes*: my first cinematic love. Marlon Brando in his
sweat-stained singlet in *A Streetcar Named Desire*. And, yes,
the brittleness of Jane Fonda in *Klute*. (A true cineaste must
be bisexual, whatever the object choice of her or his desire
in the bedroom. Those who parse film into defined genres,
who can only watch war films or action films or horror, or
only romantic comedies or European love stories or tragic
dramas, I do not understand them. All of us who love cinema

experience an electric charge of recognition in that moment in Jean Cocteau's *Orphée* when Orpheus is kissing his own image in the mirror and he sinks into Hades, into Eden, into Paradise: do we not all lean forward excitedly in our seats, knowing that Cocteau has returned us to one of our earliest memories? And the magical hand that grips Orpheus's wrist and drags him into Hades—is it not sometimes male and sometimes female? It is a travesty to know only a homosexual or a heterosexual cinema.)

The name of the video, that prosaic and unexceptional pornographic film in which I first encountered Paul Carrigan, doesn't matter. It is his presence that is significant. I was enthralled by him and thus he pulled me through the mirror.

Let me describe him as I first saw him. His beauty is defined by unselfconsciousness. He is handsome, but it is an attractiveness that is not extraordinary. It is the moment of looking across at a fellow passenger on a train or a tram, turning back and glancing at the person standing behind you in a queue, walking past a tradesman talking on a phone, his hand idly scratching the back of his neck as he talks, and finding yourself enraptured by the beauty of the everyday. To find the astonishing in the quotidian is the most exceptional of opportunities. There, before you, on a suburban street or a crowded train, is the hand reaching out to draw you into the enchanted mirror. Most of us turn away. We return to scrolling on our phones or looking out the window, fantasising of kings and queens, athletes and supermodels, of gods and goddesses—fairytales that are in fact more commonplace than a glimpse of the sublime in the ordinary. Paul Carrigan is of that order of beauty. You might not observe him in a casual glance, but if your eyes do settle on him, if you inhale his beauty, you fall in love.

In the hundreds of pornographic scenes I watched him in between the early 1990s and the start of the new millennium, he doesn't shave his body, his pubis or his arse. His weight fluctuates. His cock is of average girth and length. His acting is stilted, but there is a playful recognition of his own limitations that is charming and endearing. He does not sculpt or adorn or exaggerate his own body. It is this very simplicity that first stirred my attraction. Simple masculinity, as with simple femininity, fascinates. Paul Carrigan doesn't try to be a man. He just is. Which means he can be a man even when getting fucked. He can't betray his maleness.

Sometimes, when speaking to other homosexual men of my adoration of Paul Carrigan, they scowl or frown or purse their lips in disdain. 'He does nothing for me.' I always feel the heat of jealousy and envy in their spite. They hate that he doesn't have to try to be male.

I know nothing of the real Paul Carrigan. Is Paul even his real name? I very much doubt it. Once, over ten years ago now, I awoke at 3 am with a scene so clear before me that it had exorcised the shadows of the night. My vision was a screen. It is late morning on the Pacific Coast, and in long shot we see a man and his son at work, and I heard a whisper of music, the lilt of the Van Morrison song. Stirred by my agitation, Simon ordered me out of bed. 'Go and write,' he snapped tersely. He has learnt to read my body, and he was alerted to the urgency of a story I needed to tell. I stumbled to the study, fired up the computer and wrote the first scene of a film I wished to direct. And I knew the name of the actor I wanted to play the father; an actor who could convey generosity and mettle without compromising either virtue. So, that night, I gave the lead character his name: Paul Carrigan. He had broken free from the pornographic shadows, was no longer a mere body onto which I could project my fantasies and desires. I started to write a story about a man who loved his wife and loved his son. The title of the story was drawn from the whisper I heard on awakening. In 15-pt Times New Roman, bold, I typed: '*Sweet Thing*'.

We begin somewhere on the Pacific Coast of northern New South Wales. The first scene of the movie or the play, the first chapter of the novel, begins with a man in his late forties, a man called Paul, working with his twenty-year-old son, Neal, placing new tiles on the roof of a cabin. If it were a film, we would observe the bond between father and son from the intimate silence of the physical work. It is late winter, there is no hard sun, yet the sky is clear, and the men's bodies are perspiring from their exertions. If a play, Paul would be communicating his love for his son in an opening soliloquy, expressing the pride and awe he feels at being this young man's parent. If a novel, there is the dispassionate and precise observation of a narrator.

The family own a clutch of cabins on this fertile rise, shacks that they rent out to tourists. They love their life on the coast, but years of drought and fire have taken their toll on the business. There are constant, seemingly never-ending expenses, and they have had to remortgage the property. That is why Paul and Neal are repairing the cabin roof themselves rather than paying a tradesman. Father and son pause in their work when they notice a car winding up the hillside towards them. It is Jenna, Paul's wife and Neal's mother, returning from errands in town. Jenna has been to the post office to collect the mail, and as they sort through it after lunch they find among the bills and bank statements a letter from Los Angeles.

We know already, by his accent, that Paul is American. He and Jenna recognise the sender's handwriting and they are both intrigued and disturbed. They don't open the letter, which is addressed to the two of them, immediately. They wait until Neal has finished his lunch and returned to work—Paul says, 'I'll see you up there in a moment'—and only then do they read it, Jenna sitting on a stool at the kitchen island bench and Paul looking over her shoulder. If a film, I would cut to the writer of the letter, a man called Jackson, an ageing but still attractive and flamboyant queen, the tight curls of his once-black hair looking like they have been powdered with fine ash. He would be reciting the letter straight to camera, so we hear his voice and his intentions. If a play, the actor would appear on stage as Paul and Jenna are cast in half-shadow. And if a novel or a story, I would include the letter in the text, but in between the paragraphs—at suggestive moments—I would have the narrator indicate something of what Jenna or Paul are thinking as they read it. What memories are disturbed or ignited by Jackson's correspondence? Part of the challenge I would set myself as a writer would be whether or not to reveal directly that Jackson is African American—as I have done now—or to do it through language and oblique description. But that is something to be explored in the actual labour of the writing. At the moment, what you need to know is that the letter reveals a little of how Paul and Jenna and Jackson met, when they were all working in the pornographic industry in Los Angeles, at the end of the VHS era, just before the digital age and the internet brought that period to an end. Jenna was a young Australian woman trying to make a living in the US. Jackson worked for a pornographic video company. Paul was working in gay porn because it paid better for men than straight porn. He and Jenna met shooting a bisexual scene and they fell in love. There were years of elation, and there were years of confusion and dissolution and hard drugs. Then Jenna got pregnant and decided to return home. Paul chose to follow her. They came to Australia, got clean, had their child and left that world behind.

Jackson begins the correspondence by chiding them both for refusing the allure of the internet. 'Not even one social media account,' he complains, but his outrage is sly, feigned. 'Are you fucking dinosaurs?' The next words he penned have torn the paper. 'But who the fuck am I to judge? You should see *me*—I look like my fucking granddaddy!' Still, he has managed to track them down, for an offer has come through. Jackson has been smart, he has been careful with his money, and he has bought the rights to the pornographic films produced by the studios he worked for in the 1990s. Now he has been approached by a rich elderly gentleman who has been obsessed with Paul since first seeing him in a video where he was young, so very ordinary yet so very handsome, his masculinity unadorned and unselfconscious. This elderly gentleman wants to fly Paul to California to spend three nights with him. The elderly gentleman desires sex, but he has made it clear that there will be nothing sordid or disgusting about the favours he demands. 'Very old fashioned language,' writes Jackson—and in the film, at this moment, he would be sneering. 'Clearly some old Confederate queen, thinks he's fucking Bette Davis!' For those three nights with Paul, he is prepared to pay one hundred and eighty thousand US dollars.

And I know what I must do now as a writer. I must leave some room for suspense. A reader needs a moment to breathe. I understand this. I often castigate novelists for those endless chapters without pause, the refusal to allow even a calculated break between paragraphs, a small oasis of blank white space among pages littered with the black grains of words.

There is no humidity in the air that coils and whispers as it comes off the inlet and from the ocean. I glance at the time on the laptop, then save the document and close the lid. My stomach growls; hunger is insistent. But I don't give in to it just yet. I stand on the verandah. Among the graceful limbs of the frangipani, I see a glorious flash of blue-black. A male bowerbird is silently commanding the highest branches of the tree. With the midday sun at its zenith, even the irksome chatter of the lorikeets has been silenced. A roiling thicket of white cloud is descending slowly over the town and the inlet. Soon the world will be covered in its pale shadow. I inhale the sweet, cool air; the same ocean air that Neal and Paul breathe in as they work on the cabin's roof. I can see Paul clearly, for I see the ageing Paul Carrigan. If *Sweet Thing* were a film, I would want him to play the part. I watch the unfolding cumulus gather heft and force. It is an idea that I have carried for a long time now. Maybe the actor and myself are both too old for that imaginary film. So, a play? A novel? I try to imagine Jenna, to see Neal. At the moment they are hidden, like the bowerbird in the tree. I see only glimmers, a flash of their faces and physiques. Yet I can hear them. Jenna's voice is raspy—she is a smoker—and yet it is deep and warm. Her son has inherited that voice. There is a sonorous clarity to his tones. Yet he is gentle. His voice is masculine and gentle. It is Simon's voice. I fell immediately in love with Simon's voice.

In the pantry I reach for a can of cannellini beans. I drain them and wash them. I finely chop a long green chilli and mince two cloves of garlic. I am less fastidious with the parsley. The hunger is overwhelming now; it is making me impatient. I put the ingredients in a bowl, douse them with olive oil, season them and squeeze half a lemon over it all. Then, as the oil and juice seeps through the bean salad, I grill two slices of toast with cheese: now I am salivating.

It is a deeply satisfying lunch. I brew myself a small coffee, and I light a cigarette. The first plunge of smoke down my lungs is glorious. Paul's voice is still in my head and I begin to type.

I saw a crab chase an octopus this morning. I was walking back from the ocean beach along the boardwalk. The sun was beating serenely as I approached the end of the walk and I stopped to lean on the wooden railing, looking out across to the town, watching the pelicans gliding lazily across the crystalline surface of the inlet. The tide was receding; I was conscious of a subtle recalibration, an almost imperceptible shifting under my feet. I looked down between the solid planks of the boardwalk and the waters were serpentine, slithering as they were sucked out to sea. And at that moment I heard the splashing. A crab the size of my hand, its ivory case speckled with russet dashes, was darting and upsetting mud and sand in the shallows. Its forward thrusts seemed aggressive, until I noticed a further upsetting of sludge beneath the almost transparent surface of the water;

the cloudy scattering dissolved, and the long tentacles and suckers of the octopus were revealed. Two or three of its tentacles were approaching the crustacean, and in order to escape the crab started digging furiously into the mud. Yet as it dug, the octopus moved towards it and the crab was again forced to scramble away. For the longest moment, maintaining a wary distance, both creatures were still. Then the octopus lunged towards the crab once more and the dance continued.

A few times, people stopped and leant on the railing: a handsome young couple, she pointing excitedly at the battling creatures, speaking in what I presumed to be Mandarin; her beau not answering, his eyes hidden by tight-fitting black sunglasses, only nodding now and then. And there was an elderly woman walking an alert and confident terrier. She stopped beside me and we watched the scene for some moments. 'Those two are always at it,' she said before offering a cheerful, 'Good day'—the two words clearly enunciated—and recommencing her walk.

Not long after, a cormorant dived into the water, alarming the octopus. The frightened creature fled into the shadows beneath the boardwalk and disappeared from my view. The cormorant pecked at the crab and then, disappointed, perched daintily on one thin leg, its face turned away from the crustacean in disdain. The crab was still. Then, with fraught digging, it vanished into the wet mud. I resumed my walk home.

I had enjoyed the almost balletic contest between the two creatures, yet there had also been something daunting in the relentless concentration of their warring. To expunge the detritus of overburdened language, to sequester myself from the prescriptions and interdictions of Ideology and Morality, I wanted to see if the world of the immediate senses could act as a conduit to liberate my writing. Of course, this could only succeed if I avoided the capitulation to capitalised Nature: Nature understood through Ideology and Morality. That was a trick the mind often played, a seductive dog whistle. 'Trust me,' consciousness whispers. 'I am more reliable than those senses which depend on the frail, vulnerable physical body. I will remain at the end.' For isn't that the temptation of the mind, its trump card? Your body will fail you and die. Only I will continue. Mind, Soul, Meaning. History, Revolution, Revelation.

An octopus stirred the waters chasing a crab. The crab's shell was a glinting ivory and its markings were as magnificent as jewels sitting gracefully on a woman's full décolletage.

I strode up the hill to the house, where I charged into the kitchen, poured and drank eagerly from a glass of water—so eagerly that the liquid spilt and ran down my chin and throat—and then I hurried downstairs to call Simon.

He was at work. 'How is it up there?'

'Good. It's a beautiful morning.' And then, in a rush: 'On the way back from the beach I saw an octopus and a crab chasing each other. I lost all sense of time watching them. You would have loved it.'

'Who won?'

'A cormorant.'

'What?'

'A cormorant dived into the water and spoilt their fun.'

He laughed, then said, 'It must have been play. They wouldn't prey on each other, would they?' There was a pause, and then he added, 'I miss you. I wish I was there.'

'I miss you too.' Then I said, 'I love you," and he answered, 'I love you too.'

I put the phone down and climbed the stairs. As I was approaching the final step, I remembered that I had intended to check my emails. I had left them unanswered for two days now.

The coffee pot was whistling. I didn't return downstairs.

●

After lunch, Paul and Jenna go to their bedroom and discuss the astounding offer. 'One hundred and eighty thousand dollars,' Paul keeps repeating. 'One hundred and eighty thousand dollars.'

Jenna is sitting silently at the end of the bed.

Paul's face, his body, are vivid: I see and hear Paul Carrigan as I create him. The character of Jenna is still trapped in the imaginary netherworld; she has yet to fully emerge from the other side of the mirror. So, what I see when I imagine her is a shade. It is not a shadow that is frightened or timid. I know that she is regarding me from the other side, that she is bemused by my attempts to locate her. I cannot use the force of my desire to bring her forth. I walk closer to the mirror and peer into it. I see that her lips are full, pink, that she has shunned lipstick and any other kind of make-up. There is a defiance in that decision. She has shed many skins, this woman. I am sure of it. One of those she has discarded represents those years in the pornographic industry.

I see her in the gloaming of the other world. An almost imperceptible shaking of her head. Jenna is not ashamed of her past. She is reconciled to it and part of this reconciliation comes from the fact that she escaped, that she has her love with Paul and she has her son. She is not a dogmatic Christian, though her mother's Catholicism remains an anchor to her: as a girl and young woman it was a constraint; with age it has come to be a mooring. She is thankful to a notion of God and believes she owes God her gratitude: she didn't contract HIV when working in the porn industry, and she didn't succumb to the siren call of heroin.

Jenna has moved closer to me. Or I have moved closer to her. I imitate Jean Marais, Cocteau's lover and muse, and as Marais does in the director's *Orphée*, I place my cheek to the cold mirror.

To create Jenna, I am unable to use the force that is the erotic and that is desire and therefore will—for a writer is the god of their creation; and is it not the first understanding we glean from the Jewish scriptures, that Creation itself was a force of will?—and so I will desire her as Paul. I will possess Paul and enter his body and through him I will know Jenna.

He places a hand on her shoulder. He kisses the top of her head gently, and sits down beside her. 'I will do whatever you want. I want you to choose and I want you to know that whatever you choose will be right and I will never doubt that choice. Do you trust me?'

She turns and looks at this man. There is now more grey than black in his stubble, and his hair is thinning. He has been lax in the application of sunscreen on the sides of his neck and the skin there, always so pale, has been burnt red and is peeling, stippling. She takes his hand, squeezes it, and answers directly, 'Yes, I do trust you.'

She knows and he knows that she has not yet given an answer. What they do is make love. He initiates it. Releasing his hand from her grip, he begins to rub softly at the crotch of her jeans. He leans into her, he sniffs, and there is that most miraculous of perfumes: that of woman. How many decades has he been making love to this woman, and yet still the scent astonishes him? He distinguishes nothing of man in it. He is now aroused. His hand reaches into her jeans, his fingers tousle the sleek delicate strands that shelter her cunt, and he grasps her reciprocal arousal from how moist and warm the flesh is there, and from the rising odour, mucid in its intensity, and the corresponding rankness of his own smell; whether it is the saline bitterness of cum or the ammonic whiff of cunt juice, for Paul the perfume of sex is that of the sea. His cock is all blood now and he is hard.

She shudders as he whispers in her ear: 'I want to eat you out.'

•

When the idea for *Sweet Thing* first came to me as a film, I knew that for it to work it would need to be cast with actors from pornography. My fantasy was, of course, that Paul Carrigan would play the husband. I wanted an Australian actor to play Jenna, but it had to be an actress who was comfortable with sex on screen. Unlike the majority of pornography, the sex was not to be the centre of the film, but I didn't want to banish the physicality of sex from the lives I was detailing. It would be a betrayal of the story I wanted to tell, and of my unwavering faith in the truth of erotics, to do otherwise. Yet I understand that there is an audacity in my being the storyteller and using the real bodies of actors to communicate such truth. This is why they needed to be actors who understood pornography and were not frightened by pornography and were not censors of pornography.

This would be so much harder to achieve on stage. There are actors who are ravishing to the camera, who can charm and capture an audience from the first frame, but on stage, unable to rely on the transfiguration that is made possible by the lens, they disappear, become tiny, even ludicrous. And I can't conceive of a non-pornographic actor trusting either their collaborators or their audience to commit to the physical and existential nakedness required to perform sex on stage. If it has been done, it is only in the most extreme forms of performance art, and always with a deliberate hostility towards the audience. That's the closest the pornographic sex act comes to theatre: performance artists and strippers can hardly conceal their contempt for those who are watching them. So it is almost impossible to conceive of real sex in theatre. I suspect it can only really work—here is a revolution waiting to happen!—if a porn actor who has startling talent as a writer and director creates their own play.

If not a film, and not theatre, is it that *Sweet Thing* is a novel?

•

Paul's face, his lips, his tongue are smeared with the silken moisture from Jenna. He has given himself over to delighting her, becoming subservient to her in servicing her—and yet there is also a power in the purposefulness of his lovemaking. For the longest time he uses only his tongue and his face, his unshaven bristles, to lick and rub and press against her labia; he then pushes her legs apart, to open up her cunt to him, and for his lips, his mouth, his chin to penetrate further.

Jenna can feel the orgasm build, senses it from deep within her belly, and she clenches her teeth, not wanting to release it yet. Paul's chin has pushed further into her and the stubble scrapes against the tenderness of her clit. She moans loudly now: that tiny inkling of pain only deepens her pleasure. She looks down. Her husband's large hands are pushing against her thighs, his face is buried within her, and she observes a small circular patch of nakedness at his crown; Paul is ageing. She knows this, of course she does, but it is only now looking down at him that this physical change is exposed. The tide of her orgasm begins to recede but, as if sensing her faint withdrawal, Paul releases the grip on her left thigh and brings his hand to his mouth. He moistens his thumb, then, with Jenna still staring down at him, he gently rubs it across her cunt's lips then pushes it in, and he is rubbing and pushing, the action expert and seamless, so that Jenna feels the assault on her clit as one continuous movement, and she is lying back on the bed now and there are visions in her mind and she submits to them. Her son's friend Arlo is on top of her, looking at her shyly, and she slips the T-shirt off the youth and there is the subtle reddish fuzz over his nipples and down his belly; the fortification of her memory's desire comes from an afternoon two or three years ago when they were all down at the beach and Arlo had awkwardly draped a white towel around himself as he undid his khaki shorts and slipped into his blue-and-white-checked board shorts, and there had been a moment—Jenna had already changed into her swimsuit at home and she was applying lotion to Paul's back and happened to glance up—when Arlo released the beach towel just as he pulled up on the elastic of his shorts, and in that moment Jenna had spotted the dazzling and shocking burst of ginger pubes and the bulge of his cock; and it is this moment that she returns to now and she imagines that it is Arlo's cock that is slipping into her cunt and that he is fucking her, and as the waves of the fantasy lift her higher she can no longer tell whether it is Paul's thumb or his finger or his tongue—for now it is all of them—that are bringing her to climax and she urges, almost hisses, 'Faster, do it faster,' and it is to Paul and it is to Arlo. She comes.

She bucks her pelvis in a spasm of ecstasy and now Paul gathers her tight in his arms, his face still inside her, his eyes stinging from the damp fluids that trickle from her. He swallows, the taste sour and almost noxious, so he is close to gagging, but in that swallowing he can taste the saltiness of her sweat and of her skin and he rises, his face is in her face, and he kisses her so that Jenna too tastes herself in his kiss and with one hand grinding at her erect and raw clitoris and the other clutching her husband's hard cock she says to him, 'Come—please fucking come!'

He spills all over her hand; he shakes his cock and drops of semen fall into the black of her pubes, onto her belly. He gently flops on top of her. The cum is almost immediately cold and clammy. Their skins stick together. He is breathing heavily. She is rubbing at his hair.

'I think you should do it,' she says. 'I mean, I think we should do it. We need the money.'

She senses his nodding, and she realises, immediately and with such profound certainty that she doesn't know how she could have failed to perceive it while he was fucking her, that this was the reason they hadn't fallen into the pleasurable but ordinary pattern of their lovemaking. He hadn't suckled on her breasts; he hadn't put his cock inside her. He had wanted to lose himself in her cunt, that which no man possessed, that which belonged to her and to women. She wondered, without jealousy, certainly without unease, just in genuine affectionate curiosity, whether he had been intent only on pleasing her and tasting her and honouring her cunt, or if his keenness had been made sweeter by the knowledge that in a week or so he might be kissing a man's mouth, sucking a man's cock, fucking a man's hole?

'Are you sure?' His question is muffled. His face is squashed between her arm and her breast.

They are both thinking of that heaven-sent sum: one hundred and eighty thousand US dollars.

•

There is no silence whatsoever here in this house perched on the top of a rise overlooking the coves and wharfs of an inlet and then beyond that the vast expanse of ocean: there is always a reminder of birdsong, the boom and then plashing of the waters, the mutterings and callings of the winds; and the human isn't silent either: the rumble of vans and cars can be heard on the distant highway, and when a truck or a bus crosses the narrow girth of the bridge there is the swinging and reverberating of steel, the sound a synonym of the pealing of bells. And isn't there too, amid all this, the tapping of my fingers across the keyboard? This fervent action and the resulting muted banging have attracted the interest of a white cockatoo. I don't know how long it has been perched on one of the chairs opposite me, but as soon as I look up and notice it, it squawks. I watch it but make no move; realising that I will not feed it, the bird releases an exasperated shorter call, the white feathers ripple and rearrange themselves in a flurry of shaking, and then it is gone, diving into the air and flying to the distant trees in an action so expert and swift my consciousness has had no time to register it. It was sitting across from me, staring at me, and then, without warning, it is gliding towards the sparse canopies of the gum trees that stand sentinel on the shore of the inlet.

So, there is no silence, but there is a great peace. And in that peace, memory has the freedom to wander and to meander in ways that it cannot in the frenzy of movement and the discord of communication that is the city. In trying to understand Paul's love and desire for his wife, I had to become this heterosexual man and make his eyes mine and make his lips mine and make his tongue mine and make his senses mine and make his hands and his cock mine. It is not a fashionable idea to assert, but in that moment of being Paul, becoming my character, I was emancipated from identity. Yet, as I concentrated on making love to Jenna, to smelling her, being overwhelmed by her secretions and her flesh and her shape and her mystery, my memory detached itself from me. I was not unconscious of this separation. But I refused to be distracted by it. I wanted to complete making love, having sex. I wanted to fuck Jenna, to bring her to climax.

The fucking is done. I turn to memory. And begin to follow Her. (I have no answer to the question of why I designate memory as feminine. It is instinctual. If I am to personify Her, it is indeed María Casares I see before me, the figure of Death in Cocteau's *Orphée*, the deity who can navigate the two worlds either side of the mirror, and who leads Orpheus to the Underworld. It certainly will not satisfy either Politics or Psychology to add that Casares's appearance in that film has always reminded me of how my mother appeared to me in my earliest recollections. She and the actress share a Mediterranean heritage and the same dark hair, the same dark complexion. Our earliest memories, now forgotten, are created in the bond when our mother's body belonged to us and our bodies belonged to her. I offer this as an aside that has no resolution, for there is no answer—no Genesis story and no Year Zero—to the origin of memory. What is important is that memory is feminine.)

At the tip of consciousness, and then becoming vivid and clear as I finish writing the first sex scene in *Sweet Thing*,

I glimpse myself as a very young boy, standing at the urinal in the toilet block at Richmond North Primary School. It must be very early in the afternoon and it must be early summer, for the brick toilet has no roof and the light is everywhere and the shadows are short. I am wearing pants that my mother has sewn for me, utilising her skills as a seamstress to save money. She has fashioned these trousers for me from some old work pants she wore when working at the biscuit factory by the river. They are an ugly brown, almost orange, and the material is thick and uncomfortable; it scratches at my skin. But the most annoying thing about these pants is that there is no fly or zipper at the front. The zipper is to the side, because they were originally women's trousers and my mother did not think of changing them to suit her son. It doesn't matter when I sit down to shit, but it is humiliating at a urinal. I can't unzip; I have to drop my pants like I'm a preschooler. Fortunately, the toilet block is deserted; I must have asked permission to leave class. I would not have dared to come into the toilet during recess or lunchtime, certainly not to piss standing up. I undo the zip at my side, drop my pants and start to urinate.

I hear brutal laughter. I whip around to see where it's coming from, and as I do my piss slashes in a long arc across the aluminium sheeting and then onto the red Northcote brick of the toilet wall. I am burning with humiliation: are there three or are there four boys howling in laughter, pointing to my naked buttocks and the last dribbling of piss that is leaking shamefully onto my thighs and shoes?

They begin a chant: 'Chris wears girl's pants! Chris wears girl's pants!'

We are so very young, mere children, but we know how to cause pain. In their horrible mocking, I also recognise that the secret I have been so desperate to keep—that my trousers are not only hand-me-downs but were indeed once women's pants—is no secret at all. It is this, I think, more than my being caught naked, which causes me to augment my humiliation further. I start to wail. The boys are now quaking with laughter.

'What is going on here, lads?'

Mr Clifford has come in. The world shifts; everything changes. Surely the darkness that falls over the scene is only my remembrance of the shade cast by the teacher as he walked into the toilet block. Yet it seems that on his arrival a shadow fell across the earth. I can't conceive now what it was that he observed. There was I, still bawling, scrambling to pull up my underwear and pants in one movement. There were the frightened faces of the other young boys, their hilarity abruptly ended by the appearance of our teacher, by the fury on the man's face; one of the boys also started to cry. With a rapid gesture, Mr Clifford manages to strike lightly the faces of all the other boys. And with his punishment of them, he becomes a hero to me.

It's hard to make generations younger than mine understand the purity of punishment that involves violence. Our present age prefers masochism to sadism. Yet through so simply and swiftly reprimanding the other boys for their brutality, justice had been served and all ill-will and hatred was dissolved. I am not forgetting the perspective of the other boys: the clean, sharp rebuke was also perceived as just by them; I have no recollection of them seeking to take revenge on me afterwards.

My crying stopped immediately. I looked up at Mr Clifford.

I had two teachers called Mr Clifford. The first was this man who avenged me one afternoon when I was a young child. The second was a PE teacher at the suburban high school I started attending halfway through the eighth grade. Clearly, it is not an uncommon Anglo-Saxon name, but to my ears it always sounded mysterious: the acute snap of those harsh consonants at the end of each syllable, and the allegorical strength of them. The cliff and the ford, both suggestions of nature at its most imposing.

Not long after starting at the new school, I read Emily Brontë's *Wuthering Heights*, and I wonder now if I did not draw a connection between her Heathcliff and my Clifford? Heathcliff's savagery is inhuman. I recently reread the novel and have been struck anew by his callousness. However, once more I forgive him, and once more the cruelty recedes in the face of the erotic charge of his unrelenting will. Over two centuries have passed since its composition, and it remains the most mercurial and strange of European novels. Unlike the French—unlike, say, Rimbaud or Baudelaire—Brontë doesn't set out to write evil with the studied diligence of a student. She is no fallen Christian. She is pagan. Her Cathy's desire is for the brute, the avenger.

As is my desire. In the moment he punishes the boys, Mr Clifford becomes a hero. Yet I wrote above that there were two Mr Cliffords. Were they both heroes? Certainly not.

Here, I must make a necessary intervention. The two men—in the act of mimesis that is recollection, and which is also imagination—resemble Paul Carrigan. And Paul Carrigan resembles my Simon. These are my willing connections between men of real flesh and real blood but also of representation and memory and symbol: I affirm those correlations in the work of fiction. The men of real blood, real flesh—the teachers, Simon, a pornographic actor who used the pseudonym Paul Carrigan—have this in common: their voices are deep and melodic, confidently masculine but with no trace of aggression. I fell in love first with their voices: Mr Clifford declaring, 'What is going on here, lads?'; Simon's voice on the phone asking if he might come to look at the spare room we have advertised, a voice so resonant that I assume he is an adult and so am shocked when he comes for the interview and he is only my age, eighteen, and, also like me, a student. And a young porn actor's first few lines of dialogue, delivered clumsily, in the flattened vowels of the North American, but with a charming grace; his half-smile is bemused, and so is his tone. Their voices connects them, as does their descent from one of the most beautiful examples of miscegenation: when the Celtic race was ravaged by a Nordic people.

And the second Mr Clifford? His voice? I can't recall it at all. But, then, I was never in love with the second Mr Clifford.

I have been lost in reverie. When I look up from the screen, I can see that a light grey mist has settled over the double peak of the mountain at the end of the inlet. The light is still potent here on this side of the water, it is still warm. But the verandah is now in total shade. The afternoon is falling quickly.

A stirring of my cock. Inevitably. In returning to the men above I am returning to the first naive yet powerful comprehensions of desire. I cup the crotch of my jeans, shudder at the charge that shoots through me as I squeeze my cock.

Mr Clifford stands tall above me.

'Are you okay, son?'

The charge of that word—*son*—shoots right through the boy. Very soon, in a quarter of an hour, I will go and masturbate. I will not have access to my trove of pornographic videos and images. I will use only imagination. I will return to this moment and I will kneel before my teacher and I will unbutton the fly of his trousers and I will take his penis in my mouth.

This did not happen. It is only fantasy. Yet the child desired it.

•

Mr Clifford stands tall above me.

'Are you okay, son?'

It may have been another day, but in the editing room that is memory, all of this occurs on a single day. Mr Clifford takes my hand and leads me to the tap. He watches me as I wash my face, scrub at the salty evidence of my treacherous girlish tears. He drops my hand as we leave the toilet. It is a very hot summer's day; the asphalt surface of the schoolyard is scorching, I can feel it even through the soles of my shoes. The reflected light hurts our eyes.

Our class is cleaning the schoolyard, for this is the 1970s and there is still a deliberately martial component to school and education. Some of the children are bent over, picking up scraps of litter and dead leaves, pushing them into large white garbage bags. A quartet, all girls, are raking the sand beneath the swings and monkey bars. The boys who laughed at me all have brooms and they are busy sweeping. Two brooms rest against the red-brick wall of the toilet block. The large white outline of a circle is painted high on the brick, with a red dot at its centre. We do not have hoops. The dot forms the target for our ball games. Mr Clifford takes the brooms and hands one to me. He starts sweeping and I know that I am meant to follow his example and so I do. After a short while Mr Clifford stops and watches me. I have been imitating the actions of my mother when she cleans the house in the evenings or on Saturday mornings, those times when she is not working at the factory. Yet my teacher comes over to me, gently takes the broom and says, 'You're doing it wrong. Let me show you.'

I had been pushing the broom forwards. Mr Clifford shows me how to sweep in a circle, bringing the detritus and rubbish into one central spot so it's easier to pick it up with the dustpan and brush and tip it into the garbage bag. At first, I am embarrassed that I have failed at such a simple task, but my teacher's instructions are patient, mild, and very soon I am exhilarated that I am doing as he wishes. This is one of the most resilient of my memories: Mr Clifford standing above me, watching me sweep, his arms crossed, and the sun behind him, keeping me in cool shadow. In protecting me from the boys, in being gentle with me and also in instructing me, he becomes a father. The authority of work will from this moment remain intrinsic to my desire and to my falling in love. Simon, too, is capable and efficient at tasks of labour, and he is an instinctive and productive gardener—as was my father. And I will be delighted when I discover through my research that Paul Carrigan also worked as a technician and gaffer on film sets.

The second Mr Clifford has a body of sculptured finesse. He looks like the models who appear on TV and in advertising. He is beautiful; objectively, that is a fact. Yet almost immediately there is a distrust between us. He is my sports teacher and he is annoyed by my lack of physical grace. I admire the rigour of his body, his muscular physique, but that appreciation doesn't overwhelm me. His body is almost too faultless, as if imitating the ideals of manliness. There is something studied about it and, because of that, something desperate in its calculation.

A year or so after finishing high school, I go to order a drink at the bar of a gay club and this Mr Clifford is sitting there. Many men are looking in his direction, desiring him. We glance at each other and then almost immediately look away. We have always been wary of one another: we recognised each other's fragility. That immaculate toned body, those long splendid legs, a torso without flab or fat: what did it matter? I perceived that his manliness was a pose and a performance and a pleading. He might as well have been wearing girl's pants.

•

It is dark when I rise from the bed. There is only the faint tremulous amber illumination from a streetlight. A crust of dry semen on my pubes, a fine silvery streak across my belly; in the faint light it glistens like a slug's trail.

I have a quick shower before preparing dinner.

At the exact moment a shaft of sunlight hurls through a dense thicket of cloud, five dolphins are bounding in and out of the water. They swim in a thrilling communion, the five of them leaping and diving in unison. In the brief instance that they are under the direct glare of the sun, their polished flesh is a gleaming cobalt. When they next emerge, it is into the shadow of the clouds and their skin is metallic grey.

They are only twenty-five metres or so from where we are walking along the shore, and they too are heading south. Andrea and I interrupt our leisurely stroll, our conversation, to watch them.

With their being so close, I have the sensation that their bright eyes are sizing us up, taking in the strangeness of our clumsy ambulatory forms. The ocean too is remarkably still, and it is as if the creatures have seized on the opportunity to frolic in the benign calm of the day. They slip and rise, and within a few minutes they have raced far ahead of us. We resume walking.

'You can see why I live here, can't you?'

I nod. I almost blurt out that Simon and I are thinking of buying a house up here on the south coast, with the intention of moving here permanently when he retires from work. But he and I have long ago settled on the dream of where we would live; it is the town where I have come to work for a fortnight, the town at the head of the inlet. Andrea lives seventy-five kilometres or so further north. Her town, too, is beautiful; this stretch of coast is equally unspoilt. But it is not the place that Simon and I discovered together and so it is not *our* town. In mornings of narcotic stillness that comes after sex, his head lying on my chest, the vinegary scent of his semen still on my tongue, we lazily discuss our dream of living by the Pacific Ocean, of being far away from family and friends, whom we love, but we love each other and the seclusion of being a couple more: on such mornings, we don't need anyone else in this world.

Twenty-five years ago, we were heading home from a weekend in Sydney, having decided that instead of taking the Hume Highway, that boring, straight road, we would drive back slowly, deliberately indolently, via the longer coast route. It was late summer and so it was still light when we drove that evening across the town's elegant steel bridge and parked the car outside the fish-and-chip shop at the crest of the hill above the town. We ate the greasy, delicious food sitting on the lawn behind the shops, on one side the wild infinity of the ocean, and on the other the becalmed waters of the inlet; the sun was just about to disappear behind the twin-peaked mountain.

Simon said, 'I could live here.'

When we awoke next morning and I pulled back the curtains of the colourless motel in which we were staying, the light of the sun and the ocean exploded into the room.

I turned to Simon and said, 'I could definitely live here.'

He replied, 'We could live here.'

It occurred to me his response was a question.

We nodded to each other and it became one more thing that we shared and that discreetly separated us from friends and family.

Andrea had fallen in love with the town she now lives in fifteen years ago, three years after a wearying divorce and a year after her son had left Sydney to begin a degree at a university in Canberra. Her attachment to this place is shaped by her own history. Her coming here has been a resurrection of sorts. She is as steadfastly loyal to her chosen home as Simon and I are to our dream.

She takes my hand. 'I'm sorry that I was so brutal last night. If you want to write about beauty, then you should.'

•

She had cooked a marvellous dinner—lightly grilled kingfish with a lemony vinaigrette and a pungently dressed niçoise salad. Her deck runs along the side of the house. There is no sea view but the sound from the ocean is always discernible, and sitting there one looks over the dense canopy of forest. It is alive with the music of birds and often the discordant clicking symphony of cicadas, the interruption of the deep eruct of frogs. We had finished dinner, washed up and returned to the verandah. Andrea lit a mosquito coil and the odour was first abrasive and tart and then beguiling and finally undetectable. Over dinner we had gossiped about mutual friends and spoken of our respective families and her work as a public servant, and it was only now that the subject turned to my work.

'What are you working on?' she asked excitedly. 'What's it about? There's so much that has happened and is happening.'

She started listing events on her fingers: crisis and revolution, war and bushfires, coronavirus and the political turmoil in the US.

I interrupted her inventory. 'I'm writing about beauty.'

She stared at me, puzzled. 'Is this an essay?'

Is it an essay?

'A novel,' I answered, after a pause. 'Or let's just call it a book.' We heard a faint wind stir and chop the treetops. The light was at a dull final gasp; the foliage had disappeared into the encroaching blackness of the night.

'I am writing a book about beauty.'

My declaration was too forced, too defensive; even I could hear the whine of apology within it.

Two long fingers were draped lazily around the stem of Andrea's wineglass; her fingernails were clipped short, unpainted. She was looking straight out into the nightscape, her long face illuminated by the skipping glow from a candle. The sharp, unrepentant angles of her face—the prominent forehead, the abrupt slopes of her cheeks and the arrogant point of her chin—had always been her most striking feature. Andrea had never been pretty. That word always seemed too insipid for her. One was simply arrested by the confronting power of her face. One had to look at her, to seriously study her without looking away, to appreciate that she was indeed good-looking. Even now, with age softening her and unpityingly erasing her distinctiveness—the flushed fleshiness of her cheeks, the stark grey of the deliberately short crop which had replaced the thick straight falls and folds of black hair that had accentuated the boldness of her facial features—she still carried herself with the confident aplomb of someone who was accustomed to being looked at.

And with looking at her, I was emboldened.

'I am writing a book about beauty. I want it to be simple, almost straightforward in its intent. If I were a poet, it would be easier. Or if I were a musician. It is harder to distil beauty into prose. The novel is treacherous.'

She sipped from her glass. A globule of wine slipped onto her lip and she wiped at it. I discerned once more, as I did in that moment I first laid eyes on her, decades ago, the oblong slash of her wide mouth. Now, as then, her full lips were painted scarlet.

She turned to me. 'Why is it treacherous?'

'It is a siren's call, always whispering in my ear, "You can change the world."'

'And you no longer want to change the world?'

The air was still, and the sun was gone. The horizon had merged into the night. There was the convulsive flutter of a moth, the crackle from the candle's flame, and the rustle of some nocturnal creature foraging through invisible under-growth. Faint, the most distant of sounds, was the rumble of the surf from the far end of the peninsula.

'No,' I answered finally. 'I don't want to change the world.' I reached for a cigarette. 'That doesn't mean I don't want things about this world to change.'

'But you want to leave the actual work of change to others, is that it?'

The pomposity of her response made me laugh out loud. The lighter snapped, the blue flame shot forth and ignited the dry tobacco. The smoke filled my mouth and rushed down to the depths of my lungs. My laughter, and the smoke, filled the deck.

I gestured, letting the arc from the glow of my cigarette take in the universe.

'You asked me why the novel is treacherous, and I am trying to explain it to you.' I was sitting up straight now, the laughter gone. 'I know that there is so much happening that should concern me.' I shut my eyes and recited her list. 'Crisis and revolution, war and bushfires, the pandemic and the shifts in the superpowers. All that and more. But there is nothing I can offer anymore to illuminate any of that. And these days, when I read novels that are all crisis and revolution, war and bushfires, I am nauseated by their arrogance and their naivety. Every bloody novelist sounds the same now, whether they are American or Austrian or Angolan or Andalusian or Australian. All the same cant, all the same desire to shape the world to their academic whims and aspirations. All this compassion and all this outrage and all this empathy and all this sorrow and all this fear and all this moralising and not one sentence of surprise in any of it.' I puffed furiously at my cigarette. 'Not one moment of beauty. I don't want to write that fucking novel.'

And then I add, emphatically: 'I'm fucking sick of that novel.'

Andrea's hands are deep in her jacket pockets. A chill has risen. I get up to grab my jumper from inside.

She looks up at me. 'Should?'

I don't understand.

'Should,' she repeats. 'You said there is so much happening that *should* concern you. That implies it no longer does.'

A certain precipice: it is there before me, conjured by her questioning. I know exactly how to retreat from plummeting over its edge; I have been doing it for years now. I can agree that indeed the world is hierarchical and unjust, hazardous and ugly; I have been agreeing to it for a generation now, and increment by increment and timid sentence by timid sentence I have been substituting moralism for imagination.

I do not retreat. I look down, into the void, and the urge to jump, which is the desire to leap and to flee, overwhelms me.

I look up, into the sky. A faint iridescence of cloud veils the low half-moon; the play between light and reflection whisks the droplets of ice into a spray that capers across the night. The budding moon has reilluminated the world and now on the distant horizon of the ocean there is a shimmering glow, a pulse of silver-blue light. And in the plum-black sky the triumphant brilliance of the flickering stars; unlike those muted by the mechanical tyranny of the city, their fire pulses through the firmament. Not order but variation; and not injustice but nature; and not hazard but the infinite possibilities of accident and chaos: untameable and sublime and frightening and exhilarating beauty.

Are my eyes equal fire as I turn to Andrea? 'Of course, I don't want to change it,' I exclaim. 'I love this world.'

It is as if I have slapped her. There is a long silence between us, disturbed only by the rustle of cloth as she tightens her shawl around her body, the cooing of some marsupial in the bush below.

'We have grown old,' she announces suddenly. 'And you have grown soft.'

I am absolutely still, but it is as if my soul inside my body is mimicking the motions of withdrawal; I can feel the pull on the muscles of my calves and the stretch of the tendons in my feet as I prepare to step back from the cliff's edge. I force my spirit to remain steadfast.

'Maybe I have. I am certainly tired of outrage and anger. That's not a world I want to inhabit any longer. And yes, I am happy in my life and home with Simon. I won't apologise for that.'

Her response is swift and furious. 'I'm not asking you to apologise for it.'

I am not in a mood to be conciliatory. 'Yes, you are.'

She is visibly shaken by my response. Her body tightens and then is released when a flush of anger animates her face.

'Nothing illuminating can come from contentment, Christo. If you are happy with the beauty of the world'—and she has snarled in her enunciation of that word, *beauty*—'then stop writing novels and leave it to people who know suffering and oppression and anger and know that beauty is not enough.'

'No.'

'What?' And now her outrage is not feigned: it is real, it is ferocious.

'I am not going to stop writing.'

She sculls the last of her wine and rises. I hear the clink of the wine bottle, the slamming of the fridge door. She returns and sloshes wine into my glass before refilling hers equally haphazardly. She is standing, looking into the night.

'I think we have to rip the pen out of the white man's hand,' she says.

And I have leapt into the great emptiness and I am flying. 'Enough with that moronic, undergraduate sloganeering. You can rip the pen or keyboard from my white man's hand, but what are you proposing in its stead? The perpetual adolescent whine of victimhood? How more tedious can the contemporary novel become? You can't deify suffering as integral to art and then at the same moment demand safety as a right. I go into a bookshop these days and it is as if the shelves are filled with the agonised and narcissistic rantings of teenagers.'

I look up at her. And there is something Homeric and grand in her straight-backed virtue, in the dramatic lines and arcs of her face. The grey nimbus of her hair advances the heroism of her bearing. Her very carriage is a rebuke to me. Age has not softened her at all.

She sits down. She takes a sip of wine.

'You can't write about beauty,' she says calmly. 'You don't have that talent.'

And now she bores deeper.

'You have a particular skill: to take the contemporary world and create characters that articulate the thoughts and fears we don't dare speak aloud. That's the most powerful aspect of your writing, that emotional and unrepentant honesty. It's truly exhilarating, and even though you've been doing it for years, that rawness doesn't feel diluted.'

She now turns to me. Her coal-black eyes are still cold.

'But that rawness is also your greatest weakness. You're shit at metaphor, and there's nothing elegiac in your sentences and in your rhythms. Reflect the world back at us, Christo, that's your talent. Leave beauty to the poets.'

Humiliation is a flame that ignites within and then detonates; it scorches my flesh. My skin is on fire. I distil my wrath and my hurt by focusing on everything I despise or scorn in Andrea. If this might seem an act that requires determined meditation, that needs the luxury of time, I assert that it is not so. That is the wonderment of a friendship that has lasted as long as ours has done; the strength of friendship, as it is with family, is measured in tolerance. When I speak—and I do not require the stimulant of nicotine or of alcohol; my wineglass and cigarettes are now untouched—it is with a measured and unhurried firmness.

'That may be so, Andrea, I might not have the talent required. I will find out in the doing, I suppose. That's part of the craft of being a writer.'

She stirs as if to interrupt, and by the tremulous smile on her face I suspect an apology will be forthcoming. I do not let her speak.

'I don't care about politics anymore, and truth be told I don't think I have for a long time. I'm tired of being angry all the time. I could cope with the anger when I was younger, and maybe I'm fooling myself and my memory is false, but I also remember lots of joy and laughter and celebration in our politics. Fuck!' And as I release the expletive, I slap the table, startling her. 'Even at the height of AIDS, even amid that tragedy, we fucking laughed and danced. That isn't what politics is anymore. It's just one long endless and wearying moan. And our secret terror is that most of us know we have nothing really to moan about. Not here, not in this place.'

Again, she jerks forwards, needing to interject, and again I continue regardless, my voice rising as I concentrate my words to achieve the effect I desire: that she undergoes the same shame I have just experienced.

'I look at us and I wonder what all those years of our anger have been for. You had a good partner in Seb; he is a good man. So he wasn't as educated as you wanted him to be, he wasn't quick-witted. But he was kind and he was generous. Yet it wasn't enough, was it?'

I turn to her. She is looking away, her chin raised now in stony anger.

'Don't you think there's something masochistic and adolescent in the left politics we were part of? In feminism? In all that queer shit? All that anti-colonialist lamentation? We were parsing, parsing, parsing until we were left with nothing at all.'

And now, the realisation of what I am going to say dawns before I utter the words; my anger is depleting.

'I'm glad I've got Simon, someone I love. I'm glad I have a home. I'm glad I live in a nation that doesn't terrorise me.'

When I turn to her this time, I am not a combatant.

'How long have we got, Andrea? Twenty years, if we're lucky?' I rap the underside of the table with my knuckles. 'Thirty, if we're really fortunate?'

There is a bang and then a scratching and scrambling on the shingles of the roof above. A possum has leapt from a tree onto the house.

'Both of us know how quickly time goes. Think about Matteo. I remember holding him when he was only a few days old. That was twenty years ago.' I click my fingers. 'It went by so very quickly.'

The mention of her son has stirred us both. Andrea is scratching at the base of her glass with her nails, as if she is considering whether to drink the last of the wine. Then, with a swift and furious motion, she lifts the glass to her mouth and swallows.

'You've never forgiven me for leaving Seb.'

I sigh in genuine surrender.

'That's not fair, Andrea. I supported you throughout the separation and divorce.'

'But you think I made a mistake?'

In the pause, the faint lowing of the waves.

'Yes,' I answer. 'I think you made a mistake.'

She stands up, her shawl still knotted firmly around her, and there are flecks of light and planes of dark shadow across her resolute form. I am again reminded of an ancient deity; a caryatid.

'Will you clean up?'

I nod.

'Goodnight.'

There is no embrace, no kiss. I smoke a cigarette while her shadow is visible in the smoky glass of the bathroom window, the jerking motions of her flossing and brushing her teeth. I carry the glasses to the sink, wash the dishes, dry them. I do a quick sweep of the deck and then I grab my jacket, turn on the sensor light, and descend the stairs. I walk towards the sound of the ocean.

Andrea's home sits two blocks back from the sea and there is a narrow path between two of her neighbours' houses that leads down to the beach. In the moonlight, there is a shimmering ashen film across the water. As soon as I feel the crunch of sand beneath my feet, I grasp the firm branch of a coastal wattle for balance and remove my shoes and socks. I roll up the bottoms of my jeans and walk to the water's edge. The tide is only just beginning its retreat and the sand is damp and cold. When the first dash of water rolls across my naked feet I shiver, but I stay fixed, unmoving, feel the pleasure of my feet sinking into the silt. The roiling vapour of the Milky Way unfurls above me. Around it and beyond it the stars are ablaze.

I know that sleep will be hard tonight. Here, on the beach, the only sound the rapturous bellowing of the ocean, Andrea's cutting words don't matter. The eternal motion of the waves mocks the petty fragility of my ego. Yet I know that once I slip into the bed she has made up for me in her spare room, her derision of my writing will return to peck at me. Steadily, the damp grit of the sand rolling beneath my feet, the waves splashing and teasing, I walk the length of the beach and I don't think about our argument and I don't dwell on her reproach. Instead, I focus on the task of making Paul's wife, Jenna, and his son, Neal, real and concrete.

Creating Paul has been simple. I have had the voice and the body and the persona of an actor to be the mould from which I have first cast the character. With Jenna, I know her face. It is a face, and also a beauty, formed in the cauldron of Scottish sombreness and Irish verve with a dash of English delicacy. A prole face and a hard face but also one capable of a bracing vigour and cheek. Jenna has smoked too many cigarettes, and though she has tempered her smoking now, she knows that she will never quit. She started drinking with her mother at twelve. At fourteen, her first boyfriend, older, nineteen and already an apprentice and a wage-earner, introduced her to grass. By the time she was seventeen she was using amphetamines daily. She's smart, and she has always known she was smart, but she needed to leave home as soon as she could, no longer able to bear the histrionic bitterness of her mother. For Jenna's mother hated the world. Hated men for abandoning her. Hated bosses for exploiting her. Hated her children for defying her. Jenna knew that her mother had a point. Yes, Jenna's dumb-fuck father had left her with two infants to raise on her own. Yes, employers took advantage of her need and always underpaid her. Yes, Jenna and her brother rarely cleaned up around the house. All this was true; but also true was the fact that their mother was a terrible drunk and a perpetual victim who had never grown up. Everything was someone else's fault. She was never to blame. Jenna knew that she *must* not grow up to become her mother.

I know Jenna. She quits school as soon as she can so she can work and save. She leaves home at eighteen, moves from Melbourne to Queensland, and by twenty has made a small fortune dealing drugs. To escape the tyranny and lazy misogyny of the Surfers Paradise underworld, she buys a one-way ticket to Los Angeles. She has always wanted to see Hollywood. She is attractive, unafraid, and in that enormous—too enormous—city, she uses her body to survive. She marries a closeted real estate agent whose parents are from Ecuador. He supplies her with cocaine and facilitates her getting a green card. She gives him cover with his family and supplies him with rent boys she knows from drinking at West Hollywood bars. Drunk one night, impetuous and brave from the cocaine, and anxious because of her rapidly depleting finances—LA is expensive, so much more expensive than Surfers Paradise—she tells an attractive, elegant older man that, yes, she'll do a porn scene in his next picture. She does one more. And then another. She and Miguel finalise the divorce. She signs a contract with a studio. She meets Paul, and he makes her laugh. And for him, her honesty is revelatory. One stoned warm Los Angeles night, a party raging on the beach, techno music slamming into the night, he recalls how, on the set of a bisexual scene they were filming, she got into an argument with another actress about Spielberg's *The Color Purple*. Jenna said it was shit and the other woman, nodding, said, 'Yeah, right, the book was better.' And Paul, laughing, continues, 'And you said, "Nah, the book was shit as well."' Shaking his head in astonishment, earnest now, he says, 'And I thought, Wow, you Aussies don't hide behind bullshit. We Americans go on about honesty and our feelings and being straight talkers, but you Aussies really are like that.' He adds, 'That's when I knew I was falling in love with you.'

A necessary aside here, as I approach the rocks at the north end of the beach. Some years ago, I was invited to a writers' festival in New York City. Caro, a friend from Australia, was the festival director, and she invited Simon and I to hear Richard Ford interviewing Shirley Hazzard. Adoring the work of both writers, we accepted gratefully. But Ford's questions were lazy and uninspiring, and Hazzard seemed alternately anxious and bored. Afterwards, as all around us writers from across the English-speaking world were lining up to compliment these two literary giants, Simon and I decided to head off and grab some dinner. Caro saw us leaving and, beaming, she said, 'Wasn't that fantastic?' I must have grimaced, for she asked, 'You didn't think so?' Simon, always direct and never obsequious, said, 'It was really dull.' I had to agree. And Caro laughed and said, 'I've been living in the States too long.' She hugged us both. 'It's the one thing I miss about Australia: that people don't bullshit you.'

It seems right that I have Paul deliver a version of these words to Jenna. And it seems right that he is unafraid of this cultural trait, that it intrigues and charms him. It is the thread of veracity that gives authority and authenticity to the lovers I am sculpting.

There is one other thing I know about Jenna: she is a Christian. When she fell pregnant to Paul, she considered having an abortion. It would have been her third. Instead, she decided to give up drugs and keep the child. She returned to the calming rituals of her ancestral faith. Jenna doesn't care for intellectual justifications of doctrine and she is uninterested in the cosmography of the Bible. If challenged, she would readily admit that she thinks vast portions of the books within it are nonsense, as is the notion of an external heaven and hell. Jenna *knows* that they are real and here on earth. But she believes that it is only through prayer and the loving intercession of Virgin and Son that she and Paul have given up drugs.

Does Paul share her beliefs? He might call himself an atheist, but I do wonder if anyone born in America can truly be said to be so. Even their most vehement atheists seem evangelical. Black and white, native and immigrant, the whole nation seems to me to be drunk on puritanism. He might claim to be an unbeliever, but Paul shares his countrymen's fearful veneration of the Lord of judgement and vengeance.

There is a melancholy sadness buried deep within Paul, even though he believes he lives a fortunate life with his wife and son, in a beautiful home in a country free of the chaos of his birthplace. He works hard, and money has always been tight, but he knows he is blessed.

I have reached the rocks. I settle on an isolated outcrop that, in the darkness, resembles a flat-topped mountain emerging out of the sea of sand. In the time it has taken me to walk the length of the beach the earth has tilted; the moon is further to the west and the stars seem close enough to touch. There is also now a rising swell visible on the silver crests of the waves in the distance, and a reverberant emulation to the waves as they break on the shore, as if wanting to defy the manifest law of the tide. I glimpse Paul. Sometimes, when he can't sleep, he stealthily rises from their bed, pulls on a T-shirt and shorts, and drives down to the beach. He sits on a rock exactly like this one, cold and solitary, and looks out at the same ocean, the waters advancing then receding, in one motion touching the borders of his birthplace and in the next kissing the fringes of his new home. The eternal cycle calms him. I will have him drive down to the rocks on the night before he has to leave for Brisbane to fly to Los Angeles. He will inhale the rhythms and spray of the waves and he will be certain that he will indeed return.

I leap off the rock and tramp back across the sand, following the line of the tide. My feet have grown accustomed to the cold of the ocean.

I have Paul, and I am closer now to Jenna. I need to make flesh and spirit of their son. Even when the idea for this story first came to me, stirred by the emotions and rapture of Van Morrison's song, and wanting to extract Paul Carrigan from the flat and ugly pixilated brume of the VHS tape, I knew that their son would be called Neal and that he would be a good man. I was in my early forties then, and by that age all the furious anger of the past had begun to ebb. I no longer desired to be at war over my sexuality, and I had long abandoned the Manichean simplifications of progressive politics. There is not one particular face or person I conjure to create Neal; rather, he is the measure in a duet, an essential peace between the ostinato pounding of a drum and the meandering noodling of a horn. The drums are the boys in high school whom I feared and desired. Apprehensive of what I assumed to be their blithe masculinity, I arrogantly decried them as thick-skulled, as barbaric, as ignorant and parochial. In turn, made insecure by my immersion in books, they responded with contempt: I was the poofter wog. They reduced me to those ugly stereotypes, and I hated them. Yet now, thinking back on those young men, I also recall their resolute loyalty to one another. They were not only cruel. So: they are the drum.

The horns are my nephews and the sons of my friends; all adults now. I like these young men. Their bravado is measured, and gentler than that of the boys I went to high school with. Yet their masculinity is straightforward. I am thinking of two nephews in particular, whose strength comes from their calm and from the fact that they still labour with their hands. Such a potent phrase—*labour with their hands*—it is also one that occasions suspicion nowadays, seen as idolising some atavistic notions of work and of men. But I have always been mistrustful of soft hands, including my own. Though my own labours and my own choices have exiled me from the working-class life I was born into—only the bourgeoisie have soft hands, and only the bourgeoisie believe that rough hands belong only to men; my mother's loving touch on my cheek is harsh: her hands are rough and calloused from her work on the assembly lines—my love for the bruised and scarred and hardened palm and fingers of a hand reconnects me to this past. It is a prejudice, I freely admit this, but I could not love a man with soft hands. Simon doesn't have soft hands. His father was a builder's labourer and he taught his son to hammer and saw and drill and lift and heave from childhood. When Simon touches me, when his hands trace my spine, when they rest on my arse, when they cradle my face, they scratch even as they offer balm.

Neal has Simon's hands. He is fair and tall and kind and strong, just like my nephews. And whether I have imagined it as a film or play or novel, one thing that has remained constant is that *Sweet Thing* always opens with Paul and his son retiling the cabin roof. We first see Neal labouring.

The other thing I have always known about Neal is that he is wise beyond his twenty years. It is not an intellectual or schooled wisdom. He would never think to be unkind or dismissive to someone over abstract principle: his wisdom takes the form of empathy. It is a quality that I wish I had had as a young man, but few of us are capable of such acumen in our youth. I think Neal has had to learn compassion from an early age because Jenna and Paul made the decision not to lie to him about their past. They didn't want to live their lives in terror of the infinite portals of the digital age. Neal was fourteen when they explained to him that for a time they had worked in pornography. Once, six or so months after that evening, he typed the pseudonym his mother had used into a search engine. He could not bear to click on any of the video links. He instinctively understood that to see his mother naked and used by other men would in some sense damn him. I am not sure if Neal has any religious feeling, but I think even those of us most adamantly secular know that there is a truth to the notion of damnation: that there are acts and experiences that can corrupt us, that can steal from us the possibility of ever attaining peace. He never searched for that name again.

He did the same with Paul's screen name a few weeks later. He was puzzled by how many gay pornographic films his father had made, but he did not feel the nausea and danger that overcame him when he hesitated over the links to his mother's films. He watched a few minutes of his father sucking off a man with detachment and some confusion. He was glad that he was neither aroused nor disgusted. He switched off the computer. The next day, as Paul was driving him to school, he asked his father, 'Are you gay?' Paul stopped the car and explained to his son that he was bisexual, but that for the longest time now he and Jenna had been emotionally monogamous. 'Sometimes we stray; that's kinda normal. But it's very rare, I promise you that. We would never put our marriage and you at risk.' He cautiously placed his arm around his son's shoulder. Neal did not push him away. 'Your mother and I will never stop being in love with each other, and we will never, ever stop being so proud of our son. You know that, right, buddy?' Neal had nodded, for he did know. But still, he wanted to understand the confusion that he had felt watching his father have sex with another man.

'But why did you do gay porn?'

'Well, son, it paid better.' Then Paul laughed, a little bitterly. 'And for the most part, the guys shooting gay porn were nicer than the pricks doing the straight porn. Not always, but more often.'

That made less sense. But Neal could not quite formulate the questions that followed from his father's observations. Instead, he offered a weak smile and hugged the schoolbag that was resting on his lap. I'm too young, he thought. I'm too young to understand all this.

Paul leaned across and kissed his son. He started the car.

I sit on a desolate, sandy knoll at the end of the beach and I use my handkerchief to dust down my feet and ankles. Paul will drive to the ocean to find peace. Jenna will visit a small

Catholic church in one of the highland towns when she needs succour. And Neal will find haven in the shed, measuring and sawing and carving and polishing and burnishing the hard redwood that he is using to build a boat. Knowing this about them now, I can return to Andrea's house and the possibility of sleep.

Before I climb into the bed, I search for my notebook in my rucksack and I write their names. Next to Paul I write the word, *Ocean*. Next to Jenna's, *Church*. And next to Neal's, *Shed*.

When I lay my head on the pillow, Andrea's words return and with them that knotting of my stomach. I am not capable of writing beauty. But the words do not terrorise me. I am astonished. The next moment is my yawning, my awakening, and the touch of the bright morning sun scuffing at my face.

●

'I'm sorry that I was so brutal last night. If you want to write about beauty, then you should.'

I look down at Andrea's hand gripping mine. We are on the same beach that I walked along last night. It wears a starkly different aspect in daylight. The rocks that had seemed black and menacing now reveal brilliant seams of saffron and ebony. There had been a claustrophobic intensity to the darkened beach; the extravagant, glimmering stars had seemed so low in the heavens. Now, near noon, the sky seemed to have been tossed an impossible distance beyond us, its canopy vast and infinite. The ocean without end meets the infinite sky. Andrea's hand is moist, as is mine. I bring her hand to my lips, and I kiss it. Then I can release it.

'Don't worry about it,' I say. 'I apologise as well. It was a silly argument.'

She swoops and picks up a pebble, its smooth grey surface marked by what looks like a greenish-blue cross. She rubs it against her jacket's sleeve and then puts it into her pocket.

'I wouldn't characterise it as silly,' she says, turning to me, her face serious. 'I think it's been so long since we have spent time together that we rushed the conversation. I had no idea that you no longer consider yourself left-wing. It came as a surprise.'

I hope that my silence doesn't appear mutinous. The truth is that I am craving to return to the splendid house I have rented, with its wide-open deck, its view of the inlet and its glimpse of the ocean. I am tired of talk.

I kick my bare feet into weak, crashing waves; an arc of wet sand drizzles the path ahead.

'I don't know if I have abandoned being left-wing,' I begin tentatively. And then, breathing in the invigorating blast of wind that is now racing headlong towards us from around the cove, I continue. 'But I think now there are worlds and experiences beyond politics that also matter.'

'So, everything is not political?'

'God, no!'

She stops, is looking out across the water. 'It is so bloody beautiful here.'

Beside her, I nod.

'Christo,' she says, and I hear the tiredness in her voice, 'I don't know who I would be without my anger.'

My impulse, which I know I must resist, is to blurt out, 'Why should politics only be anger? Why must it always be outrage and vengeance?' And then I think of where she has worked the last two decades. Shelters. The majority of my friend's life has been spent working to give shelter. Women and children unluckily bonded to savage men. Five hard years in a community in the outback. The last decade and a half with asylum seekers and refugees seeking papers and a final destination. She was surrounded by anger. She breathed it in daily, was made exultant by it and was galvanised by it. But it is a bitter diet. I keep my mouth shut and stare with her out to the sea.

'I thought it was a reprimand, what you said about beauty. It hurt.' She raises her hand, still not looking at me, so that I won't interrupt. 'I know you didn't mean it that way. You have no idea how much I envy you. My god, I would love to be a writer. I want to be a writer. It's a dream I've carried with me all my life. And in a few years I'll be sixty, and I've done fuck all about it. And so, when I asked what you were writing about and your answer seemed so cavalier—*I'm writing about beauty*—I was furious.' She turns to me now. 'I was jealous.'

There is a very subtle pleading in her eyes, something almost coquettish in her anxious mien, as if I am a much older man from whom she awaits a gift. I smile feebly, and return my gaze to the horizon. In the distance, there is a becalmed slick of water; the blue of this portion of sea is lighter, fainter than the dark hues all around it, and a white bird—possibly an osprey or maybe only a seagull; it is too far out to tell—sits contentedly, bobbing on the gentle swell. I can't imagine my friend as a writer, certainly not a writer of fiction. I don't think Andrea could ever stop looking over her shoulder as she wrote, wondering what the world—her friends, her colleagues, her clients, her son, her ex-husband, her family, her mentors and her idols and her enemies—would be thinking of what she was writing and the characters she was creating. I don't think Andrea could ever stop herself from second-guessing her reader's reaction. It is cruel, but I know that Andrea's writing would be pallid and timid and limp.

'You can always write,' I say. 'That's the great thing about both writing and painting: you can start at any age.'

She beams. My affirmation, though a lie, is sincere.

After a leisurely and delicious lunch at a cafe overlooking the mouth of the river, we stop in her town's bookshop and graze the shelves. I find a new edition of Yourcenar's *Memoirs of Hadrian* and I ask Andrea if she has read it. She shakes her head and I offer to buy it for her, declaring that the writing is some of the finest crafted I have ever read. Just as I reach the counter she calls out, 'Oh, I really wanted to read this book; I've heard terrific things about it. Lots of our friends love it.'

I look over at the book she is holding. It is non-fiction, something American, something earnest and angry. I return the Yourcenar to the shelf and take the American book. 'I'll buy you this one.'

It's a release, the drive home. The sun warms my naked arms. I play no music and I listen to no podcast; I watch the forests and the farmlands, those patches of concentrated green and tame yellow, go by. I follow the serpentine winding of the peninsula and cross the bridge over the Tuross River. The water is still; the narrowing band of white silt forms the firmest of borders. A flock of white cockatoos tear across the sky, heading into the inland forest. And then, moments later, a diagonal of black cockatoos follows until, in a moment of splendid riposte and a miracle of shared instinct, the black birds abruptly change direction and sweep up the river towards the sea.

It is still afternoon when I reach the house. I rush in, grab my bathers and a towel, apply some sunscreen and drive straight down to the beach. The water is freezing, and for a moment the shock of it scalds my skin. I resist the pummel of the elements and keep diving under. In a few strokes, my teeth have stopped their chattering and I am swimming in the deep.

The inlet flows into the ocean through a narrow entrance formed by two artificially constructed spits. Each long wall consists of giant quarry rocks, except for the furthest tip of each buttress, where enormous concrete dolosse, their forms imitating giant anchors, have been sealed into the rock face; the stone, scored by sun and sea and salt, has worn to a brilliant ochre colour. On days when the wind is raging and insistent, the mouth there has a portent of a hellish gate, with the pounding, untameable waves beating on the fortifications. Once past the mouth of this narrow ingress, the waters subside and, though the squall blasts across the rocks, the inlet sea is imperturbable.

Today, the ocean is also peaceful. I had mechanically, impatiently, brushed my teeth as soon as I had awoken in the morning, and I am dressed in the T-shirt I had slept in last night. I march along the boardwalk, walk onto the protected cove of the inner arm of the inlet's entrance, fling off my sandals, strip off my T-shirt and, braving the chill in the air, refusing to be cowed, I plunge into the sea. The water is immediately icy, and it flays at my skin. But my strokes, never graceful or stately, are powerful and charging, and when my lungs demand breath and I break the surface, I turn around and the beach is distant, and my feet cannot touch ground. There is one other swimmer paddling near the shore. I lie on my back and release a defiant and exhilarant roar.

For some years now I have been concerned about my expulsion from the world of dreams. I know that they have not vanished from my life completely, and there are many mornings when I awake and there are snatches of colour or shape just receding from my consciousness. Sometimes it is a face that is at the edge of vanishing; at other times a sentiment or an emotion affects the whole of the day, yet remains resistant to naming and precise categorisation. But the actual content and visual sweep of the dreams, the images and the tableaux, they themselves have begun to disappear. Yet for the last few nights, I have recalled my dreams.

I have never been the kind of writer, or the kind of person, who is diligent in recording and imitating the fantastical life of the unconscious; and certainly, I have never thought of dreams as auguries. Yet I respect the fathomless depths of that world, and when I was very young, the disappearance into fancy and illusion and whimsy were essential to joy.

Even as a child, I recognised that there was an integral connection between this world of imagination and speculation, and those subterranean spheres named Hades or the netherworld or even Hell—an understanding gleaned from the petrifying terrors of my nightmares and by the shaming, disturbing visions of desire: if we accept the Monotheistic and the Feminist injunctions and warnings against lust, then we must also concede that there is Original Sin. I know from my own dreams, my own fantasias and even the coded sketches I would secretly write and draw in my school exercise books, that there is no such thing as an innocent childhood. Awed and filled with trepidation about this other world—and to some extent I still am, for I still approach it with caution, and I whisper prayers and have a plethora of superstitious tics and rituals to ward off destruction—I nevertheless was fascinated by and drawn to it. Isn't this in part what made me straighten in the cinema seat when I saw Jean Marais as Orpheus approach the mirror in Cocteau's film? The underworld is the homeland of the imagination.

Though my swimming strokes are not elegant, they are strong, and it is in water where I feel most content with and proud of my body. On land, I enumerate all my physical faults with an assiduous, if not corrosive, determination. On land, I deem my body weak. But in the water I marvel at the ability of this body to master motion and direction, to form communion with wave and with water. And the sea is on the other side of the mirror; it is a world in which the ground beneath has fallen away. It is no accident, therefore, that as I slog and beat and play with the water, I am thinking of dreams.

Since being here, at this place by the ocean—and separated from another netherworld, the dictatorial and bureaucratic digital world of the computer and the phone—I have awakened with clear memories of my dreams. The last few mornings I have risen with recollections that form stories and form scenes. Even those which have disturbed me have also thrilled me with their immediacy, their vitality. I have not been exiled from that world. I can approach the mirror.

It is not only the unconscious dream; it is also the return to the means by which memory and recollection have been increasingly present and vivid these last few days, assuming real force and potency in my waking life. These moments that break the temporal veil between the past and the present might be even more significant and inspiring for a writer and an artist than the unfathomable, sprawling canvases of the imagination in sleep.

This morning, striding down the boardwalk, I was fourteen again. I am returned to sitting alone on the bus. All the other students—for it is three-thirty in the afternoon and we are all on our way home from school—are sitting together, jostling each other, laughing and teasing and making fart noises, and the girls are whispering about the boys and the boys are showing off to the girls, when one of the older boys, large and mean, sneers at me, 'Why you sitting alone, Bruno?'

He then pinches his nose and answers his own question. 'I know. 'Cause you smell.'

The other kids on the bus laugh.

On the boardwalk, the memory flashes past and that old hurt is gone. The emotion I return to now is gratitude. For just as the teasing laughter was fading and the girls were returning to gossiping and the boys were returning to bragging, someone plonked himself down next to me. A boy in my class called Clark.

It must have been summer or late spring, because we are all in short sleeves or have our jumper sleeves pushed up. Clark had very white skin.

A woman walking an eager labrador puppy passed me, and I stopped to pat the dog. The woman and I exchange cordial greetings and my thoughts of Clark were gone.

His face returns to me as I swim. On the walk back to the house, I remember more. He becomes solid and real. All other inspirations for Neal—my nephews, the boys I feared yet also hungered for in high school—have been tangential and oblique. The kindness of that small gesture, Clark sitting next to me on the bus: from that seed I will germinate Neal.

It is not yet mid-morning and the gum trees and spindly shrubs that hug the road that runs alongside the boardwalk cast shadows, and in their shade the air is nippy, occasionally piercing. I have draped the wet towel around my neck and my skin there has become ice from the damp. Yet the jolt of discomfort is not unpleasant; if anything, it offers a piquant reminder of the sensual pleasures of the world around me. I round a bend and suddenly the bright sun is tumbling across the inlet, the luminosity such that the town seems held in a fine opaque haze, cradled in the very source of the light. A pod of pelicans is gliding smoothly on the water and then, in unison, there is a wild flapping and calling and they shoot across the inlet, making their way to the summoning horizon, gradually and triumphantly gaining speed and height as they soar. The waters are their highways. They follow the bend of the inlet's mouth and, on reaching the open sea, they rise higher and begin to recede from view. My heart is pounding with an electric momentum, and the joy I feel banishes the cold. The sun's embrace, which holds the town, is also holding me; I am cocooned in its warmth. As I trudge up the hill to the house, a delicate sheen of perspiration across my shoulders and back, I offer a prayer of gratitude. To the sun? To the world? To God? Possibly all of these. The love and contentment I am experiencing reminds me of Andrea, and I am chastened by the recollection of her unsmiling, wounded face. I want to be reconciled to her, out of another form of love, which is the love of friendship; we share so much, including memories that bind our old age to our youth, a rare gift; we are also not as unlike as the pettiness of the other night's argument suggested. Yet, I love the world and I don't believe that it owes me forgiveness. It is an exhilarating realisation and my gratitude swells.

At the crest of the hill, just before turning into the lane that leads to the house, I halt and look back down the slope. The tide is out, and the mangroves rise craggy and knitted from the muddy embankment. The water's surface is a clear jade; underneath, the shadows of the oyster beds are visible. The fierce sunlight bounds off the girders and the upper rails of the bridge. And the infinite ocean is an azure glory. As the sun cradles all this aspect, at the edge of my vision is the verdant frame of the eucalypts and forest she-oaks. The world is as beautiful as I have ever witnessed it.

I offer one more silent thanks.

The moment when Clark resisted the pull of peer oppro-brium and sat next to me on the bus could not have been the first time we talked. Surely, we must have exchanged a few words before then. But in this release of memory occasioned by my retreat from both the city and the screen, that afternoon on the bus is the most present and powerful of recollections. I make it our first meeting. Integral to this freedom I am experiencing over the last few days is the reminder of the corporeal force of memory. The boy—for we are only thir-teen or fourteen—sits down next to me, and I recall the scrape of his creased white shirt on my skin. And there is a distinct and faintly unpleasant odour as well; of sweat, salty and fusty. His face is surprisingly agreeable. I realise this only now, in returning to memory, for I don't think I thought him attractive back then. I was still enchanted by the cheerful masculinity of Stavros, of my father and my uncles and their friends: a sunnily unabashed Mediterranean maleness. It had only been a few months since we moved house from the city to the suburbs, and my understanding of the world was still that of the migrant working-class streets I had grown up in. At night, my hand between my legs, it was Stavros's odours I was inhaling. Yet Clark had indeed been a comely youth, I recognise now, and it was only the casual meanness of the schoolyard that made us all blind to his winsome appearance and his generous spirit. He had a particularly hurtful nickname, to do with his unfortunate habit of sneezing and blowing his nose on the sleeves of his jumper or his shirt. Again, it is only now, returning as an adult to these scenes, that I realise all of this takes place in the late spring months, when the school year is nearly over, and the child is clearly burdened with hay fever. Even that day, sitting next to me, I am disgusted by the yellowish snot dripping from his nostril. He snorts, swipes his arm across his nose. From the back of the bus, one of the older girls calls out the nickname. The other students point and jeer. Clark sits placidly beside me, a weary grin on his face.

They distrusted us both because we were working class. I didn't understand that then. Working class: such a loaded and beleaguered term, such a convoluted history! The tussle over ownership of that designation is ongoing, even by those—left, right, in the middle and even outside the fucking circle—who argue the term is redundant or corrupted, but I will not be ensnared by the temptations of consciousness, of underlining and capitalising and rarefying. The antipodean world in which I grew up didn't have the violence and exclusions of class and caste that one finds in Europe or in Asia. If I only comprehend the cause of the other children's suspicion of me now, decades later, then it must have been equally indistinct to those who taunted me and Clark, who mocked me as Bruno—that was the smallness of that past world, in which all wog boys were called Bruno and all wog girls were Maria—and him as Snotface. If he and I had been reassuringly handsome, and certainly if we had ability in sports, I think we may have found some accept-ance. The distrust was merely superficial. In Europe and in Asia, class hatred is manifested deep in the body, running in the blood, and so feels as instinctual as racism; and, as with the racism, there is a literal physical recoil of the flesh when classes bump against one another. I was a migrant's son newly arrived in the suburbs from the mysterious and dangerous inner city. This was just before the dawn of gentrification: a young boy in my class, Peter, asked me in all seriousness, 'What was it like growing up in a brothel?' He had taken his parents' dismissal of the city as full of whorehouses and gambling dens as gospel. And Clark's mother was unmarried, and they lived in state housing. To my young eyes, their home was indistinguishable from all the other houses in the street, no different from the bland brick-veneer house that my parents had just bought; it was not the tower blocks I was familiar with from the city. Yet just the whispered knowledge that it was a 'commission house' was enough to set it apart. Clark sitting down next to me on the bus was a gallant and fraternal act of kindness. I will insist on this. He must, however, have also had an inherent sympathy for what connected us, an instinct that guided his kindness and his decision.

I wonder now why I didn't fall in love with Clark. The answer to that might be quite simple: I had more need of a friend. Our skins did touch, and the warmth of his skin against mine is undoubtedly a sensual memory. Perhaps it was a risk neither of us was prepared to take at that time.

He was proudly protective of his mother, as I was of mine. This too we had in common.

If Clark were a fiction, I would kiss him hard on the lips. I would not rewrite his smell, his scent. I would uphold it as pungent and sharp and even a little offensive. But I would disappear into the force of that kiss and I would understand the smell as arousing.

In a pub in one of the coastal towns near his home, Neal will kiss his girlfriend. He will kiss her hard. She will be conscious of the sour stink of alcohol and something gamey on his breath from the meat pie he had just eaten, and thus she will be resistant initially; but when, chastened, he pulls back, she will draw him closer and she will allow herself to fall into his kiss.

That night he will tell her for the first time that his mother and his father used to act in pornographic videos back in the US. She will tentatively—and shocked by her own excitement—ask him if he has ever watched any of them. 'Once,' he'll answer. 'But I'm never going to do it again.' They will be lying next to each other on a hillock that rises to a cliff that looks over the wondrous ocean. She will be silent, and Neal will think she has fallen asleep while looking at the stars. But then she will clutch his hand. 'You're kind,' she will say. And he will know she doesn't love him as he loves her.

The next day Jenna will drive her husband to Brisbane to catch a flight to LA.

I put on a coffee and head downstairs to phone Simon. He answers on the first ring. As always, when I call him at the office, his voice is a little distant, somewhat hushed. He doesn't want work to intrude on the intimacy between us. He asks me how the writing is going, and I answer that I am still not sure. 'I am writing about my past,' I explain. 'It clearly is as much memoir as it is fiction. The writing of one demands the same craft one uses for the other.'

'And *Sweet Thing*?'

'I am still thinking about that,' I answer. 'Taking notes, making some sketches. But I can't stop thinking that the book I need to write is about beauty.'

There is a pause. And then he asks, 'Are you enjoying it?'

'Being here? Yes, very much. I miss you.'

He laughs quietly. 'Thanks. But I didn't mean that. Are you enjoying the writing? That's what you wanted from going away.'

I walk over to the door; on the neatly mown lawn, there is a small quivering rabbit basking in the sun. I tell Simon and this time his laugh is loud and warm.

'I wish I was there,' he sighs.

I tell him I am enjoying writing.

I step out onto the patch of gravel outside the granny flat, taking care to shut the door quietly so as not to disturb the rabbit on the grass. Its fur is a golden colour, but the coarseness of the hair makes it seem speckled by white dust. I gently inch forwards, but the crunch of my footsteps on the pebbles startles the animal and with three swift leaps it has disappeared into the shrubbery at the edge of the lawn. There is a rustling, and from the thin branches of the lemon myrtle there is a trembling, a further swishing of leaves and twigs, and a yellow-and-bronze-striped honeyeater darts into the air. For a moment it hovers above the tree, then with a determined flap of its wings it flies under the Hills hoist and over the neighbour's yard.

As soon as the coffee has brewed, I take it back downstairs and sit on the lawn. I strip off my shirt, fold it into a pillow and lay my head on it. I close my eyes and concentrate on the delicious prickle of the grass on my shoulders, on the backs of my thighs and on my calves. Any morning dew has evaporated. The earth beneath me is warm. Simon's question returns to me and I am intrigued that he has understood something of what I am doing, even though I have not till this moment articulated it to myself. There is a vital connection between the beauty I am seeking and the pleasure that I have been trying to find again in my writing. This is why there is a ruthlessness in my intent to strip all moral and political purpose from the books that I am trying to imagine and to shape and to create. I am also constantly reminded of the essential relationship between sensuality and the imagination, of how the senses feed the act of creation. The sharp tickle of the grass on my skin, the strange juxtaposition of the blooming and the fetid in its aroma. I can hear a murmuring; the distant pound of the ocean, of course, and also the trill of the birds, but isn't there also an even more remote lowing? No wonder the world's first people believed that gods or titans lived in the Underworld. I turn my face so the grass scratches softly at my cheek and I open my eyes. I can see the veins in the individual leaves.

I have always understood the connection between my writing and the sensual world. In the city, sequestered from nature, the force of it seems only to be the erotic. But that is merely one face of the sensual.

I turn to look at the sky. It is a joy, I wish I had said to Simon, now that I am looking up at that colossal glass vault, so commanding and so humbling in its clarity; it is a joy to animate characters with my breath: giving birth to Paul and Jenna and Neal. Playing God. I reach out my hand, pretend to touch the sky. The glare of the sun is blinding.

As a child I would lie in my father's garden, amid the leeks and the delicate flowering beanstalks that he tied to posts with shoelaces. I would lie between the plants and pretend I was in an enormous forest, and I would look up between the leaves and the branches and this same sun would burn its form into my eyes. I would then close my eyes and pretend that the charge from the light was a form of divination, that a god had reached down his hand and was offering me a gift. And from this gift arose stories and scene after scene of films that I would one day direct. In my room, under my bed, I hid the exercise books in which I tried to harness this energy bestowed on me by the gods and write the words and draw the images that would one day be novels and stories, films and plays. It always seemed a gruelling and impossible task: all those hundreds of characters and ever-evolving stories, often reduced to a mere title that I wrote on a single page.

How to make real the transformation that occurred whenever I surrendered to my secret dreaming as I lay in my father's garden? I have returned as an adult to that house where I grew up. The backyard is narrow; the vegetable plot must have been small and paltry. Yet I had hidden within it and it had been the most luscious and impenetrable of forests. I had made it so.

I run my fingers along the blades of grass, I sniff at the residue on my fingers. It is musty, clearly of the earth. I raise my arm again and this time it is myself I can smell, the moist heady pong of the sweat from my armpits. Lazily, I run one finger along the damp hair there and then lift it to my lips, wipe the moisture across them.

There must be a chemical, an organic foundation to desire. In some ways that is a ridiculous question to ponder, for the intuitive, even obvious response is of course: reproduction is biology. But we live in an age estranged from the world. We live in our heads and we live in our screens. There is an ugly rancour that refutes the link between biology and sex, as if that reminder will have us fall off the edge of what is our world, plummet into the unpalatable recognition that we are as much animal as soul. Those who rail against the biology of gender and sex are as suspicious and hateful towards the body as were the most pious of early Christian moralists. I rub my palm into my armpit, collect the sweat and cover my face with my hand. I inhale deeply. To remind myself I am also flesh.

Was my sexuality formed as an infant in the domestic opera of the little worker's cottage in Melbourne where I grew up, in those early years when my family all slept in the same room? Or was there an element in the protein of my genes, one that has travelled across eons, that formed me as a homosexual from the moment I was germinating in the womb? I have always supposed that it is a combination of nature and nurture that forms us; all other iterations of this argument now bore me—and to dwell on them would be to move me further away from the purpose of the book I want to write.

I now swipe my fingers over the hairs of my other armpit. It is some ancient ritual I am enacting.

Stavros's smell, the release of him through the sweat that poured from his skin, that formed a glistening shield on his chest, that he washed away with sponge and water as I watched him in the bathroom; and also the way his odours wrapped themselves around me as I sat on his lap and lay in his arms: to have known this is a boon. Only a few years later, now firmly aware that there was a joy to this sensual world that was both delightful and also dangerous, arousing but also taboo, I would watch my father and my uncles, my older cousins and their friends, wash in the toilet blocks after a day of swimming in the sea and I would be transfixed by the flushes of hair revealed under their arms as they raised them to wash the salt and grit from their hair, stand there astonished at the audacity of the thick black pelts above their cocks and under their balls.

I hoist myself to my feet. A memory has intruded, slowly taking shape and form, and I am suddenly conscious that there are neighbours on either side of this house, that there are other properties on this hill and that the sun is in command and all is visible. Where I need to delve now is secret.

•

The peninsula beaches of Melbourne are not dangerous; they are sea, not ocean. On hot summer weekends a caravan would set off at dawn from our houses in the inner city, heading east to the coastal townships of Rosebud, Rye and Dromana. My mother and Aunt Irene would have been up late the night before, past midnight, preparing and baking the pies and roasted vegetables that would form part of our lunchtime meal at the beach. Even so, even having had so little sleep, it would be the women who would wake my brother and me in the morning, and we, shocked by the outrage of the early hour, would moan and close our eyes, demand to be left to sleep. My mother and aunt would have none of that. They would call us ungrateful animals, spoilt and soft. *Australezoi*. Australians, not Greeks. Often, my father or Uncle George would enter, and one of them would lift me in his arms and the other would lift my brother, and they would tickle us and nuzzle our chests and our necks with their unshaven chins, and even though we didn't want to—we wanted to sleep, we demanded to sleep!—we would both break out into delirious laughter. We were awake. And I would be rushing to the bathroom to brush my teeth and run water across my hair before combing it straight.

I am holding my father's hand. We are standing on the small brick wall he has built around the vegetable patch. The moon is high in the sky and the world is dark, yet I know it is not night, that something else is emerging. 'Listen,' my father whispers. He points across the low corrugated-tin rooftops of our neighbours' houses, points to what seems a grim, black horizon. 'Listen,' he repeats. The light softly creeps into being. First, a vague mist that seems to emanate from the bowels of the earth; then that vapour deepens and becomes milky, and there are yellow and orange lines and splashes in the sky and it is no longer black and it is waves of lilac and plum-coloured swirls, and then I see it, the first thin rays of the sun, and simultaneously I understand my father's instruction: I am not only seeing dawn, I am listening to it. One by one, the birds of the city form a chorus. The emerging day has a boom to it, the world now feels replete with motion and each movement has a sound. My father lifts me off the low wall and pushes me gently towards the outhouse. As I sit on the toilet in the darkness, thin sheets of light streaming through the planks, I hear the toot of a car horn. Uncle Elias, Aunt Diamanda and my cousins have arrived to pick us up. When I push through the outhouse door, night has vanished. All is sun and light.

This is the first dawn I remember.

I wish to sketch this next sequence as deftly and as accurately as possible, even though I know that writing can never be so forensic, cannot ever be evidence. My account will remain unchallenged, no reader or critic can take on the role of the prosecutor. They only have my words to go on; there are no other witnesses. This is why all utopians distrust the poets. The poet is treacherous, a challenge and a rebuke to the collective, to the nation, to faith and to creed. Is this why I am retreating into the far interior of the house, away from the light and into the shadows, not wanting anyone to see me? I have taken my laptop and am sitting on a sofa in the living room under a framed reproduction of Manet's *The House at Rueil,* a magnificent painting that also mocked those wishing to ascribe revolutionary intent to art, that lent the radicalism of the Impressionist's technique to the representation of that most abhorred of bourgeois delights, middle-class domesticity. How I revere this painting: the pallid greens and blues that shimmer and come to vital life the closer you draw to the canvas; the house that is sturdy and large, a little untidy, the gardens a little unkempt, that suggestion of a summer dwelling, a well-loved family retreat; and the obtruding tree trunk that divides the canvas and is a most audacious presumption: it is what makes the painting one of the most perfect works of art I know. 'Nature intrudes,' I can hear Manet whispering. 'Nature doesn't adhere to your visions or your beliefs or your sentiments.' It is this wilfulness that the poet and nature share, and it is why I detest the taming intent of that label, Mother Nature: let us make her nurturing and sweet, the goddess of ecological purity. She is nothing like that! She doesn't give a fuck for purity and care, for compassion and justice, for fidelity and communion. She can conjure an annihilating wave from the deepest ocean; she can make mountains collapse and the earth rip open. She is no simpering mother. Manet understood her: that protruding trunk is Mother Nature's scandalous swinging cock; this mother has power. I sit under the painting. I know what I am about to do is perfidious.

That day, four cars form the caravan heading to the beach. In a few years, when my parents move us to the outer suburbs, my mother—who will still have her job in the auto parts factory in Richmond—will learn to drive. My father, who is a maestro when it comes to the garden, who knows how to cajole and to encourage and how to work and stir the earth, has no talent for the mechanical. He will never learn to drive a car. So, my family, my parents and my brother and myself, are picked up in Uncle Elias's grey-panelled station wagon. That scent of sweating vinyl and Marlboro cigarettes and petrol! I sniff, and I revive it all. Let me orchestrate it thus: my uncle is driving. My cousin Vicky is sitting in the front, between my uncle and my father. My brother is in the back seat, between my mother and my aunt. And I am with my cousin Bill in the rear of the wagon. I love the tumble and unsteadiness of being in that enormous cavity. I even relish the abrupt and terrifying moments when the car jerks to a halt and Bill and I are flung into one another or slammed into the interior walls. Our mothers reach for us frantically, screaming at my uncle to slow down, take care, and pleading with God to keep us from crashing. Bill and I are hooting with laughter, exhilarated.

I must be eleven. Am I eleven or am I twelve? I have developed the first scant traces of hair across my pubis. They disappoint me, for unlike the dense and potent fur I spy when I sneak glances at the older boys and men in the change rooms at the public pool, the hair that has begun to grow is sparse, a few curl-tipped seeds.

We stop outside Uncle Nikos's house. He is not really my uncle. He and my father met when they sailed on the same ship from Athens to Melbourne. Yet, I have been raised to regard Nikos as family. He was, and remains, my favourite uncle.

It is astonishing what one is sure of in memory, and what remains blurred and opaque, only intermittently discernible through the darkened glass of the mirror where the present kisses the past. I am certain, definite, that there are four cars in the convoy; yet I struggle to remember who else was with us that Sunday summer morning. What is vivid is the solid and heavy heat of the day. It is still early as the four cars turn onto Dandenong Road, yet the heat in the back of the station wagon is already overbearing. Bill and I are sweating. The light is uncompromising, refracting and ricocheting off the asphalt roads, the concrete walls of the warehouses and factories along the highway. When the cars finally turn towards the sea, when they park alongside each other under the enormous shelter of a Moreton Bay fig, we children clamber from them, calling for our togs and towels. Our mothers hush us, urge us to be patient, but that seems impossible. The sea is just visible, dashes of blue and slashes of white, between the thick verdure of the trees. The light is so brilliant it seems austere. And there is no wind. That too lends a solemnity to the day.

The beaches along that western-facing flank of the peninsula, segregated from the ocean by the enormous arms of the bay, are unthreatening. There must have been adults on the shore, or even beside us as we waded out into the water, but all I remember is the squealing and teasing and laughter of us children. So shallow are these waters that we had to slog for what seemed like miles before the water covered our shins, but once the tepid waves started nipping at our knees, at our thighs, there was a rapid drop and the water was at our chests, then our necks. And we older ones, emboldened by the certificates we had earned at swim school, dived and tumbled and swam out to the point where our toes could only just scratch the sand. We were thrilled by our own daring. Our screams must have rung out across the whole of the bay that day.

Hours in the water: that is how I remember the summers of my childhood. There must be other cultures in other parts of the world where children experience this festal communion in water. But this continent has space: the vastness of its land and coast, and the sparseness of its population. I am inside the body of that young child—am I twelve? I think I must be twelve years—and my strokes are clumsy rather than confident, but they are efficient, and I swim out further and the water is in my eyes and the sun is high and it is like daggers if I look up at it but I kick my feet as I was instructed at swim school and I remember how to breathe and I am in deep now and to verify my courage I stop swimming, I tread water and I look back at the beach. How distant it is! Uncle Elias, the best and bravest of the adult swimmers, is the only person who is further out than I am. My brother, my cousins and our friends are bobbing up and down closer to the shore, all of us lost in our individual daydreams. From the apex of the sky to the fringe of the horizon to the remote glimpse of the shore, I am cradled in an impossible space. It is not frightening at all.

I look up from the laptop. There is the faintest of cramps across the back muscle of my left thigh. I have been sitting crookedly. I massage my leg, stand and walk out to the deck. It is afternoon and the deck is in shadow. A large, thick cloud mass, white on its crest and grey wet slate on its undersides, is rolling towards the sun. Soon the world will be in its shadow. Yet, for the moment, the inlet sea flickers and sparks and the ocean behind the treetops is a deep blue. My hands tighten on the wooden railing of the balcony. My destiny was written, decided and weaved that long-ago summer day. I was never frightened by this ocean. Simon and I dream of living together by this ocean. I cannot conceive of a life far from it. This is my home. Even when I have detested it or been angered by it or have been ashamed of it, this has always been my home. I was never going to do what my mother and father did; I was never to leave home and be a migrant. The dreams I entertained in youth were mere whimsy.

I flick the lighter: the sharp click of the flint wheel, the gasp of flame and the whoosh as the tobacco ignites. I laugh to myself. So many decades to realise this truth. My hand reaches out, as if my fingers could touch that distant water. These seas, this ocean, this has always been my home.

Butting out the cigarette, I go inside to fetch the computer and bring it out to the deck. I don't need to hide what I am about to write from the world.

Uncle Nikos was, and remains, my favourite uncle. It is possible that his not being a blood relation is central to the bond we share. Whereas my adoration for Stavros seems imbued with an intense sacred power—my attention to him was indeed reverential, and my child's insistence that we every day enact the same performance: me watching him wash, handing him his towel, glimpsing his reflection in the small, cracked mirror on his bureau as he splashed those drops of cologne over his face and body, all surely arose from a devotion to ritual—it was a brief infatuation. Stavros disappeared from my life when he became engaged and moved into his own home. Uncle Nikos, though, has always been there. Our affection is mutual. I think he delighted in my love for storytelling, how I badgered him for tales of his village life, and I in turn always thought him an attentive and uncondescending adult figure. Later, in my adolescence and then in my early adulthood, this fondness between us would be strengthened by a shared pleasure in arguing over politics, in the cama- raderie of the coffee table. He also took great pride in my studiousness and in my love of letters. In fact, when I was accepted into university he wept with joy. Such opportunities were not available to him, a child of poverty and occupation and civil war; he was only allowed to complete his primary education before being sent off to work. I detected in the vehemence of his reaction a secret, almost shameful dream he must have cherished: that he could have lived a life in which he was a scholar.

There is another memory to do with my Uncle Nikos and the beach, though it is highly likely that these events did not all occur on the same day. We spent many days together at the sea. Yet in the resurrection of memory, it is as if the two recollections are conjoined, as if some supernatural force links them both. I have always been fascinated by the ancient myth of the Fates, of how the trajectory of our lives is dependent on their sewing and their weaving, how their needles and yarn craft our lives. The original Greek word, *moïra*, is one of the first words I recall hearing. Fate, making meaning out of accident, was a central belief for both my parents and all the adults of their circle, migrants who had pitched into the future by sailing to a distant, unknown country. Even Nikos, proudly and arrogantly secular, dismissive of super- stition, he too believed in Fate. So, I see the goddess taking the cloth, threading her needle and stitching together two moments that will bind my uncle and myself together for eternity. The point of her needle pierces the fabric.

I am sure it is another day, and that I am younger than twelve. Not much younger, but my body is still a child's body, no sabotaging of its innocence by those ugly bristles above my cock that I will try to hide from the other boys when we are changing into our swimmers. It is, however, also a summer's day and, again, we have been at the beach. It is time to leave and we have all crammed into the red-brick shower block. My father and Uncle Nikos turn on the taps and we boys squeal and scream as the freezing water rains down on our heads and our shoulders. We kick off our bathers and furiously scrub under our arms, our groins, between our thighs, watching as the sand swirls around our feet and dribbles down the drain. I turn. And I see my Uncle Nikos naked.

Most memories are ghosts. They reside deep in the netherworld, and even when one calls them up, demands that they emerge, often they can be glimpsed only vaguely, darkly. The mirror is stained, soiled, cracked.

That is not true for this moment.

On the deck I inhale, and I close my eyes. Not tightly; not so that the vista before me becomes a churning cauldron of reds and yellows and streaks of white in black, that cosmos which has so delighted me from childhood. Instead, with a gentle blink, I ensure that my recollection is indeed still whole and complete.

I can see my Uncle Nikos as if I am viewing a sculpture, a late classical god moulded from bronze. He hasn't noticed my gaze. He is grinning, my father has made some joke, and my uncle has his arm raised, letting the water rinse his armpits. His fur there is not heavy and the hair on his chest and belly too is sparse. He has not yet grown fat. He is taller than my father and his chest is expansive and powerful as he stands with his feet apart. One hand is raised above him and the other is lifting his full round testicles, and he begins soaping his cock and balls. He is tanned a honeyed brown by the sun and the skin that was protected by his bathers is shockingly white. His penis is stout and the bush of his pubes is thickly clotted and raven black. There is a moment when he looks across at us children and he catches my eyes. He winks at me.

I can spend eternity in that moment: neither of us is startled, or ashamed.

This glimpse of my uncle is precious to me. Alongside Stavros's smell, it is a kindle to all desire: it will stimulate dreams and yearnings, and therefore galvanise imagination. Nikos's nakedness was shocking and there is something of terror in that experience. I was—and there is no other word, for the moment was both sensual and sacred and forged a union between those two elements that can never be broken—transfixed by his beauty. This dizzying enthralment of the male body as something solid and imperfect, coarse and alive and rough-hewn, will remain with me for life and will make me impervious to the charms of the effete and the pretty. It will determine the men I fall in love with and desire, and for the works of art I will adore and the films that will captivate me.

I am in danger of sanctifying beauty and I do not wish to do that, to capitalise it and make it Beauty and therefore make it inapproachable and distant. Let me consecrate this memory instead . . .

. . . we are at the beach, we have all had a splendid lunch on the blankets that our mothers laid over the earth. We ate the pies they had baked the night before, and the breads and the sweets, and our mouths were full of the tastes of feta and walnuts and honey. Under the shade of the Moreton Bay figs our fathers drank wine and they smoked, while our mothers packed away the soiled plates and cutlery, and shoved all the waste into plastic bags, and then slowly, one by one, we all fell asleep.

What an exquisite sight that must have been, a contented repose after simple pleasure. I am remembering it all as if I am directing a film, an overhead shot where the camera peers down between the branches at the bodies, large and small, male and female, adult and child, some stretched out in luxurious isolation on their beach towels, some huddled together on blankets, and though all are in the shade, the sun occasionally breaks through the canopy and speckles of silver light fall on the sleeping bodies.

Then one of us children, impatient to return to the beach, called out: 'Can we swim now? Is the hour over?' (For we had all been taught that one could not go into the water immediately after eating, or you risked being assaulted by a horrendous cramp and drowning.) And a mother or a father propped themselves up on an elbow, searched for their watch and announced, 'Yes, we can go swimming.' And the children grew excited and the men jumped to their feet and the women adjusted their swimmers. But my Uncle Nikos, he was stretched out on his blanket, his yawn long and magnificent, his hands clasped behind his head; and with the turning of the world and the shifting of the sky, shafts of sunlight pierced the trees, and the unexpected light made the hairs of his armpit glint. I remember that golden hue so very clearly. Even half a century later, I can touch those hairs, I can still see a drop of sweat clinging to one of them. And can I recall the smell? I think I can. And though I was metres away from my uncle, surely too far, I smell salt, the salt of sweat and sea. And Uncle Nikos drawls lazily, 'I'm going to stay here. I'll sleep some more.' And immediately, without thinking—it is an instinct not a calculation—I declare: 'Me too! I'm going to swim later.'

Nikos glances over at me, and he winks.

My mother asks, 'Are you sure?'

And Nikos replies with a laugh, 'Get lost, woman, Christo and I don't need any of you.'

It is true, we required nothing else of life. Let me be clear: there was nothing perverse in my uncle's mischievous dismissal of the others. The nature of our love was a deeply gentle affection.

The procession of adults and children marched through the shrubbery onto the beach. I was lying on my stomach, listening to the crackle of the leaves, the scratch of the sand and gravel. The sound disappeared and what remained was a faint and soothing whistle in the trees. A wind had lifted; and almost as soon as it surged, it disappeared, and the leaves were once again still. There was only the quiet rasping of Nikos's long snores. With my chin on my arms, I gazed at the sleeping man. I can reproduce him faithfully: there was the round protuberant chin that quivered with each snore; there was the dark blush of bristle on his high, arched Slavic cheeks; there were white spots and marks, faded sunburns, on that dark ochre skin across his shoulders; his right hand rested on the heaving and retreating chest; the scant hairs across the slight mound of his belly were black: his was a strength and solidity that seemed to me, looking at him lying there, to have sprung from the earth. His tight blue bathers revealed the solidness of his cock, the fullness of his balls; a clutch of coiled black hairs protruded from under the tight elastic. Carefully, so very slowly, I released one of my hands from underneath my head and with care, as if the limb was now separate from myself, I followed its skulking movement as it crept across the grass, as it ended up between my legs, as it cupped the still damp crotch of my bathers. I started to rub.

And the *moïras*, the laughing Fates, they have stitched these memories together. My hand sliding against my now-hard cock as I recalled the heaviness of my uncle's penis when I peeked at it in the shower block, the weight of his balls, the alarming thickness of the hair that crowned them both. His snores had softened; his eyes were still closed. My rubbing became so frantic it started to hurt. My thumb pulled at the elastic of my bathers and my erect child's penis sprung out. My hand formed a fist around it. I was looking at Nikos's sleeping body stretched out on the blanket, yet I was also kneeling before him in that toilet block.

I jerked; a warm thick clag shot out and splattered across the grass. My body shuddered again, a glorious unnerving convulsion, and a thick paste of semen oozed all over my hand. Mortified, I pulled my bathers over my shame and started vigorously wiping my wet palm on the grass. There was a rustling. My uncle was sitting up and looking over at me kindly.

'Christo,' he said quietly, 'we'll go for a swim.' There was the slightest of pauses, and then he added: 'Do you need to go to the toilet?'

I nodded.

I stood at the sink in the toilet block and scrubbed at my hands for an age, washing them again and again. The semen, this strange substance emitted from inside of me but which

seemed an alien matter implanted in me by some malig-
nant devil, had dried so quickly on my skin. I scratched and
scratched at it, trying to eradicate the last telltale signs of
my wickedness. He must have seen me. He must hate me.
He must despise me.

I walked from the toilet block back to our haven underneath the trees. My uncle was standing, smoking, gazing out
over the shrubs to the sea. As soon as he heard me approach,
he swung around, and he was beaming. He strode towards
me, embraced me, then lifted me high so that the sea was
surrounding us, the clarity of the blue was emanating from
both of us. I was so very high in his arms. He kissed me
hard on my belly, and the hard bristles of his cheeks stung.
One last squeeze and he lowered me gently back to earth.

'We should join the others.'

He quickly rubbed lotion over my body, my chest and
belly, my arms and thighs, gently slapped it over my cheeks,
my face. He poured the oozing white paste into my palm,
turned and ordered me to rub it into his back. The skin there
was rough, not smooth at all, and red where his shoulders
were peeling. But the rest of him was a deep cinnamon. My
hands were now diligently rubbing lotion at the base of his
spine. There were spirals of short black hairs on his lower
back. I remember they disgusted me. They formed a sparse
trail that descended into the back of his bathers. There, the
hair was thicker, longer. I stopped my rubbing in the lotion.
He reached around, grabbed my hand, squeezed it. Then he

released it and leapt up, shouting, 'Let's go swimming!' And we raced down to the shore.

This is a precious recollection, and I guard it jealously. It is not embalmed. I return to this moment again and again, and through the years and the different stages of my life, it is always a rediscovery. I always recall the soothing coolness of the shade under those heavy-limbed trees. But while I remember them as those giant fig trees, there are times I wonder: were they cedars? I have recounted this story and made it sinister, exaggerated the peril that is always assumed when an adult and a child share a sensual bliss. This betrayal of the experience was short-lived; I only represented it as such to, first, justify the puritan dogmas of religion that condemns the flesh, and then to acquiesce to the equally priggish orthodoxies of politics that disavows subtlety in the erotic. It is a relief to have abandoned both God and ideology.

I return to it, this exquisite moment, this ever-changing remembrance, because it formed me as a writer. As a person as well, of course. The whole afternoon does now seem redolent of being in the garden, in Eden, for I think I shared eternity in that moment with my uncle. It was unquestionably sensual: the smells of it, the sensations of it, my fingers on his skin, his on mine, the shade, the hardness of my dick as I watched him sleep, the distant bashing of the surf; unquestionably sensual because it was all so absolutely alive. Nothing evil or sinister or hurtful occurred, however it was the crucible of my sexuality. My uncle understood my love for him and, further, my desire for him, and he did not push me away. This was an initiation. If we had lived in an ancient world ruled by ancient gods, all of us would undergo such rituals to bridge the passage between leaving childhood and becoming adult. Nikos offered me his hand and supported me as I leapt across the divide. All else around me was making the erotic shameful. He did not, and though it took years to really ferment and seed, his grace gave me courage. I honour him for initiating me into manhood by idealising him as the perfect man.

As a writer, the moments we return to, that we change, that we exalt, that we sometimes dishonour and betray, are what the craft of fiction is about. This is why it is indeed treacherous, and why the lying poet is to be expelled from all utopias. This is the first moment I can remember in which I understood fully, even in the moment of its happening, that truth and imagination are enemies.

To my ear, the writing of that final sentence—the bearing down on the keys as I type, *truth and imagination are enemies*—seems a loud and assertive jangling. Not offensive; an exhilarating and defiant resounding. I shut down the computer. It had been my intention to check my emails for the first time in days. But having returned to Nikos and to my own emerging, the thought of entering that inert, meagre world is unbearable. I drive to the beach.

Like the child I once was, I run jubilantly into the water. The first smash of the waves across my crotch and belly and chest slice me open: the water is icy. But with the first dive, the first plunge underneath and then the sluicing through the water, emerging to the sun and sky, the cold is vanquished. I dive once more, sense the force of a rip as it sucks me towards it and I resist, struggle to stand and plant myself in the churning, shifting sand beneath the water. I stagger away from the rip and I am safe.

And I know why I have once more returned to the garden: I can see Paul getting on the plane; I am in his head as he finds himself in the decadent comfort of the business-class seat that a stranger has secured for him, a stranger who has fallen in love with him from a distance after seeing his spectral image on VHS and DVD. As the plane shudders, accelerates, Paul utters a swift and heartfelt prayer. He prays to a God he doesn't believe in, pleads with this supernatural being to keep his wife and son safe.

He drinks the glass of champagne offered just before take-off, and he drinks a whisky before the first meal. The fog of the alcohol allays his fears. He wonders what the stranger looks like. Fat or thin? Attractive or ugly? Old, certainly old, older even than Paul is himself. He reminds himself of the outlandish amount of money he is receiving. He doesn't lie to himself. He knows it is not only the money. It is mostly the money but not only the money. The life he has on the Pacific coast of Australia is a good one. But this is an adventure. And it is his own: it belongs only to him. He loves his wife and he loves his child but it is thrilling to be by himself, on this plane, in this luxury, where he can recline the seat and lie in it as if it were a bed. He is thousands of feet up in the air. Above the clouds. Heading to America, heading home for the first time in twenty years. He lets out an inadvertent giggle. He awaits his meal and doesn't think of the stranger again.

For a few minutes the sea has been calm. But I see the tumult in the far distance, just below the horizon. I tread water. I know if I straighten my legs, I can touch the seabed. I paddle, feel the touch of the sun; and then the waves return, bigger and more ferocious than before. I slip into the gap between them and swim hard until I am riding the crest of a wave. I abandon my struggle and the wave, that giant's fist, grips me and lifts me high into the sky and then dumps me into the water. I spit brine from my mouth, it gushes from my nostrils, I am heaving from the loss of breath and my right knee is grazed from where it slammed into the sand. None of that matters. I turn and face the ocean and sky. I know what the stranger who has hired Paul looks like; he will be older, of course, much older. But I know the roughness of his skin, I know his face and his eyes. I will make him Nikos.

I still have an hour, possibly longer, before the sun sets. I dash back into the water.

Last night, I cooked a simple meal—stir-frying some local prawns with garlic and crushed lemongrass and preparing a white bean and red onion salad—and ate it on the deck, flicking through a newspaper till I found the puzzles page. I then methodically went through the cryptic crossword, managing to get all of it out but one clue. I had already spoken to Simon before dinner, so I decided against going downstairs again for my phone and instead made a mental note to ask him about the crossword when we speak tomorrow. Once dinner was finished, I sat out a little longer on the deck, drank another glass of wine and only with the seemingly abrupt fall of the dark did I retire inside. I went through the clutch of DVDs I had brought with me, but I was in no mood for any of them. I searched for and found a USB in the pocket of my rucksack. The television belonging to the rental property was small, but it was a recent model and it could read the information on the memory stick. I used the remote to scroll through the various options. Again, none of the movies I had stored there appealed. Instead, I started James Agee's *A Death in the Family*. It is a book I last read in my twenties, and I had only the faintest, most spectral memories of it. I knew that I had admired it on that first reading, and now I was immediately immersed in the recounting of a past life and a past history written with ruthless eloquence and an equally potent vigour. I brushed my teeth, and I went to bed early to read some more. I didn't want to put the book down, but within the hour my eyes grew heavy and my attention drifted. I switched off the bedside light. I was asleep and then I was awake. Dawn had not yet arrived. I read the book for another hour, then I rose from the bed, had breakfast and showered.

I was ready for a walk by 7 am. At that hour, even though the streaks of russet cloud across the slowly flaring sky promised that it would be a warm spring day, the air outside was still frosty. I put on a woollen jumper and regretted that I had not packed a scarf. There was a sharp slap in the morning air as I ran down the stairs. Descending the hill, the light on the horizon, floating serenely above the ocean, was already a dazzling white, though the inlet was still doused in tints of grey, in patches of shadow. Maintaining a brisk pace, my attention wavered between the emerging of day all around me and the recollection of the words I had read last night and first thing in the morning. What is exhilarating about Agee's prose is that there is not a whiff of condescension about it. Whether writing from the perspective of a child or that of the child's mother or aunt, the language always honours the character. And though the novel describes the absolute terror of death, and of how accident, ruthless and unforeseen, can scupper the unremarkable, gentle drift of life, the tragedy does not overwhelm. Is this stoic pragmatism something unique to the US? To its people as well as its artists, I mean? It's refreshing, even if that spirit now seems to belong to the same distant past from which Agee's novel emerges. I recall the children, the old woman, in the film script that Agee wrote for Charles Laughton, *The Night of the Hunter.* I first saw it when I was very young, and I thought the young boy's determined protection of his sister, and the resourcefulness of his attempts to evade his stepdad, the psychotic preacher played by Robert Mitchum, were heroic. The film doesn't ignore the boy's real terror. It is frightening. But he uses his wits. That very phrase seems indubitably American. Your wits, your innate strengths, are more important than the class or caste you are born into. But that was the past; even the Americans don't believe that anymore.

Walking to the front beach, I find myself whistling the hymn that Lillian Gish sings in the film. The main surf beach is at the opposite end of the town to where I am staying. But it is early enough, and I feel energetic enough, for the walk. I have my second coffee of the morning at a cafe perched at the highest point of the town with a magnificent view of the ocean. The air now is crystal in its clarity, and I know it cannot be true but, as I sip my coffee and follow the meandering line of the coast heading north, I believe that I can see Sydney in the distance. Impossible. It is a five-hour car-ride away. That is part of the allure of where I am: heading to a metropolis is not something that can be done on a whim. Canberra is the closest city, yet that drive is nearly three hours. As long as I ignore my phone, the urban stridor cannot reach me.

Simon and I are growing increasingly fatigued by the city. I was tempted to describe it as an alienation, however the weight of that word is not quite right. He and I are both children of the city, born into it, into its laneways and traffic and crowds. I whined at my parents' decision to move us to the suburbs when I was a teenager. I had no patience for all that space; for the longest time that space was indeed estranging. I couldn't wait to return to the city, to its brashness and aliveness. It is impossible to live a life without regrets. Thankfully, the majority of mine are in a minor key. When a face, a voice, a word or a sensation animates a shameful recollection, it causes a slight sting, like a subcutaneous injection, and is quickly forgotten. There are regrets, however, misdeeds and failures, that leave a deep, lifelong scar. At sixteen, a few years after the move, I raged against my father, called him vile names for having taken us from the city to the bland conformity of suburbia. We were in the garden, he was using old shoelaces to tie the fledging tomato stalks, and he tried to explain to me that what he now had—a house with a bedroom each for his children, a garden with which to feed his family—had been his one dream since he was a boy. I had already visited Greece once and seen where my father had been raised. His village was high in the mountains, so that even at the height of summer a bracing draught blustered across the slopes. A cottage made of rock and stone, a hearth and then a room in which a shepherd family of eleven children lived. Some of them slept with the animals at night, even in the infernal cold of mid-winter. But I was only ten years old, and a child raised in consumerist comfort cannot comprehend the profundity of poverty. It would take many more returns to my parents' homeland to even come close to glimpsing that truth, and it is one that I am destined to perceive through a glass darkly. At sixteen, and yelling insults at my father, I didn't think of that small damp cottage on the side of the mountain, surrounded by pine forest. I only thought of myself. 'What a pissy little dream,' I scoffed, flinging my arms wide to take in the whole of this detested suburbia. 'I'd be embarrassed if *this* was all I wanted from life.'

This memory isn't a mere sting. It can still slam me like a punch. My father had been wounded and reduced to silence by my insults. He continued toiling. I apologised to him when I was an adult and had finally come to understand shame and understand regret. But the memory of my ignorance and self-righteousness is still chastening.

I am passing an unadorned, handsome white weatherboard chapel. I whisper, in Greek, 'I am sorry.'

And now Simon and I are older than my father was when I insulted him. And Simon and I too dream of space. We were born in the city, but we are both children of peasants.

It might be that it is the thought of blood, of how it has a song and how that chorus of ancestors is one of the hardest of superstitions to forsake, that decides me against strolling along the immense expanse of the shore. Instead, I take off my shoes and socks, roll up the bottoms of my trackpants and walk across the sand towards the headland on the southern side of the long beach. There is the faint outline of a cenotaph on top of the hill, where a cemetery sits. I take the risk that there will be a path leading to it from the beach. Is it the recollection of my father? My feet plash and kick in the shallows, my step is determined. It is as if my body, my blood, needs a simple communion with the dead.

There is a path, steep but well beaten, that climbs to the cemetery. The graves are mostly modest headstones—there are no elaborate and baroque tombs—and the graves themselves are level with the ground. I walk along them. There is a white wooden cross, scarred by rain and sun so that the paint is scabbed and peeling, lending the crucifix a wounded dignity. A clutch of cheap toys are scattered around the base: a doll, a Disney figurine and a yo-yo; a sad-eyed rabbit puppet.

A woman's name is marked on the cross, her twenty-seven years of life, and the terse words *Our beloved wife and mother forever* are carved across it. Three iris stems are strewn across the grave, their flowers only just budded. The earth is covered by a layer of gravel, the stones neatly brushed and levelled. She has been dead five years but clearly has not been forgotten. I look across to the startling drop of the cliff. There is a quickening wind; to the south, dark clouds are amassing, gathering speed.

There is one Orthodox Christian grave, and the photo of the woman who is buried there shows a face that is dignified and resigned. According to the inscription on the headstone, she was born in Rhodes. I wonder about the possibilities in her story. Again, I glance down at the startling immensity of the sea below. In the end, she has been returned to the water. A different water, a fiercer god than the docile deities of the Mediterranean Sea; yet, it is a return.

The cemetery itself is divided into two by an unsealed road. The graves are older higher up the rise, and I follow a ragged dirt path that runs along the back of the plots. Very soon I find myself within a copse of tall spotted gums. Within this sanctuary, both wind and light fall away. The path drops quickly, and the soil there is damp, muddy in places, but I follow its descent and I can hear the grumble of the sea. The path ends at a ledge, and I leap onto sand.

At the far end of the beach there is an outcrop of giant boulders, their shadows black against the gleaming sapphire of the sky. As I approach them, I see that the flat top of the tallest rock is home to a squad of seabirds: cormorants, albatrosses and gulls. There is indeed a soldiery aspect to their occupation of the rock. I am the only other animal on the beach, yet they do not start crying or screeching as I come closer. They are secure on their rampart. A shadow dips and then disappears over the water. I glance up and an eagle is hovering, its enormous wingspan ominous and wondrous at the same time. I regret that I was born in an ungallant age, a prosaic and not heroic era, and thus I cannot read fortune or peril in its flight.

The tide is out, and I can walk among the rocks and boulders at the end of the cove. They are of volcanic origin, and the black rock is still glistening from the dew of high tide. Deep pools have formed between the rocks and there are miniature solar systems within them: a school of silver fish, crabs with the thinnest of gangling legs and the tiniest of sea anemones. The water there is clear, and I kneel by the edge of one pool and push my face beneath the surface. The cold is abrupt, yet tantalising, and I am giggling to myself as I emerge in a rush from the water: for an instant, I was a child. Again, a reminder of how those excursions to the sea forged and directed my imagination. I look down at the pool and already my devastating disruption of its world is forgotten. The ripples, the displaced silt, all of it is beginning to settle. The little fish and crustaceans that darted away when I thrust my face into the water have returned and are swimming calmly. My finger hovers over the surface but I don't wish to be a cruel god again. I do not disturb them.

The argent-winged eagle is no longer above us. It is further out, over the sea. A precipitous, spinning dive and it emerges from the water with the glint of silver in its beak; it returns to the heavens and, as it does, drops of blood and flesh fall from the fish it has taken; they fall softly, as rain, back to the sea.

I shudder. Not afraid; just aware of the profound amorality of nature.

I climb across a small bank of rocks and drop into the next cove. And if I cannot read the omens of the skies and the birds, I realise I have been given a gift in what I find there. There is another outcrop of boulders, this time in the centre of the beach, its form more slender and seemingly precarious than the eyrie of the birds. This protrusion of rock does not seem to be formed by the crashing down onto earth of one immense boulder, quite the opposite; it is as if some demonic infant was using the stones and boulders of the beach around it to build this lopsided formation; the middle of the rock, for example, seems larger than its bottom. It is this unevenness that lends an upsetting volatility to this ancient figure. As I approach it, it seems to shift and change shape.

Alongside this tower, shaped in some antediluvian forge by a primordial god and then hurled onto this lonely antipodean shore with such force that it seems to have been blasted into the landscape, there stands a shorter, more symmetrical outcrop. It too has emerged from a furnace; its surfaces are heavy and black. It rises sharply, with the faintest of curvature, as if it wishes to bend towards the larger structure.

Once, travelling through Italy as a young man, I saw Constantin Brancusi's *Bird in Flight* at the Peggy Guggenheim Collection in Venice. I was enraptured. Metal wrought into spirit by an artist's invention. Bronze brought alive. So captivated was I by its beauty that I leant in and grazed it with my lips. It was the slightest kiss and I meant it as gratitude. Of course, the guards, once notified of my transgression, escorted me roughly out of the museum. But I was whistling as they flung me through the doors. What did I care? I had kissed Creation.

Here on the beach, I am returned to the sculpture: the same graceful curl, the same intimation of a birth, of a force emerging. I walk near to the rock formations, study them, but then my attention is caught by the magnificence of the sea. The bay is small, a pearl-shaped cradling, and the calm quartz of the water has a lightness and a depth that reminds me of the impossible blue with which one painted the ocean as a child. I drop my runners near the rocks and run to the water, let it gurgle and tickle and lap at my feet. Ahead, across the infinite expanse of cobalt majesty, the sky is clear, the illumination absolute. I turn around to survey the position of the sun, which is still to reach its zenith, when my attention is caught by a titan that rises from the sand. It is an illusion formed by my standing at an oblique angle to the two boulders. Yet knowing this does not dispel the awe I experience. The two stone forms no longer seem separated; the squatter figure appears joined to its giant sibling to form the front leg of the colossus that now dominates the shore. And what seemed a jumble of lopsided shapes and outcrops of the larger rock now form the head and the neck, the chest and the torso of the giant. He does seem to be lunging forwards, there are even massive arms at his side, as if he has broken free from an underground prison and is taking his first liberated strides on the earth. I am absolutely still. I do not wish to ruin this wondrous hallucination.

It is male. It is my creation and I make him male. More so, like the Fates sewing together patches of time, I am drawing together the pieces of fabric, laying them alongside one another this way then that, testing how to stitch them together. My mind is a tangle—the titan on the beach; Nikos lying outstretched on the grass; and Paul's plane landing in Los Angeles, his clearing customs, his thrill at hearing the American accent all around him and apprehension of who will be waiting in the arrivals hall, the man who is willing to pay that astonishing amount of money—all of this is a whirl inside my head.

I return to the water. The eternal rhythms of the ocean, the dragging out and the hurrying in of the invincible waves return me to peace and to clarity.

I know that the man who will be waiting for Paul on the other side of the gate at Los Angeles airport will be modelled on Nikos. I will imbue him with my uncle's strength. He will have his form. And that form is sturdiness, a toughness that is working-class and masculine. As yet I don't know the man's name. I fix my eyes on the sprinting waves. Conrad. I have received his name. He will have been christened Kostas, after a grandfather who first came to the United States from Greece, but he has always been called Conrad, a good and unpretentious if proudly American name. He is now rich, but he was not born wealthy. He has worked; he has scarred and toughened hands. I return my gaze to the colossus. There again, the premonition of movement, of solidity, of strength. I have started stitching the fabric together.

Art is akin to alchemy. An improbable undertaking. Some claim that inspiration comes in a moment, bestowed by the gods, perhaps, or springing forth from a dream. Others appeal to the merit of craft, and they suggest that only labour results in artistic revelation. This tug of war between dedication and chance, akin to that perpetual struggle between nature and nurture, will never reach a truce. I squat on the shore, an activity that does indeed now require effort from me. For some of us, age creeps inwards out, and I identify my oncoming frailty in the depletion of my steadiness and in the weakening of my bones. Yet I force myself to this crouch, skim my hand across the surface of a small pool and, bringing it to my nostrils, inhale the pungent brine. That physical sensation brings clarity to consciousness: it is between the singular moment and the perpetual grind that story is formed. For over a decade *Sweet Thing* has been fermenting. I can claim that imagination is a cellar deep in the earth, and it is from there that dreams and fantasias emerge. Haven't I avowed this already? Beyond the mirror, Orpheus descends; he does not climb to the netherworld. Every time I have placed a copy of Van Morrison's *Astral Weeks* on the turntable or into the CD slot over the last ten years, Paul and Jenna and Neal have been developing shape, gaining voice, shimmering spectres between this world and the world beneath—but they have been trapped beneath the murky glass and I have struggled to perceive their reflections. I haven't been able to extend my hand to lift them to this side of the mirror. Occasionally, very occasionally, I have sketched notes or drafted scenes to further animate my creatures. But I haven't found the means to release them into being: when I am asked about the book I am working on, I don't speak their names. In part, it is because the story emerges from another underworld, that of pornography, and it is the one stumbling block of the Anglo-Saxon's language, usually so dexterous and malleable, so gleefully promiscuous in borrowing and stealing from everywhere, that it fears the erotic. The language distrusts the human body. It can exalt and rhapsodise nature, a tamed and serene nature, but it resists venerating the human form. Therefore pornography, always lurking in the shadows, even in the dazzling unnatural light of the digital age, is a language English still stumbles over. *Sweet Thing* emerges from that shame and that obsession.

I shield my eyes. There is a glint in the water, and then a dark shadow passes underneath. A quickening of my heart. Is it a shark? The waves break into drizzles of foam and the shadow is gone. I mouth a quick thanksgiving, as if the depths have again come to my aid. I don't wish to domesticate pornography but to shed another form of light on it, less blinding.

So, ten years of thinking about it: but it is only at this moment on the beach, coming across the colossus—how long has he been in the act of emerging here in this isolated cove? Centuries? A millennium?—that a character who has hitherto resolutely, defiantly refused my entreaties has finally chosen to step into the light. He is still at a distance, but I peer into the mirror, my face touches the cold glass, and I glimpse him. He has the form of my uncle and now I have given him a name. Accident and endeavour. That is the singularity of our alchemy.

Walking up the short but steep incline back to the cemetery, along the main beach and then cutting through town towards the bridge across the inlet, I find that all of nature has receded and it is the first encounter between Paul and Conrad that I see. The automatic doors with the stippled large block type reading LAX slide open, and Paul, wheeling his small suitcase, peers anxiously at the faces crowded around the barrier. Jackson had explained in his last email that Conrad would be waiting for him. There are limousine drivers in their mafioso-style suits, holding boards with names written in English or Chinese, occasionally Arabic. Conrad will not be one of them. There is a moment when Paul sees his name but doesn't recognise it. It is handwritten, in a formal black script, on a white sheet of paper. It is not, of course, his real name; it is the name that he used when he was working in pornography. It is not Paul Carrigan that the man is seeking—it is Sean Garner.

And it is as I am approaching the bridge, the rusting steel cables trembling, shimmering, as a large truck pounds across it, that I swiftly choose Paul's porn name, in homage to a young child's love of Sean Connery as James Bond and the attractive gambler and gunslinger that James Garner played in *Maverick*. In fact, I embellish this further; it is while watching *Maverick* on TV as a child, in the small house in Sacramento that belonged to his grandpa—always too hot, always too draughty and too dusty, always stinking of mildew—that the young Paul senses his cock stirring, hardening, like when his mother's boyfriends fling him their porno magazines to look at; the same warm feeling in his crotch as when he sees the naked women and girls in the magazines. Lying on his stomach on the floor, Paul will wiggle, enjoying the friction of his groin along the rug; and then he is returned to the show he is watching. I think all of this in a rush as I cross the bridge. The first thing I will do when I reach the house is type the name into the document on my laptop.

There is a moment where Paul doesn't recognise his name. Then his eyes shift back to the white sheet.

That's right, he tells himself, I'm Sean, not Paul.

And then he notices the man's hands. They have the same shape as Nikos's hands, in that they are large, the fingers broad and thick. They are not attractive hands, there is nothing genteel about them. What Paul recognises in them is what reassured me as a child: the certainty of aptitude and momentum in such hands. Conrad is old, and Nikos's hands were still those of a young man that day on the beach when, in my secret masturbation, I buttressed the love between us and made it unperishable.

I do understand that this love, while eternal in the sense that it lives within me and cannot die, and so can only be extinguished at my last breath, is also solitary and belongs to me; I have never spoken to Nikos about it and I would not dare: it would shame him and I would shame myself. There isn't even a language with which to speak it, and anyway, he is an old, old man now, older even than the age I have made Conrad. His love and affection for me is still undoubted. The nature of my love remains solitary, onanistic; it is, then, of a different order from the love I share with Simon, which is a blessing passed between us daily, in our kisses and our embraces, and even in our conflicts, our crude and embarrassing squabbles; and just as the love is passed between us in the spittle of our kiss, it is also apportioned in how our bodies lie alongside each other at night when we are asleep, from the sweat off our skin. In such a way the love between us forms a universe, it is always in motion and forever expanding. It does not pivot on one precise moment—that afternoon at the beach, alone together—as does the love I have for Nikos. It must be a rule of masturbatory love that it eternally swivels on the limitation of the singular instance, an endless and continuous repetition. Here I do it again, I am revisiting the occurrence by distilling it in the moment when Paul recognises the vigour emanating from Conrad's hands.

'Hello, I'm Sean.'

I can hear my blood propelling through my body as I ascend the steep hill. I wrench myself from fantasy, from this first encounter between the men, and return to the world, immediate and concrete and sensual, all around me. The course of my blood in my veins. The sweat at the small of my back, trickling down the cleft of my buttocks, moist under my arms. The swollen clouds, slate grey, are now mustering overhead. I reach the summit and, before turning into the lane I look back, down the hill, and the sky above the ocean is darkening. I am hoping it will rain. I will not leave the desk that I have made of the long hardwood table on the deck. I will write the encounter between Paul and Conrad. I stop myself thinking of it any further. The task now is to release them from my fancies and daydreaming. To do so I need to sit down, either with pen and notebook, or with my laptop open. Only that will unlock the postern between imagination and creation.

Lost in my musings, I had not remembered to stop at the shop near the bridge to buy fish. For lunch I break four eggs into a bowl, pour in some soy sauce, some pepper, whisk the mixture furiously and quickly. I slice a red onion, a clove of garlic, and finely chop a long green chilli. In a few minutes the omelette is ready.

Over lunch, I do not think about work. Instead I read yesterday's paper; all that news of the world and the gossip of celebrity boring me, and I turn again to the crossword. The final clue remains elusive. As soon as I have finished eating, I put on the coffee then go downstairs for the phone and call Simon. As soon as he hears my voice, he says, 'You seem happy.'

'I think I know what I'm doing.'

'With the book?'

'Yes. With the book.'

'Good.'

'I nearly got out yesterday's cryptic, but there's one bloody clue I can't get.'

'What is it?'

I hesitate; my mind settles, recalls.

'Plant in a rut must flourish,' I say.

And almost immediately, with only the most minimal pause, he answers: 'Nasturtium.'

'I fucking love you!'

We laugh out loud.

When I end the call, my finger moves to the blue icon for email. I tap on it. But the messages—first one downloading, then another and another until there are dozens—can only be distractions. I switch off the phone without reading them, put it on the table. I walk back upstairs.

The coffee pot is sputtering and wheezing, and I go into the kitchen and switch off the gas. I pour the thick coffee into a small cup, take it outside. The clouds overhead are still not black but there are streaks of the dark shadow of rain over the ocean.

I sip my coffee and smoke a cigarette. When it is nearly burnt to the filter, I stub it out in the ashtray. I flick open the lid of the computer. I start to type and there are the sounds of small detonations, bursts of crackling and cracking across the tin sheets of the verandah's roof. The first spit of rain has arrived. Within minutes it builds to a crescendo. The world is lost in the drumming of the rain.

'Hello, I'm Sean.'

The elderly man's handshake is strong and assured, and the grip is maintained for exactly the right length of time: released too early and it would betray uncertainty, held too long and it would imply aggression.

'I'm Conrad.' He indicates Paul's suitcase. 'Would you like some assistance with that?'

'No, I'm okay.'

'Good, let's go to the car.'

Paul extends the case's handle, adjusts the light pack on his back, and follows Conrad out through the airport's sliding doors. The dry smoggy Los Angeles air smacks his face. He has forgotten the parched astringency of the city's pollution, the impenetrable shade that hangs low in the sky, the drab fungal cast a perpetual awning shielding the sun. He thinks back to the brilliant blue-green shades of the Australian coast he'd left only a day ago: how much more splendid, unspoilt, is the landscape on the western rim of the Pacific basin. As he walks behind Conrad, he hears the American accent in its varied tones and pitches, and delights in the brazen assuredness with which the taxi and Uber drivers honk their horns. A very obese man in a shiny brown business suit, the jacket so tight around his astounding belly that it seems impossible the buttons haven't popped, has one hand resting on his luggage while the other holds a phone jammed tight against his ear. 'There just ain't no way, baby,' he booms. 'There just ain't no way!' As he and Conrad stop at a pedestrian crossing, Paul is jostled by a young woman who pushes her luggage trolley straight across the road without pausing. On the other side she spins around and calls, 'Sorry, honey!' and then strides into the car park. Her insouciance makes Paul want to laugh out loud.

And it is black. LA, America, is full of black people. He has forgotten that too, and he is delighted by it. The Australian cities he has visited are not exactly white. Brisbane, Sydney and Melbourne: whenever he is in the heart of those cities he is aware of how Asian they are. But they are certainly not black. He is home. And there is no other place in the world like America. This is confirmed when they reach Conrad's car, a sleek, black and expensive SUV which looks—though Paul is no expert on cars—brand-new. It sports a large Stars and Stripes bumper with the caption: GOD BLESS AMERICA. Yes, he is home.

Conrad presses a button on his key to open the trunk, then takes Paul's suitcase and effortlessly swings it up and in. Paul is struck by the man's agility, which belies his age. And Conrad is attractive, and that is a relief. Jenna had speculated that the john would be fat and ugly, with terrible breath and incontinence issues. It had been a surprise how quickly they had resumed the merciless teasing of young kids working in porn.

Conrad closes the trunk and turns to Paul. 'Now, we're heading to Santa Barbara. I know you've had a long flight, though, so I'd be happy to spend the night in a hotel here in the city.' Conrad's cheeks are flushed, as if he is embarrassed by the rush of words. His eyes, deep-set and black, are imploring. 'Really, Sean, whatever you want, I'm happy to accommodate.'

That's right. He is no longer Paul; he must remember he is Sean. He feels a flush of pleasure. It has been a long time since he has been Sean, since he has had that boldness and that conceit.

Opening the passenger-side door, he winks at the old man.

'Let's head north straight away. I've always liked Santa Barbara.'

'Greenville, South Carolina.' Replying to Sean's question, Conrad's face breaks into a proud smile. 'Born there, raised there, gonna die there. It's a good place. It's given me a good life.'

Sean is enjoying listening to the laconic melodiousness of the southern accent. Not that Conrad is a big talker. As soon as they had started to slowly edge into the long exit road leading out of LAX and bleeding into the city's jumbled asphalt and concrete capillaries, Conrad had flicked a button on the digital screen on the dashboard and the car had been flooded by caressing, aerating piano music. Sean had been surprised by the choice, given Conrad's unpretentious drawl and casual attire—black denim jeans, a red-and-ivory-striped Miller ranch shirt with the sleeves rolled up to the elbows. Neither Sean nor Jenna had been raised with an appreciation of classical music, and if he were honest, Sean found the heavy pomposity of it—particularly those belting, crashing symphonies—tedious. But the piece they are listening to now is gentle. The touch of the pianist's fingers on the keys is light, entrancing, and the music has a plaintive, melancholy air.

'This is beautiful.'

'Chopin,' Conrad tells him, pronouncing the composer's name with a distinct Carolingian softness. There is a slight tension. Sean notices it in the stretching of the muscles along the old man's throat, as if he had been about to say something more and then thought better of it. The silence which had been companionable and easy only a moment before now is strained. Sean focuses on the music instead. Its simplicity, the plangent unhurried notes, is soothing.

They are on the freeway now. He rests his head against the passenger window and gazes through the windshield at the dance of the cars and vans and trucks: sometimes accelerating, darting between lanes, sometimes slowing to a crawl. The world seems to pulsate, a reverberation that is everywhere, and he is reminded that there are millions and millions of people all around him, that this city shifts and rushes forwards and hurls and vaults and rages every single second of the day and night. In Australia, he can drive for an hour and see no one else on the road. That is impossible here. No wonder the fear of earthquakes and seismic calamity are ever-present in Los Angeles: the city never stops moving, racing, charging. It all rushes back; Sean remembered: living here had always felt like being on the brink of a great quaking.

He awakes with a jolt. The car is parked in the lot of a twenty-four-hour diner, the name of the restaurant—*Annie's*—cut out in a continuous italic scroll from a metal sheet which soars above the building. Yawning, discombobulated, not sure where he is, Sean glances around. Through the rear window he sees the sheen of blue ocean. And looking straight ahead he sees Conrad returning to the car, a paper bag in one hand, sturdily balancing a cardboard tray with two takeaway coffees in the other. That's right. He is in America.

The old man, seeing that Sean is awake, gives him a warm and gracious smile.

They resume their journey. The music, while still calm, unadorned yet elegant, no longer seems pensive. Perhaps the short sleep has lightened Sean's mood, or maybe it is a different composer. Sipping his coffee, the air outside the car less dense and suffocating now that they have finally been released from the city, Sean studies the man beside him as he drives. The coast highway has narrowed, begun to wind, and Conrad's grip is tighter on the wheel, his attention fully on the road.

The potency of Conrad's hands. The hands of a man who was no stranger to work. The tanned skin is scarred and weathered, speckled with the pink and brown blotches of age. The tufts of hair on the knuckles of the man's broad fingers startle Sean; the hair there is thick, still black, even though the hair on Conrad's head, clipped short in a crew cut, is completely silvery grey, and the light dusting of hair visible beneath the open collar of his shirt is white. And though the skin is withered, his hands hold the wheel firmly, the tendons and muscles are taut; there is nothing frail about them.

And all at once, thrusting through him as if pierced by a sword, so excruciating and staggering is the onslaught, he thinks of his son, of Neal's lean body, his son's strength and beauty forged from work and from the morning hours in the surf. He had texted Jenna before his flight departed Brisbane, and then had not thought of her again. This is not a cause for guilt; he knows it is not a betrayal. Though it has not been articulated between them, since the arrival of Jackson's letter they have both fallen into occasional daydreams, imagining a life without each other. They are to be apart for a fortnight.

Jenna's response when he mused that he might stay on an extra week or so, reacquaint himself with LA, was to nod in amenable agreement. Without needing to speak about it, they are each grateful for the respite. There is no sense of disloyalty about this, as Sean knows without question that he will return to his wife and their life together. But to have forgotten Neal, even for a few hours, seems a shameful treachery.

'Are you okay?'

Conrad had asked the question abruptly, almost rudely, but Sean is not at all perturbed by his sharp tone. He realises his expression of pain, his wincing, must have alarmed the other man, but he understands that for men of Conrad's generation emotions such as fear, anxiety and confusion need to be expressed in a combative form so as not to expose weakness.

Sean raises a hand and begins massaging his neck, pretending that his discomfort is merely physical. 'Sleeping on a plane is murder on the body.'

'Was it comfortable? I've heard Qantas are excellent, but I've never done such a long flight.'

'It was great. Absolutely great.'

The answer pleases Conrad and they lapse back into silence. Sean is about to disturb it, to thank the man for arranging the comfort of a business-class flight, then he remembers that this is a business transaction, and with that thought a sourness seems to enter the roomy cabin of the SUV. Sean drops his hand, shifts his body away from the older man. He notices the ugly fold of skin under Conard's firm jaw, as wrinkled and flabby as a chicken's wattle. That release of odium energises Sean, makes him stretch his legs, pushing his feet hard against the floor of the car; he thrusts his chest out, enjoying the sensation of dominating and filling space. Doing so, his hand slides against the coarse grey cotton of his sweatpants and rubs against his phone, the sharp corner of his cigarette pack. Sean indicates the green exit sign ahead.

'Can we make a stop? I need to phone home. And I need a cigarette.'

He suspects that the old man detests smoking, yet Conrad's response is courteous and immediate. He nods and, flicking on the indicator, begins to merge into the exit lane.

Sean smokes, Paul doesn't. He had been surprised by the immediate impulse to buy the cigarettes as soon as he had noticed the kiosk near the exit doors at LAX. He hasn't smoked for more than twenty years. Jenna had given up while pregnant with Neal, and he had decided to quit in support. The cravings had been awful for a fortnight, tempered and manageable for the next year and then had largely vanished. Of course, they smoked dope, which probably helped. But he has not missed the poisonous rasp of cigarettes. And then there had been the kiosk. He had asked Conrad to wait, then went straight up to the counter and asked for a pack of Lucky Strikes Blue.

He sucks hard on the cigarette, texting his son, leaning against the bonnet of the car. It is a Lexus, he notices for the first time. It seems an odd choice: Conrad seems the kind of man who'd drive an American car. He glances over his shoulder. Conrad is sitting behind the wheel, scrolling through his phone. The old man suddenly looks up and smiles, seeming almost bashful, unsure of himself. Sean releases a long stream of smoke from the corner of his mouth, returns to the phone. He has already sent the text. He is performing.

Returning to the car, he feels a little ashamed of the stench of the smoke on his clothes, on his breath. He hadn't meant to do it, but as soon as he has taken his seat he says, 'Thank you.'

There was wealth in Australia, of course there was; the island continent was one of the richest nations on the planet. But the scale was so very different from the ostentatiousness and indulgence of American affluence. It is still afternoon as they approach Santa Barbara, but even in the white foam of the blazing afternoon light the wedge of city sprouting between the mountains and the incandescent blue ocean is a glittering, coruscating treasure box of turrets and spires. Sean experiences an urge to giggle with childish glee in appreciation of the vulgarity and the daring. No one did give a fuck. Ultramodern geometric structures built into the hills, with floor-to-ceiling tinted windows; high-gated villas modelled on Teutonic fortresses and palaces; and, high on one of the slopes, a bulky, square whitewashed mansion with steep minarets rising from every corner, the tiles alternately crimson and alabaster.

For a moment, Sean is overwhelmed: he is jet-lagged, confused as to the role he is meant to play over the next few days—the contract had stipulated that Conrad requires Sean's services for three nights—and disorientated by the strangeness of returning to a country that, it hits him now with an accelerating and perplexing force, he loves very much. So he is relieved when, rather than driving into the heart of Santa Barbara—into the crowds, into the noise, into all that animation—Conrad turns off onto a small road that rises towards the mountains north of town. He stops the car in front of a thick metal gate set in the soft yellow bricks of a hacienda-style wall and reaches into the glove compartment, finds a key and clicks its button. The gate rumbles, the panels separate, and he steers the car smoothly into the driveway.

'Here we are.'

For a moment, neither of the men move. The house, at first glance, is unprepossessing: a wide garage next to a squat rectangular two-storey building, its rendered walls painted a dull, unattractive cream. Yet, the frames around the windows and front door are made of red hardwood. The steel-panelled gate they had entered is not cheap. And beyond the narrow strip of hedged garden to the side of the garage, there is a glimpse to the Pacific Ocean beyond.

'Is this your place?'

Conrad's laugh is full-throated, masculine and rumbling, and dispels Sean's wariness.

'No, Sean, I have to admit I'm not much one for California. But I thought I'd rent a place here.' And now he turns away, his chin lowered, once again looking abashed. 'I know it's a long journey I've asked you to undertake.'

There is something sweet about the old man's shyness and old-world courteousness. Sean stretches out a hand, drops it on the crotch of Conrad's jeans.

It is a mistake. The man almost leaps out of his seat; and indeed, the back of his head bangs against the headrest of the driver's seat with such force that for a few seconds the seat ricochets back and forth. Mortified, Sean withdraws his hand. There is only the sound of the old man's quickened breaths. Sean's cheeks, his neck, are hot with embarrassment.

Conrad, still looking ahead, as if not daring to face Sean, says quietly, 'I guess we should unpack.' He presses a button on the keys and beneath them there is a mechanical whirring from the engine, the car trembles gently and behind them the lid of the trunk slowly starts to rise.

Sean's eyes fly open. The room is in complete darkness. There is the sound of the rolling, purring waves—the ocean winds are gentle this night—and a faint subdued music. He sits up in the bed. He is still in his T-shirt, in the grey ugly sweatpants he had worn on the flight. He sniffs under his arms. The stench is concentrated: he reeks. Of course, he hasn't showered; he hadn't meant to fall asleep. Jenna had been forceful in her instructions. Get into the rhythm as soon as you get there. Don't fall asleep until it's night-time. Well, he's fucked that up. His head is clanging. Slowly, discerning a glimmer of light in the gloom, he notices a tall glass on the bedstand and he reaches for it, drinks all the water in three long gulps. He takes his phone and, as soon as he touches it, the screen is illuminated. A photograph he had taken from the verandah, looking down the green slope of the front paddock, the ocean filling half the frame; and his wife and son walking down the hill, deep in conversation, Neal's face, grinning, turned slightly askew, as if seeking his father. Over the image he reads the time: 8.45 in the evening. Sean's hand searches the cedar wood panel above his head, locates the switches. The first one lights up the whole bedroom and it is too harsh, too bright. He immediately turns it off again. He flicks the second button. A faint light beams from the ensuite. Sean stands, strips off his T-shirt and pants, kicks them into a corner. His first priority—and he experiences it as a furious, imperative need, akin to salvation—is to shower.

As the crescendo of water streams over his head and shoulders and back, he thinks back to the urge that had propelled him with such speed into the bathroom. Salvation. The potency, the danger of that word, surprises him; as has its arising, after being so long neglected. Sean has not thought of God, nor of God's absence, for decades. Jenna's faith is a constant in their life together, and he neither resents it nor envies it, but her trust in God's grace has a clarity and simplicity of purpose that he cannot reconcile with the beliefs and rituals and superstitions of his childhood, nor to the shames and the terrors of the religion his mother had espoused.

A memory invades his consciousness—and this was exactly how it is for him, he experiences the entry of the recollection to his mind's eye as a ferocious assault—and he is ten or maybe eleven and Buck, his mother's new boyfriend, is beckoning him over and Buck looks a little like Jerry Smith if the footballer had a cigarette dangling permanently from his lips and his forearms and the tops of his hands were covered in slashes of indigo, black and scarlet tattoos. He approaches the man warily and then swiftly Buck lifts both arms and the boy is shocked at the flare of orange tufts of hair underneath the man's arms. Buck holds out his fists, so close they almost graze the boy's belly. 'Look at them,' the man insists, and the boy sees that on the closed digits of the left hand the black numerals 6 6 6 have been marked between the knuckles of the index and two middle fingers, and that the middle finger of the other fist has a blue crucifix, and a scrawl of thin black ink runs across the closed fingers. It reads: *MATT HEW 8 :22.* 'Do you understand, boy?' Paul shakes his head. Buck's right hand shoots forwards and he grabs the back of the boy's head and pulls Paul into him so that his mouth and nostrils are buried in the man's sodden armpit and the stench of it is so nauseating, dank and rotting, that the boy squirms, needing to gag. The man hisses in his ear, 'There is only the Devil and there is only the Lord and men don't matter, fathers and mothers and all the rest of the stinking

vermin that crawls over this earth, none of that matters.'
And with that, Paul is released.

In the long, luxurious stream of the shower, Sean shudders.
He bangs the side of his head with his palm, as if in that
extreme action he can dislodge the unwelcome memory. He
whispers to himself, gaining stillness and resolution from its
utterance, 'Remember, you are Sean, you are not Paul.'

He turns off the taps.

The ensuite is spacious, immaculately clean. It is not only
this that lends it the air of a hotel room. It is well stocked
with toiletries that all bear the logo of a particular company,
an outline of a vine leaf set against a pale, almost opaque
jade square. The bath towel is oversized, freshly washed and
the fibres long and thick and soft. The mirror above the
basin runs the length of the wall. Sean dries himself, drops
the towel and examines his body.

He has resisted the vanity of dyeing his hair. It is his
belief—a belief shared by Jenna—that letting it go grey
naturally but keeping it cut short is a more effective amelioration of age. And indeed, a few days before the flight, he
had driven into town to get it trimmed. Nevertheless, there
is no denying that his is now an ageing body. The steady
maintenance and work required on the property have kept
him fit. He is certainly not overweight. But there is a paunch,
a double roll of fat on his midriff, and he now gives the rolls a
squeeze. He has been slack with the gym; he should take
more opportunities to go out for a morning surf with his son.

Sean turns, stretches his neck to glimpse his backside in the mirror. A faint, very faint spiderweb of hair along his lower back, disappearing in the denser bush between his buttocks. His ass isn't too bad. Definitely not a young man's ass—or *arrrse*; he speaks the word aloud, deliberately slurring and elongating it, and then chuckles to himself at the travesty he is making of the Australian accent. He had debated driving to Byron Bay to get a full wax treatment but Jenna had reminded him that one of the distinctions of his porn persona was that Sean Garner was the stereotypical man-next-door, always portraying a heterosexual Everyman—the plumber, the delivery guy, the neighbour mowing his lawn—who just happened to have sex with a man whenever the opportunity was presented to him. Sean places both hands over his chest, cups his nipples, notices the slight wobble there. He drops his hands, quickly shakes his penis and his balls. No change there.

Then he looks down, away from the mirror, and smiles ruefully. Yes, a few rebellious coils of silver hair in the thicket of his pubes.

He brushes his teeth and applies deodorant. Still naked, he quickly unpacks, finding ample space in the drawers and the closet. He decides on his black Levi jeans, the R.M. Williams brown leather belt and a simple white Bonds T-shirt. Not his dress shoes. He slides on a pair of grey ankle socks and laces up his white Puma sneakers. He takes one last look in the mirror, runs his hand across his hair, hoists up his pants and tightens the belt. He won't wear underpants. He knows that the dance of the evening, its moves and directions, will all be dictated by the client. Yet he also knows he will try and choreograph a specific moment: the old man on his knees, Sean standing over him and unzipping, his cock falling out, grunting to the old cunt, 'Suck me off!'

He gives himself a thumbs-up in the mirror and whispers, 'You'll be alright, boy, you've played this part before!'

The house is deceptive: it appears compact when first observed from the outside; but at the end of the short corridor an open archway leads into a sprawling living area, with soft light falling from the downlights in the high ceiling and from the moonbeams flowing in through the glass doors past the enormous kitchen. Outside on the patio, the perspective making him look tiny, Conrad is leaning over the railing, staring out to the ocean, dressed in a shirt and cargo shorts. Though Sean can't spot a stereo unit, piano music is tinkling through the open space. Only one small outcrop of wall, forming a narrow alcove, defies the symmetry of the open plan. Sean stands before it. On that wall is a huge print of a somewhat dilapidated rural house, lemon yellow weatherboards, a simple white-painted portico, once clearly elegant but now the beams and brickwork have aged and shifted, augmenting the impression of the building's decline. The most winsome features of the house are the cornflower blue shutters, flung open as if to announce the arrival of summer guests. A curving, irregular tree trunk cuts the view in half. The painting is familiar; Sean has seen the same print, on a smaller scale, somewhere else. He is struck now by how the artist has captured a sense of the house being on a precipice; once loved and well-tended, once a home, it is now falling—not quite, not there yet—into ruin. And Sean thinks about the money the stranger on the deck is paying him and, taking a deep breath, rolling his shoulders, he feels the onset of a swagger pitching through his body.

He is surprisingly nervous, as if this is a first date. And in some ways, it is. That makes him smile, and he thinks of his wife. There have been infidelities in their marriage—the trajectories of his and Jenna's lives had long ago dispelled the caprice of physical monogamy—yet infidelities are not affairs and the sex he's had with other people over the last twenty years has been largely anonymous, always brief, always transient.

He flings open the door to the patio and Conrad spins around. He is beaming; there is delight in those dark flashing eyes, in the wrinkled corners of his smile. The glow of the moonlight makes his cropped hair appear ivory. He is old, Sean muses, but he is attractive. Is there Italian there? Latino? Old Baptist bodies, if they don't go to fat, do get slight and desiccated. There is an indication of hardness to Conrad, nothing of the sissy about him. Sean gazes steadily at the old man, recalls the terror in Conrad's eyes when Sean had reached for his cock in the car. And even now, though clearly glad to see him, there is a hint of that same almost adolescent nerviness. Sean makes a decision. He struts up to Conrad, grabs the back of the man's head, brings their lips together.

A jolt of initial resistance—Sean feels the other man's body straining away from him—and then the release. They kiss for a long time. Sean tastes the chemical mint of toothpaste, the saltiness of the saliva; but what pleases him most is that he is aroused. It is the harshness of being with a man, the scratching of Conrad's bristled cheek against his, the grip of the man's arm around his neck and shoulder. And the mouth is hard, the lips are rough, with nothing of a woman's softness. He grinds himself against the older man, his hand disappearing under Conrad's shirt to rub the soft curls on his chest, retreating to the small pouch of the belly, dropping further to cradle the fat, squat cock. It is limp, cold. They stop kissing.

'Can we sit down?' Conrad's voice is shy, trembling. He steps away from Sean and walks over to a small portable bar at the end of the deck.

Sean doesn't move. He stares out into the darkness: the restrained swirling of the ocean, near invisible except for faint webs of silver as a wave breaks; the patches in the spray which capture the moonlight and flash a cold metallic blue before returning to shadow. There are the twinkling lights of yachts and small sailing cruisers dotted around the bay, and in the distance the lights of the town seem to pulse with a steady ominous glow. There are no stars visible. In every way, Australia now seems remote.

He adjusts his crotch. Thankfully his erection is ebbing. He is humiliated. And resentful.

'I'm sorry, Sean; I guess I'm frightened. You are the most beautiful man I have ever seen. And I'm just very frightened.' Conrad's sneering laugh, his contempt, is clearly directed at himself. 'I'm an old fool. I do apologise.'

Conrad walks over to the glass doors, pushes one ajar, presses a button on the kitchen wall. The far end of the deck is instantly bathed in a gentle amber light. For the first time, Sean notices a compact dining setting: a long rectangular table, its surface cold and gleaming, surrounded by four chairs constructed from the same dense metal. There is the steady lapping of the water from a small infinity pool at the very edge of the patio.

'Please.' Conrad gestures to the table. 'Sit. You must be famished.'

Sean is. Lowering himself into one of the chairs, he appraises the cold cuts, the breads and crackers and dips, the corn chips and salsas spread along the table. He is already salivating. He helps himself to a bread roll and, tearing off a piece, scoops up some gummy, red salsa. As he bites into it, the heat from the peppers floods his senses, rushing to his head like a drug high. He is perspiring, the sweat beading his forehead, trickling down his neck. He swallows and immediately reaches back for more.

Conrad places an open bottle of beer next to Sean's plate and then sits across from him. Sean chugs on the beer, downing almost half the bottle. He scoops up more salsa, adds thick slices of chorizo, sprinkles green chillies over it and finishes with a squeeze of lime juice. His lips, his chin, his hands are soon dripping with oil and sauce.

'Sorry,' he mumbles, his mouth full. 'You just don't get Mexican food like this where I live.'

The older man is taking an evident joy in Sean's pleasure. Conrad himself only nibbles at the food, explaining that he ate earlier, but he hadn't wanted to wake Sean from his sleep. The silence is companionable, broken only by the sounds of Sean's chewing, the unbroken purring of the pool and the occasional shout or peal of laughter from a sailing craft bobbing on the waters below.

Finally, Sean nudges back his chair and pats his belly. 'Thank you, that was terrific.'

And almost immediately, the atmosphere grows tense. The two men avoid each other's eyes. Realising that he needs to fart, Sean squeezes his stomach, his buttocks, rises and asks for the loo. Corrects himself. 'The bathroom.'

As soon as he sits on the toilet his wind breaks, and there is the squelch of wet faeces spraying into the water, splattering on the porcelain. There is one more long ugly fart, a final rumble of his stomach. Sean snatches thick wads of the toilet paper, vigorously wipes himself clean. Sordid memories return. Sordid. It is an unusual word, not one he remembers ever using before, but it is exactly the right word for his reminiscences. He used to hate it: the enemas and douching and foul pills they'd take to induce constipation; they'd tasted of wet grass. The whole rigorous regime on porn sets to conceal the treacheries of the body, the sounds and fluids and solids that the body secreted, has soured him on anal sex forever. Not even with Jenna. Standing up with his jeans around his ankles, Sean winds more toilet paper around his hand, shuffles to the small wash basin, wets the paper and, bent over, wipes the wet tissue over the inside of his buttocks, across his butt crack. He flushes the filthy mess down the toilet.

As he washes his hands, he peers at his face in the small oval mirror, takes in the puffiness below his eyes, the ruddy flush on his cheeks. Sordid. That strange word is still spinning around in his head.

Outside, Conrad has opened another beer for him. Sean sits down and grabs it gratefully.

'I was married for forty-eight years.' Conrad's laugh is dry, curt. 'To a woman,' he adds. 'I guess you have to make that clear these days.'

Sean looks up. The old man's elbows are planted on the steel tabletop, the tip of his chin resting on his fists. He is facing Sean, but his gaze is fixed over Sean's shoulder. Sean understands instinctively that part of the reason he is here, returned to America, being paid by this old gentleman, is to listen to what is now being related.

'Tania died last year. We were married when I was twenty-three. Not long back from Vietnam.'

Sean's eyes dart to the old man's face at the mention of the war. A nudge of fear, and also a sullen respect. Some of his mom's old boyfriends had been in Vietnam. From a young age, Sean had learnt to be on the alert when he heard that word. He can imagine Conrad being severe, even heartless, if he believed it necessary. Yet his isn't a cruel face.

And then Sean remembers: cruelty and ugliness can wear the most charming of guises. He needs to be on his guard. And he needs a cigarette. He pats his jean pocket, sighs with quiet relief to find that his Luckies are there.

Conrad has fallen silent. Then expertly, with a smooth gliding motion, he takes an expensive gold-plated lighter from his shorts pocket and ignites the flame. Sean draws in smoke then exhales. The older man points to one of the empty beer bottles and Sean nods curtly. It will do as an ashtray.

The old man is weighing the lighter in his hand.

'I never smoked. Tania did. Not the last twenty or so years of her life, of course, on account of our age.' He slides the lighter across the table to Sean and laughs softly. 'Though I do suspect that she had the occasional smoke for old time's sake. Always had mints in the glove box of the car. She was a good woman and I did love her, and she knew that. Three children, two girls and a boy; they've grown into fine women and a fine man. We don't see each other often.' And at this his voice falters, saddens. 'Truth be told, they didn't see much of their mom either once they grew up and left home.'

He shrugs. 'That seems the American way, ain't it? We don't know how to be close to family anymore.'

Now he is looking directly at Sean, and this makes the younger man uncomfortable. He is only half-listening to Conrad. He is thinking about how quickly and easily he has resumed smoking. The first cigarette, back at LAX, had been corrosive, the first drag unpleasant. Maybe if he had tossed it away after those first two or three puffs he'd never smoke again. But by the end of the cigarette he was aware of a pleasant but not hallucinatory sedateness; not numbness, just quiet. And just now, there was the panicked fumble for the packet, the relief that he had not left the cigarettes back in the bedroom.

Conrad's body is turned slightly away from Sean, his long thin legs exceedingly pale in the moonlight. He is looking out to the ocean. Sean reminds himself that he must pay attention to the old bastard. He has to encourage him, flatter and seduce him. He casually shifts in his seat, his knee gently grazing Conrad's leg.

Conrad turns to face him again.

'It was a good marriage, Sean, I do believe that. I carried guilt for a long time because . . .' Conrad pauses, clears his throat, then continues. 'Yes, indeed, guilt, 'cause of what God and nature had made me. Tania never said anything, and I'd like to believe she remained ignorant of the fact that I was not the man she needed me to be. Mercifully, we were able to make love, and I believe she enjoyed it. Not so often in the last many years, not so much at all. But that's no different to anyone, I guess.'

Sean, who has been smoking his cigarette in silence, is astonished by the ferocity of his contempt for the pitiful old man. Surely the damnable fool must perceive the fakery of Sean's smile? His jaw hurts from stretching it so, as if he was one of those vintage arcade laughing clowns, those gaping mouths into which he and his friends would toss pebbles and cigarette butts, used condoms and the damp stinking ends of roaches. Sean hadn't tricked much, mostly only as a favour for some of the producers he worked with, often to pay for drugs, but even with that limited experience he'd been struck by how quickly resentment and scorn flourished when sex was reduced to a mercantile transaction. Sean drops the fag end into the beer bottle; there is an abrupt fizz. No, he thinks to himself, it isn't because sex is being made commercial that gives rise to the contempt. It is when affection, intimacy, even love are being sought and bought; that is when bitterness and revulsion rises to one's throat like bile. Here is this old cunt raving on about his boring old marriage to boring old Tania who probably always knew that she'd made the mistake of marrying a faggot. If she really had been called Tania; if the old man really is named Conrad. Sean has lied about his name, after all, and presumably the old man wants to protect himself from the mercenary desires of an old porn actor. On those rare occasions when she recalled the old days in LA, Jenna always said, 'The distrust between whore and john is mutual.'

'She was very pretty.' Conrad has been scrolling through his phone. He now shows Sean a photo. 'This is when we had just got engaged.'

The picture must have been taken in the 1970s, judging by the depth and pastel brightness of the colours, undiminished by the pixilated digital reproduction. A young woman in a sleeveless, white knee-length dress with a red floral pattern is standing next to a young man in jeans and a pale blue Wrangler shirt. He has his arm draped carefully over her shoulders; there is a slight distance between them, but she has her head tilted towards the youth, and it is obvious that she trusts him. There is also something about the defiant diffidence of her stance that suggests to Sean that this was her best dress, that she had made a special effort for this photograph. Her fair, thin hair is cut in deliberate imitation of the shagginess that was so emblematic of that decade. Sean takes the phone and splays his fingers across the screen to enlarge the image. He is looking at Tania but his mother's ghost intrudes; she'd had the same layered hairstyle.

He turns his attention to the young man. So very handsome. As Sean studies the young Conrad's face he knows that this is why he is being shown the photograph; not to put a face to Tania but to see Conrad as a young man. In the photograph his hair is longer than he wears it now; it is jet-black, almost greasy, shimmering even on the phone's screen. He looks Italian but he doesn't possess the strutting virility of those Sacramento wop boys who used to fascinate Sean as a teenager. Conrad's face isn't that lean, that hungry. The cheeks are fuller, the eyes softer. When Sean was a boy there was an ad on TV all the time—was it for cigarettes?—in which a young man was getting off a scooter in a piazza in Italy somewhere. The colours were warm, all oranges and tawny reds, and there had been a real dignity to the beauty of the boy on the bike. Sean has always thought that solemnity European, definitely exotic. But here was Conrad, thoroughly American, and though the original rapture of beauty had long gone, callously assaulted by age, that poise and self-possession is still there. He doesn't begrudge the old man's vanity at all.

'She was very beautiful,' he says, handing back the phone. 'You both were.'

Conrad gets up and walks over to the bar, returning with two more beers.

'We met in high school. She was the sweetest girl.'

Conrad sits down. He twists off the caps to the beers with an almost ferocious fleetness.

'I'd had a few experiences with men when I was young. They were grubby. But I was most ashamed when I fell for a fella I was in training with in the marines. That really terrified me, made me think, my God, I really am a faggot.'

The harsh savage stress on both syllables of the word; as if he is spitting them out, has to force them from himself.

'We married when I returned from the war and I went into business with my brother. We were both auto technicians; that had been our father's work, the trade our grandpa taught himself when he first came to this country.'

'Italy?' The interjection is involuntary. Sean is still thinking of the boy on the scooter.

Conrad glances over at him. 'Papa Nick was from Greece. Don't know where from exactly. He died when I was a boy and he never was one for looking back. He loved the States.' He raises his beer bottle. 'God bless America.'

The two men clink their bottles.

Conrad takes a sip, clears his throat once more. 'My brother was smarter than me with technical stuff. He worked out a flushing system for pistons that saved on labour and saved on time. He said to me, "Connie, you have the business head—you and me are partners." I got us a patent and in time we made a lot of money. I have been very fortunate, Sean, very fortunate indeed.'

A sudden wave of sickness, as if his stomach is falling away, the vertigo located precisely in his abdomen and guts; dear Lord, is he going to vomit? Worse, shit his pants? Sean feels the wetness and heat of the sweat rising on his brow and the back of his neck. He places the cold bottle against his right cheek.

'You okay?'

Those coal-black eyes, kindness there; it augments the dignity of his features.

'I'm fine, Conrad. It's the jet lag.'

And giving it a name is a relief; the biliousness has gone.

'Money didn't come in straight away. It never does.'

Conrad is continuing his story. There is clearly a grim purpose to it. Sean wonders if he has rehearsed it, delivered his monologue in front of the mirror in preparation. Or is it a narrative so long churning in his head that it comes out clear and relentless as soon as he dares release it?

'Those first few years on the road I was unfaithful.' He swallows, takes a long swig of the beer. 'With men. Always strangers. Always brief. And then we all started hearing about this disease that was killing homosexuals in New York and San Francisco and then, it seemed, the whole world. People were saying that it was retribution from God.'

Conrad breaths in sharply.

Jenna often said, 'Only the Devil believes he knows what God thinks.' Sean now repeats those words.

The old man nods.

'I thought I had it, Sean; I thought I must have AIDS. But, worse, I thought I must've given it to Tania, and that good and faithful young woman didn't deserve it. I drove over to Charleston, went into a clinic. They said it would be some days before they rang me with the result. I waited and I prayed and I promised the Lord that if I didn't have it, I would never betray Tania again.'

Conrad sighs, a long, ravaged breath, his chest expanding, a mixture there of deep sorrow and an equally solemn pride.

'I didn't have it. And I kept my word.'

And then Conrad surprises him. The old man's fingers curl, touch his forehead, his chest, his right shoulder and then his left.

'Those poor kids dying so young . . . That was a truly wicked disease.'

And faces, memories, flashes of the past, they all whirl fast in the corner of Sean's mind. Looking at the beer bottle on the table, recalling it all. The solemnity of Aaron's funeral, the little chubby-faced youth who had so loved getting fucked. The shock of walking into the synagogue; none of them had known the self-styled 'queen of gang-bangs' was a devout Jew. Tom from Queens: now *that* gorgeous son of a bitch had the Italian swagger. Matty, all Midwestern artlessness and a raging heroin habit. Ronnie Hays, who'd transformed himself into Washington Toblerone; oh, how that had made them laugh, for it was true: his cock was as thick as a beer can and as long and dark as a chocolate bar. Annie, Jenna's best friend, had got it from sharing a needle. Sean envies Conrad, as he sometimes envies his wife, for those rituals mortared to faith. He shakes his head; and it must have been too quick, too startling a motion, for the old man is looking at him with concern. Sean waves his hand to indicate that Conrad should continue talking.

'I was tempted, so many times I was tempted.'

Having been lost in his own reverie, the man's words are confusing. Then Sean remembers: Conrad's vow to remain faithful to his wife.

'The one indiscretion I allowed myself was that from time to time I would go into shops—you know, the shops that sold dirty magazines and videos.' Conrad has now turned away from Sean again. The abrasive, wet sound of his throat clearing. The thin wrinkled skin at his throat expanding and contracting. Even in the weak light, it is clear that the man is flushed, mortified. Sean does him the kindness of looking away. He considers there is something admirable in the old man's perseverance.

'I'd walk into those stores, in the back where the'—a hesitation; then a snarl, a lash as he says the words—'where the jerk-off booths were, and I'd put the tokens in and I'd start watching. Always men. I had an unholy hunger for men.'

Sean's hand sidles towards his cigarettes. The leap of flame from the lighter, the gasp of the tobacco being lit: the sounds are brazen.

'One evening, I walk into one of those places and I collect my tokens and I go to the booth and I press the buttons and the films flash past and then I see a face.' Conrad pauses. 'I think it the most handsome face I have ever seen. Strange and even perverse as it must sound—and man, it sounds perverse my saying it now—but I swear to my Lord that it is the truth: I fell in love immediately with that face.'

There is the scraping of the chair's legs on the tiles as Conrad shifts closer. Sean looks up. The man's face is calm; the tenderest of smiles is forming on his lips.

'It was your face, Sean. You are still the most handsome man I have ever seen.'

On that final word, Conrad's voice breaks. There is a sob, quickly checked.

'I'll get us another beer,' Sean says quietly.

When he returns, Conrad is composed. He takes the bottle and drinks from it gratefully.

'I stayed in that booth for hours. Putting token after token in those slots. Not to'—Conrad coughs—'not to pleasure myself. To watch you. You were in two scenes. In the first, you are with a very pretty, smooth-skinned black man. You are sitting reading a book by an open fire and the black man comes in and he teases you, and then the two of you make love in front of the fire. I was fascinated by how much you were perspiring in that scene, Sean, and it seemed natural and so very wonderful in its naturalness. It somehow made you seem more masculine. I envied you. I envied you for your beauty and for your confidence and wondered what it must be like to go through life knowing you are beautiful and living with that confidence. It must be remarkable.'

Sean is thinking: I worry about my weight. Like all guys, I wish my cock was bigger. I have a lopsided grin, makes me look like a damn fool at times. My hair is balding up top. But yes—and it is only now, at the old man's words, that he understands it is true—he has been fortunate, from the time he was a very young boy all the way till now, as an ageing man, to have always known he was attractive. It is the only fortune he has known.

No! That isn't true. He has Jenna and Neal. He is very fortunate.

Sean says dryly, 'You're handsome too.'

At this, the old man laughs aloud. He reaches out and pats Sean on the knee. Just as swiftly, he withdraws his hand.

'Thank you, Sean. That is very kind. I didn't know it. Maybe all the difference comes from knowing it.' His voice falls to a whisper. 'I was not a courageous man. I hope in the scales of justice that I weigh on the side of the good. But I know my weaknesses. I was not a strong man. I never had that confidence.'

The lazy heat hasn't lifted. One moment, Sean experiences the heaviness as a weight on his nape, finding it almost impossible to lift his head; and then in the next moment he feels light-headed, as if a drug fugue is about to begin. He cannot feel the warmth; he is only aware that his pits are damp, that beads of sweat are dribbling slowly down his back. His shirt is clamped to his skin. He spies expanding patches of wetness every time Conrad lifts his arms.

The old man is still talking about that video he had seen in the jerk-off booth as if it were a sacred icon painted over the altar of a medieval basilica. Lost in his memories, Conrad is describing how he took note of Sean's name, how he eagerly searched for his image on the slicks of porn videos, on the covers of skin magazines on the racks of sex shops. In a monologue that has become a consecration, he talks of his love for Sean.

The object of his adoration shudders inwardly every time he hears the word. This is not love, Sean is thinking. This is so very distant from that miracle. He pities the man. Conrad has lived a wretched life.

'Anyhow'—and at this word the old man's voice is now stark, there is the tint of rage in it—'none of that matters.' Immediately, his tone softens. 'I am grateful to you, Sean, for shining light into my life. I know that I became obsessed with an image and that probably Sean is not even your name, that I know nothing about you really. But if it hadn't been for you, I don't know if I would have been strong enough to resist lust, to keep my vow to a woman I loved.' The fierceness returns and he looks at Sean directly now. His eyes are flashing and his craggy old-world face has a leonine grandeur, and Sean recalls the handsome youth in the photograph and, within the tidal assault of the jet lag, the fall into and retreat from faintness, desire for the man floods through his body for the first time.

'I loved Tania.' The old man raises his near-empty beer bottle. 'I have not had sex with anyone else for nearly forty years. I kept my vows.'

As they clink bottles, Sean's repugnance, which had stemmed from pity, vanishes. Stop thinking like a whore, he orders himself. He releases himself from Sean and is Paul. It is not for him to judge the nature of Conrad's love nor to pass judgement on Conrad and Tania's commitment to each other. Paul knows the urgency of desire, how it overwhelms and demands to be sated. Even if ridiculous, punishing and self-defeating, the man's will must be formidable and his loyalty is certainly heroic.

His fingers are shaking as he puts another cigarette to his lips: how astonishingly quick and delightful this return to addiction. The lighting of the cigarette, the first spill of smoke into his lungs, calms his nerves. Paul turns to the old man. The question has formed in his mind and he is unsure if it is the right one to ask. He is still uncertain of his role on this night, on this weekend. Is it merely to listen? Or is there more required of him; an exchange of confidences, perhaps? Paul has no intention of revealing anything about his life to the old man. He has taken his own vows.

He asks his question. 'Conrad, do you want to have sex with me?'

The old man's howl explodes in the silence. His body is doubled over in shame and in weeping, and it is almost unbearable to witness his pain.

Paul pushes back his chair, kneels before the old man and welcomes the shuddering, heaving body into his embrace. In time, the man's body gradually relaxes. Paul now feels the cold, as the gentle night breeze whips over the collar of his shirt, damp from the old man's tears.

*

Paul's eyes open to immediate wakefulness and he knows that he will not go back to sleep. The silky sheet is crumpled at his feet; he and Conrad are both naked. The old man releases long spurts of wheezy snores. They are not loud; they have the same gentle sonority as the quiet rumbling of the ocean. The light seeping in from between the curtains illuminates Conrad's body. He is turned away from Paul and the dumpy cheeks of his ass are shockingly pale and shockingly hairy. Paul is repelled.

He carefully slides out of the bed.

Conrad does not stir. Paul had offered him a sleeping pill and the man had accepted it gratefully. The effect had been almost instantaneous. Paul takes his phone from the bedstand and the screen bursts into life. The grand green and blues of the New South Wales northern coast, his wife and his son walking away, Neal turning to him. He kisses the screen. It is 4.45 am. He has slept for three or so hours. Yet he is alert; further sleep will be impossible.

He slips on a pair of jocks, pulls the T-shirt over his body.

His intention is to walk straight out to the patio, but his attention is caught once more by the immense print of the house. He walks over to it and gasps aloud at the spectre of his own reflection in the glass. It is as if the gods-defying scrambling of time occasioned by the plane travel, and the resultant exhaustion, has accelerated the vindictiveness of age. His stubble is ragged, hoary across his cheeks and chin.

His jowls sag, his gut protrudes from under the T-shirt and there is a damp stain across the front of his jocks. Gazing at himself like this hurls him back to childhood, the onset of adolescence and the nervousness and awkwardness of that age, with its insistent self-absorption: how many hours had he spent peering into the small cracked mirror in the bathroom of the tiny house in Oak Park? Peering at the pimples on his brow, at the acne bursting across his shoulder blades, lamenting the weakness of his biceps, the scrawniness of his neck. And then, in that interregnum between junior high and high school, his pride at the strengthening of his arms and legs, the tightening of his chest, the heft that came from playing football and weight training. Even then, there had still been parts of his body that disappointed him, but he now recalls his gratitude—maybe he even thanked a god—at the realisation that he was not ugly. Perhaps it is the fug of the jet lag, but it is as if the oath he half-mumbled before the broken mirror all those years ago is spoken aloud again in this room on the edge of the Pacific Ocean. 'I'd off myself if I was ugly—ugly like Bobby Cassidy or Jenkins Eriksson. I'd fucking cut my own throat.' He is now stricken by the heartlessness of those words.

Standing in front of the print, his shadow returned to faintness, he considers the painting once more. He is fairly certain that the setting is European, but it reminds him of traipsing through the well-to-do suburbs that backed onto the woods near Sacramento; the trees there resembled the one at the centre of this painting, dividing the dilapidated house in half. He remembers most the shade and darkness of those forests, the dense canopies blocking the sun. Yet on occasion, the sun broke through and the light had the brilliance the painter had captured here: the sea-green dappled luminescence of the leaves; the rays against the white stuccoed walls of a Sacramento mansion—or, in this case, the peeling weatherboards of a once-stately home—reflected back in a flash of light that seared your eyes, and for a moment the world seemed to be a detonation of overexposure. Summers in Oak Park could be sweltering, the heat dry and rough as it whipped at his body. The woods were an escape.

The market on their way to Clearlake; he must have been twelve or maybe thirteen, just about to start junior high, and while he can't remember the town they stopped in, he remembered clearly, as if this memory had the veracity of a photograph, the dull blue hills of the woods as a back-drop and old bikers beside filthy caravans, selling bundles of magazines and trinkets from the hippie era; women with wrinkled mouths and their dyed-blonde hair tied back in ponytails, cigarettes dangling from their lips, watching eagle-eyed as he flicked through crates of old LPs. His mother laughing—it seemed she was deliriously happy that day, looking so young—with her new boyfriend, Rudy, who was whippet-thin with long greasy hair but a wide and generous smile. Paul had liked Rudy, and so had Andy.

At the thought of his little brother he experiences a pain as sharp as a knife gutting him from his belly to his chest. Paul pounds his stomach; to wrestle with the memory, to beat it back in retreat.

And in a flash, it returns. Coming back from visiting Josie in Clearlake; he remembers his aunt's grimace of distaste on being introduced to Rudy, and how in that moment his mother's joy had vanished. Arriving home, he and Andy had headed to their room. When he emerged some time later to ask about dinner, his mother was already high, the tourniquet hanging limp from her arm. He watched Rudy inject himself. Piled on the low coffee table of the living room were the three art books Rudy had bought at the market. The cover of the top one featured the white falling-apart country house, the tree seeming to erupt from the centre of the earth, a surprising warmth emanating from such cool colours.

Rudy released the belt around his arm and swallowed, his tongue darting like a snake's around his chapped lips. Fell back into the sofa. Pointed at the book. Smiled at Paul.

'That there, buddy, that's by one of the greatest painters that ever lived.'

The man and the boy had looked at each other. In Paul's memory it seemed to last an eternity. It must have; he still feels locked in the scrutiny of that gaze.

And he answered: 'I don't give a fuck about some old fag painter. What's to eat?'

Paul turns away from the print. He opens the door to the patio; the night is still balmy. The waves break rhythmically below. Yet though it is not cold, he is shaking. He grabs for his cigarettes. Andy. He hadn't thought about Andy for years. It is sinful—and he can't think of another word to do his shame justice—it is sinful that he doesn't know whether his brother is alive or dead.

•

The dark has slunk in. I have been oblivious to it, lost in the writing. There is a thrilling momentum to the work when a story and its characters begin to race ahead of your hand as you scrawl across the pages, as your fingers pound the keyboard. Of course, these characters have been gestating for the longest period; when it comes to *Sweet Thing*, they have been there, behind the mirror, waiting to emerge, for over a decade now. Yet Paul's exhilaration and bewilderment at having returned to America, and the devout love Conrad has for his wife, are unexpected, startling; the emotions of the men do seem to be directing the play of my fingers across the keys. Every artist, every writer, must have an element of the superstitious to them. I do not mean in the rituals we enact before we sit down at the desk or before the canvas, the fastidiousness about using a certain kind of pen or a specific brand of oil paints. We are members of a ridiculed guild, defenders of an impossible craft: we have faith in alchemy.

My musings on the uncanny are fortified by the waning crepuscular light. There is a dull pain at the base of my skull. I have been hunched over the computer for hours, and I have forsaken all those ergonomic practices that alleviate the subtle pressures the body experiences when it is made subordinate to the mind. If aligning myself with alchemy is an expression of the wilful pride and arrogance of the writer, then that ache in my neck, the dull throbbing all along the base of my spine, the swelling of my feet, all of that is the rebellion of my ageing body—and I am reminded that I am not magician and certainly not immortal and even more adamantly that I am not indestructible. I save my work, push back my chair and stand. I raise my hands high over my head, touch the tips of the fingers of both hands to one another, and then stretch all the muscles of my body, feeling those of my abdomen twist and unfurl, my buttocks squeeze and tighten, my calves distend as I raise myself on the tips of my toes. I don't count. I hold my breath until the need to inhale air is so overwhelming that my body revolts and my feet slam onto the boards of the deck and my arms drop to my sides and I am gulping the sweet night air.

As the twilight recedes beneath the shroud of darkness, the revolution from day to night is not so much conveyed by the changes of the light—out across the town and the inlet, out to the unbroken line of the horizon, the last rays of the sun defiantly cast a burnished flame against the shadows—as by the shifts in sound. The chirps and screeches and songs of the birds have all but vanished and the burping of the frogs in the next-door neighbour's ponds has just begun. From a more distant garden, the relentless buzz of cicadas is beginning to fade. A truck rolls and thunders across the bridge and I hear the clanging of the steel girders. A crunch of brakes, the rumbling thunder of acceleration up the hill, and then that sound too vanishes. There is a rustling in the shrubs at the end of the garden, but it is all darkness in that patch and I cannot glimpse a thing. With both my hands gripping the wooden railing of the deck, I push against it. Blood thumps through my body, and the ache in my neck is gone.

Genesis, I think to myself: that is a much better word than *alchemy*. From when I first saw that word in the diaphanous thin pages of a King James Bible as a young child, it has fascinated me. Raised in the Greek language, I knew its meaning immediately. Birth. Yet there was a subtle accentuation in the English translation that was perplexing and enticing. It seemed to speak of a moment—the moment of birth—and yet also suggest an infinity, the act of birth as ceaseless and eternal. I wonder now whether the reason I never found the creation of the world in six days a stumbling block to sincere faith came from this good fortune of having Greek as my first language. The clue was there in the opening word: birth occurs in the moment and in eternity.

Conrad was being birthed as my fingers flew across the laptop's keys. He was fashioned from memories and inspirations that recede back into the furthest time, and from flashes of insight that go back merely to yesterday. My Uncle Nikos and the titan of stone on the beach beneath the cemetery both sculpted Conrad.

A callous shriek from a bat flying above. Glancing up, I spy a spit of shit; it gleams in the emerging moonlight as it hurtles to the ground. I laugh loudly. The natural world is mocking me. You are no God, it chortles.

'Whenever I begin to doubt God, son, I go and look out to the world. Always, my faith is strengthened.'

This was said to me by an old man, a Protestant minister, whose name I have sadly forgotten.

•

I was in my eighteenth year, a callow youth with a genuine inquisitiveness and a disposition towards kindness; my weaknesses at that age were ill-discipline, both in thought and in habit, and a proclivity towards dissimulation when threatened. The most shameful result of that tendency was a resulting lack in courage. I was also hungry for the world, my appetite shameless. In many ways I had been a cosseted and spoilt child, not raised with material advantage but certainly buoyed and secured in life by the sacrifice and loyalty and love of family. That is possibly the most crucial and overriding privilege, by which I mean it carries greater responsibility and sway than all those phenomena denoted by a capitalised idealism: it means more than Class, more than Gender, more than Race, more than Sexuality. More than Nation. And more than God. It is love. Anything else pales in comparison.

So, I was eighteen, and newly addicted to amphetamines. I had lost the flabbiness of adolescence and was slim, a litheness accentuating all that was most Mediterranean and Levant in my appearance: the somnolent skew of my dark eyes, the rich honey of my skin, the brilliant black of my hair. I was not handsome, but for the first time in my life I was striking, and I was learning that I could be desired. I was finally released from the long years of banishment at high school—for that was how I experienced the glacial transit of time within that institution, though I had good friends and a teacher who steered me gently yet firmly on a proper and classically cogent course. The bullying, the provincial intellectual stupor of Australian suburban mores in the last decade of the Cold War and the casual—not necessarily hateful, but certainly at times malicious—racism from some of the students meant that my years of school were experienced as a confinement. But this was now the ancient past. How wonderful is that slaughtering of time that we are capable of when we fling ourselves into the first delirious steps from youth to adulthood! I was—this needs to be repeated—hungry. I was ravenous. For drugs and dancing and sex and conversation and books and films and touch and alcohol and danger and risk. I had taken the overnight train from Melbourne to Sydney and, high on speed, I hadn't slept all night. I spent the journey talking incessantly to a steely-jawed young man, a scraggy truss of orange hairs on his chin, who was travelling to Sydney to meet a father he had not seen for a decade. Speed was his drug too, and we were riding its initial ecstatic seduction; it wasn't yet demanding recompense. We spilt out onto the platform at Central Station in the early morning, the sun so alive it burnt my eyes. The boy from the train gave me the address for a dosshouse near the station, and I secured a dormitory bed among the alcoholics who lived there. (Now, closing my eyes to the night, parsing memories, trying to find that path to the past, approaching the mirror and peering through its cracked, grimy surface, I try to recall those men. I remember the smells. Of their pissing their beds at night, of the communal shower with the stain of shit caked into the grout. Those men had seemed ancient to me and they stank of misery. I wanted nothing to do with them. I slept there, I showered and then I escaped. They must have been only in their thirties and forties, yet there was the reek of death to them. The alcohol was killing them. I was too young. I was pitiless.)

I slept, I showered, I went out and danced and took drugs and had sex. I was taken home by an agitated bald father who explained that his wife and children were visiting his sister-in-law in Grafton that weekend. When he undressed, I was appalled by the hairiness of his body. As he was fucking me, I stared at a framed photo of his sons on the bureau beside the bed. Is it a truth, did this happen, or is it a fiction I have created within memory that as he was grunting and thrusting above me, his sweat splattering my back like heavy raindrops, he reached for that photograph and turned it over? Or did I do it? He released a long hollow bellowing as he ejaculated inside me. I shuddered from the pain as his penis slid out of me. I heard him gasp. I tried to turn over, but his hand was pushing hard on my neck. 'Don't move,' he said harshly; then more quietly, 'You've shat yourself, and I think you're bleeding.'

He rang me a taxi so I could return to the city. Pushed a clump of money in my hand, much more than I needed for the cab ride. Next morning, I used that money to book a flight to Tasmania to surprise a friend who had recently moved there. She lived in Hobart but there was a cheap deal on flights to Launceston, so I booked that flight instead. I left the airport and walked towards the highway, where I began to hitchhike.

The driver who picked me up was the Protestant minister.

•

The clicking ruckus of the cicadas has ended, and the sun has been swallowed by the ocean. The world now belongs firmly to night. I used Nikos as a mould to form Conrad's body. The old man who picked me up in Launceston is the breath from which I fashioned Conrad's soul.

'Whenever I begin to doubt God, son, I go and look out to the world. Always, my faith is strengthened.'

•

I had only been hitching for half an hour or so. It was the end of winter and the sky was a sombre grey cloak draped heavily over the earth. The constant drizzle of rain seemed so light as to be negligible, so it was a shock when I realised that it had soaked through my jacket, my jumper and shirt, right through to my skin. I was relieved when the car pulled over ahead of me and came to a stop. I have no interest in cars and rarely notice models or makes. If I were to hazard a guess, I would say that the car was white, and it was a station wagon. What is much more important is that though I lacked confidence at eighteen, and though I do believe I have inherited a peasant's caution and an instinct for self-preservation from my parents—I can respect recklessness in art, and sometimes even in politics, but always from a distance, and always with initial mistrust—yet I was fearless. I had discovered hitchhiking when a teenager, my instincts always compelling me to return to the inner city where I had grown up, to turn my back on the monotonous torpor of the suburbs. I would take the train into the city, first for the cinema and then, as I got older, for sex; then, needing to get home after the trains and buses had stopped and not having money for a taxi, I discovered the utility and pleasure of hitchhiking. (Only once in all the years that I hitched—and from sixteen years of age into my early thirties I did enjoy and indulge in that freedom—did I experience terror. A man picked me up just before midnight in Sydney. As soon as I slid into the passenger seat, I had a presentiment of peril. Such intimations are not rational, and they arise from the body itself and not from consciousness; there was nothing in the man's appearance or his words to frighten me. And yet, my body immediately broke out in a cold sweat and my breathing became shallow. When the car stopped at a red light, I opened the door and jumped out. There was the screech of a car in the lane next to ours, a loud cursing, and I ran across the road without looking back. I am convinced that I escaped danger that evening. I am grateful that I was raised in my mother's religion and that through my father I know the rituals and crafts of magic, such as the banishing of the evil eye and the respect and circumspection we owe to ghosts. I have often pitied people who were not raised in such traditions. It must be a wretched impediment to be unable to comprehend evil.) So, fearlessly, I ran to the car that had stopped for me on that dismal afternoon in Launceston. There was an old man behind the wheel, a thick crest of white hair sprouting from the top of his head. He leant across and wound down the passenger-side window. 'Please take off your coat,' he said, 'and shake it.' There was no gruffness in his order; it was expressed kindly. I quickly did as he asked, then threw my pack onto the back seat and got into the car.

The heater was spluttering, and every thirty seconds or so it would emit a clicking sound, but compared to the icy cold outside, the interior was blessedly warm.

'Where are you going?'

'Hobart.'

He laughed at this. He named a place where he could drop me off. So little did I know about Tasmania on this first visit that I had no idea whether he was going in the direction I needed or not. He put on his indicator, merged into the traffic, and we were on the road.

He was distinguished. I mean by this that he was very thin, very tall and, despite his age, straight-backed. There was that pride in his bearing. I noticed too that his left hand trembled slightly where it rested on the gearstick between us. I remember clearly that he wore a smart brown suit—not the tedious and ugly brown of earth, but a fabric with a bronze sheen to it—and that it seemed, even to my ignorant eye, to be well cut. Less clear is the question of whether he wore a tie. His shirt was pale, a hint of lemon in the whiteness. No, I don't think he was wearing a tie.

In the end, he took me all the way to the capital. The exact details of how this eventuated, the precise moment when he chose to take me all the way to Hobart and the recollection of the conversation that led to that decision are all lost to me, so deeply buried and in memory that they are *literally* unfathomable. The mirror between consciousness and dream does age, it cracks and sometimes shatters so that shards fall away and there are spectres and ghosts that are lost to our perception forever. Thinking back, I am genuinely puzzled and intrigued by what the old man and the young boy—for all my vainglory and my diffident assertion of adulthood at eighteen, I was still a youth—talked about. I do know that at some point I revealed to him that I loved men.

For a while we drove in silence. And then he veered off from the main road that swept through the lush cleft of the Esk Valley and took me into abandoned ghost towns and showed me the sandstone bridges and alehouses and tollbooths built by convict labour; and he drove to the coast and introduced me to coves strewn with boulders and rocks that sparkled like underground treasure vaults on the edge of the southern ocean, buttery yellow coral clinging to stones of rich ginger colour: here, he explained, the ancient peoples of this island prayed to their gods, the sea and the sky and the earth. He was excited when I told him my name and guessed straight away that my parents were born in Greece. He had not travelled much himself; a few times off the island and only once overseas, to the Holy Land and Greece. He spoke lovingly of Athens, recalling not just the splendour of the ancient city but also the alleyways and crumbling late-nineteenth-century steps of the modern city, observing how even in the blaze of summer there was a cool shade that seemed to run back and forth between the Acropolis and Lykavittos Hill. Was it at this point he revealed he was a retired Protestant minister?

He was exceptionally kind. He paid for a wonderful meal in a small tavern overlooking the South Esk River; restaurant meals were not part of my upbringing and I was conscious that I ate so much faster than him and I remember being confused by the amount of cutlery. He told me that he had been married for over forty years to a woman he loved. It was over that meal—and it was on that day I first intuited something of the notion of friendship and love being formed over the breaking of bread, and why the ritual is integral to Christian fellowship; I tore my bread, dipped it into the remnants of sauce from our meal, and sipped my wine as he spoke—that he told me he was homosexual and had been so all his life. He loved men, he explained to me, simply and sadly, but he had made his vow of marriage to his wife, and he had not forsaken that vow. *Ever.* I remember how he spat the word. Not from regret but from conviction.

Back in the car, he said that it was probably time to drop me in Hobart. 'Your friends will be waiting for you.' And partly out of gratitude to this gentleman who had gone out of his way to show me the home he loved and introduce me to his island's beauty and history, and partly because I was so inexperienced and because there is an arrogance in the dispassion of naivety, I said to him, 'If you like, you can have sex with me.' I am embarrassed now at that wording, the insinuation that I was making a sacrifice. He laughed, sadly but lightly. He squeezed my hand. He said that if we had met even ten years earlier, when he was in his seventies, he might have taken me up on my offer, but he had lived so long in his denial now that to make love to a man would settle nothing and possibly release a deluge of sorrow. He asked if he could kiss me. In the restaurant car park, the rain pelting the windscreen, we kissed. It was decidedly strange. I had kissed older men already but not someone as old as he. I was too young and therefore callous. My imagination conjured images of skeletons and grinning skulls and carnivalesque phantoms of death. I was too young, and I feared his age: I didn't comprehend it. His tongue as it pressed against mine felt like the working of a mechanical toy. He pulled away first. He drove me to Hobart.

•

I have made him Conrad. Though I have deliberated on *Sweet Thing* for so long now, and though I have known that it is an offer from an old man that initiates the story, in all these years I have not heard the voice of this man who desires Paul. He has been silent, and I think this silence is the reason why the writing stalled. Even when thinking of it as a film, I couldn't imagine the old man's face. Unless we hear their voice, a character is trapped behind the mirror, in the furthest reaches of the shadows. Somehow, the accident of seeing the titan on the beach and it recalling Nikos, and the recollection of a gift passed between an older man and a youth, spurred this ferocious bout of writing. In that accident, there was creation.

It's paltry in comparison, but in creating Conrad I am expressing my gratitude both to Nikos and to the old man in Tasmania.

It is surely night now. A possum is scratching on the roof of the deck. There is a low din from the droning and flapping of moths and mosquitoes. I place the laptop in its sheath and go indoors.

As I open the screen door to the kitchen, all the living area is in darkness, except for a few stray beams from the streetlight that purl through the glass of the doors that overlook the front porch. They fall on the Manet print, tremble across the glass. In that dim light the colours remain hidden. Only the white of the ramshackle old house is vivid.

The diapason of the birds announces the morning, as does the tremulous ashen light that brooks the half-drawn curtains of the bedroom. The light is subordinate to the song, and amid the chorus there is one bird that calls louder than the others. It is a discordant shriek and for the first few days of my stay I found it ugly. Its complaint was the reveille that dragged me from the netherworld, returned me to awakening. Yet over the course of the week I am growing fonder of its voice and no longer find it disagreeable. There is an insistent pleading in its shrillness, as if the bird is aware that I cannot understand its language, as one finds with old people who have had no occasion to leave their mountain or valley or desert or island or outback home, so that confronted with the strangeness of the foreigner, they repeat themselves endlessly, their voices rising and becoming more querulous in their determination to be understood. *It's the day*, the bird is carolling. *It is day and the world is beginning anew.*

I raise my arms, entwine my hands and bring them behind my head. The coils of my armpits are lightly streaked with the faint dew of perspiration; the smell is sharp, unpleasant, yet satisfyingly masculine. I am thinking of Anouk Aimée and Candice Bergen.

Last night, in a small celebration of the work I did on the prospective novel, I watched two movies chosen from the clutch of DVDs I'd brought with me. The first was Jacques Demy's *Lola*, a black-and-white French film from the early sixties; the second was Mike Nichols's *Carnal Knowledge*, a movie from the USA made a decade later. It is most likely the accident of watching the films back to back that makes me think they speak to one another, that there is a call and response across the Atlantic; but I am a writer, and I believe in the utility of accident, its necessity. Both films are about the yearning young men have to live a life that is not mundane. And both films observe the incomprehension that can separate woman from man. In each case, the men fail the women through misunderstanding and ignorance; yet the films are not accusatory or bitter. Demy's film is lighter, not only because he is blither and more elegant as a filmmaker, less earnest, but also because he is younger than the Nichols who directs *Carnal Knowledge*; yet both American and French culture in the early 1960s were less aggrieved, more naive, than the partisan cultures that will emerge after May 1968 and the war in Vietnam.

I esteem both filmmakers, their quiet but staunch adherence to their respective sensibilities. I wonder if the wryness yet warmth of their perceptions comes from their both being bisexual. Demy was married to Agnès Varda, an equally brilliant filmmaker, and they were clearly devoted to one another. Yet his desire for men was accepted between them. Nichols, too, was married to women and loved men. Sex may be about power—that is the reigning ideology—however, in loving both women and men, the bisexual must glean the understanding that why we love and how we desire is not reducible to mere conquest and vanquishing. There is also surrender and concession.

I unclasp my hands, stretch them above my head, wanting to put off complete awakening; I am still half-asleep, and I know that I am lazily writing a review in my head. I jerk my right hand open, an abrupt motion that scrubs clean the words forming in consciousness. Demy and Nichols disappear, and the cluster of images from the films—Anouk Aimée getting dressed behind the folding screen of her small apartment; Jack Nicholson rubbing himself down after his shower in the college locker room—vanish too. I am returned to my body. My bladder feels swollen; the subtle pain forces me into complete wakefulness. I head to the bathroom.

The light outside is dazzling, the sky a soaring cerulean expanse. I sip my coffee and return to thinking about Anouk

Aimée and Candice Bergen. The former is the more talented actor; she convinces as the working-class dancer, Lola, and she similarly convinces as the frustrated, distrustful bourgeois wife of the filmmaker in Fellini's *8½*. Bergen never seems relaxed on screen, certainly not when she was young. She always seemed to be trying too hard. Yet her performance works in *Carnal Knowledge* because she's playing a young woman at the dawn of the sexual revolution, when the availability of contraception and the shifts in the economy will vault women out of the home and begin to free them from the mandate of their biology. The jitteriness of her constant motion, the agitation in her voice, the sense we have that she is always second-guessing herself and the resulting tentativeness, are perfect for the nascent feminist character she plays in the movie: exhilarated at the potential of what might finally be attainable, and also terrified by those possibilities.

The working-class Lola, raising a child on her own and working as an erotic dancer, has her dreams, but she knows that she has to play the cards she is dealt, and that money— who has it and especially who is born to it—is ultimately the great decider. She can't afford the rich university girl's ambitions.

The movie camera is brutally inegalitarian. It prioritises the face over the labours of skill and craft. In that glorious flourishing of cinema in the twentieth century, movie stars were the most beautiful creatures in the world. The photograph, too, is ruthless in its cold appraisal, but the movie camera caught the body in action. When we gaze at a photograph, we see ghosts. When we look up at the movement on the cinema screen, we see dreams. In her first major film role—in Sidney Lumet's relentlessly unsympathetic adaptation of Mary McCarthy's *The Group*—Bergen is one of eight young actresses and arguably the least accomplished. Yet she is clearly the one who will be the movie star. You want to reach your hand towards the dust-particled light and touch the image. Cinema is a polytheist's art; the tribute we offer the gods is both devoted and erotic.

Even though it is not yet eight o'clock, the sun is baking. There is the white stream of haze across the far ocean and impulsively I decide to forgo a morning walk and go swimming instead; that shimmering whiteness where the blue of the sky and the blue of the sea are kissing is too tempting. I gulp down my coffee, peel and eat a banana, brush my teeth, strip and put on my bathers. Slinging a beach towel over my shoulder, I shove the sunscreen, my reading glasses and a book into a cotton tote bag, grab the car keys and lock up the house. The thought of being in water so excites me that the anticipation sends jolting currents sparking across my skin.

As I descend towards the inlet and follow the curve in the road that ends at the intersection before the bridge, I see a trio of local high school students waiting for the bus. The tallest among them, a sharp-shouldered youth with lank, greasy hair, is balancing precariously with one foot on the hard edge of the kerb with his arms out, the right hand raised above his shoulder and the left hand jutting out perpendicular to his hip. A girl of the same age—sixteen, seventeen?—has her arms crossed, her head cocked to one side, watching him. Teetering in that position, he is talking furiously, as if there is something urgent that he must communicate. She seems dubious. Standing apart from them, looking out to the glistening water of the inlet, is a much younger child—he cannot be more than fourteen—whose tightly curled hair is the same blond as the girl's. He is rolling something under the sole of his shoe. Obviously, I take this all in at a glance as I drive by. Yet in that quick glimpse I have grasped that the younger boy and the girl are siblings, that the older boy is explaining a surfer's technique in order to impress the girl, and that the young boy is hurt by the refusal of the older lad to acknowledge him.

Sweet Thing will never be a movie. However, imagining it as such is the closest I have come in my life to thinking as a film director, envisaging the opening long shot of the father and the son on the roof, the screen bisected into the green of the land and the blue of the ocean. It is a scene that I have cut and recut until I know every cascade of light, every shift in point of view; when the camera needs to be still and when the camera is in motion. And that vision is difficult to forsake.

I am driving along a winding country road, keeping a watchful eye out for any wildlife that might step in front of the car, yet I am also conceiving a scene: my eyes see through the fixed rectangular frame of the movie camera and my ears record dialogue and atmos and sound.

Paul has returned to Los Angeles. We will not see any more of his interactions with Conrad, won't know how they spent their remaining time together. Paul is staring at Manet's painting of the *House at Rueil*, and then the violence of the jump cut—and it is the film editor's skill that we writers most envy, the command they have over time, their ability to wrench us from space, to hurl us into the future or fling us back into the past, to defy the commandment of temporal tense; an expert or genius writer can achieve this, but oh, what a struggle, what an effort, what a gnashing of teeth, a pulling of hair, a banging of the desk to get there; how jealous I am of the film editor's craft—and Paul is walking down a narrow corridor, brightly lit with artificial yellow light, and whereas the soundtrack to the scenes with Conrad has been austere—utilising only diegetic sound, so that the Chopin we hear never swells beyond the intimacy and estrangement between the men, and when there is silence it is only the breaking of the waves on the beach or the squalling of birds that intrudes, the sound of Paul's breathing as he gazes upon the painting—now the sound is loud: dervish, devilish techno that pounds the cochlea of the viewer, a sound so furious that it is close to pain.

And as I press down on the clutch, shift into a lower gear to round a sharp bend, I suddenly remember the first time I heard Chopin's music. It was playing in the old man's car as we drove through the Esk Valley. I asked, 'What is this?' And he answered, 'Chopin. Do you like it?' I nodded, relishing the sibilant whisper of the name, a name that was not unfamiliar, though I don't believe I had heard his music before. Silently, in the kindly stranger's car, I played with the word. *Chopin*. A word like fresh honey on the tongue.

Loud furious techno. In the audience we should feel the sound banging in our head, thumping in our blood. Paul walks through an open door and enters a crowded apartment, modern and luxurious, the living space opening up to a wide balcony, with the lights from the cluster of skyscrapers in downtown LA visible in the distance. We will never be told where the party is, but I imagine it taking place in the in-between of West and East Hollywood, in the indeterminate space between the native-born and the immigrant, the affluent and the bohemian. At some point, as Paul enters, the point of view shifts and the camera becomes subjective: we are seeing through his eyes. Everywhere there are long-limbed youths: the white women and men are tanned a uniform solarium orange, and they wear white shirts and white skirts and white minidresses as if to accentuate the synthetic colour of their skin; the black and Latino men and women are deliberately more eclectic in their choices, but whether in streetwear or expensive casual dress, they too know they are superb, desirable. In the hierarchy that is beauty, the ageing Paul doesn't rate a glance.

Yet there is not only youth. Middle-aged women, their skins overworked and over pummelled so that, whether black or white, their faces are like masks fastened over their skulls, two gashes ripped in the fabric for eyes which—black and gleaming, blue and pellucid, or chestnut and dull—seem to peer through the cage of that veneer. The ageing men all have arms and forearms and necks and shoulders and chests and abdomens and legs formed at the gymnasium, the muscles protruding, powerful; yet there is something distasteful about these engorged features, and we eye them with the suspicion we reserve for chemically enhanced vegetables on supermarket shelves; those giant pumpkins and perfectly rounded tomatoes, so extravagant in their perfect symmetry and so disappointing to taste.

We hear Paul's name spoken. The subjectivity of the camera is ruptured. Paul is beaming. And Paul and Jackson are in an embrace so consuming, so passionate, that the youths, these vain and indolent gods and goddesses, are compelled to turn and stare.

Jackson is wearing a black suit, a powder blue shirt, and a red bow tie; the apparent conservatism of his dress is subverted by the black polish painted on his elegant, manicured nails. His hair, shorn to a uniform millimetre length, is silver. He releases Paul with a tender kiss on the lips.

We become aware of two people standing beside Jackson: a man whose skin is glazed *that* orange, his muscles inflated to *that* ridiculous size; and an ageing woman with *that* face, a red-and-white checked bandana tied loosely around her thin neck. Yet their smiles temper the bizarreness of their attempts to arrest time. Their smiles are warm, and we should perceive them as sympathetic.

The woman takes a packet of Marlboro Lights from a compact white handbag with a thin gold strap.

'Do you faggots still smoke?' she asks in a sardonic drawl.

And Jackson answers, 'Does the Pope shit in the woods?'

The lights of downtown are pulsing feebly behind the heavy smog curtain of the city's night sky. I would like the viewer to experience an exhilaration at this vista, for the setting to emphasise the elation that Paul and Jackson and their friends are experiencing, smoking on the patio, reminiscing about their youth, recalling when they first became friends and started working together, when they fucked one another and made love to one another and when they got high together. 'So high we were the favoured children of the sun,' says Jackson, and the vista must seem impossible, fantastic, because it is an ugly, sprawling city and it spews and excretes into the ocean, vomits a gaseous and noxious lungful up to the sky, yet the sheer size and delirious activity of the city redeems it. So that as the quartet smoke and reaffirm old friendships, and as their memories glide from joy to sadness, as they honour lost friends and recall the ravages wrought by drugs and diseases (at some point we must hear Jackson say mournfully, 'We all had to pay our dues to the Devil; he never forgets what's owed him'), the city spread out below

217

and above them is a canopy painted in sombre and gloomy dark oil colours; except here and there, where there are thick splotches of colour, and the screen comes alive. The audience needs to see this beauty in the city to understand why Paul, in returning, is reminded of what he most loved in the country of his birth.

And then a long, soaring alto voice will shatter the soundtrack and it is the a cappella introduction to the SOS Band's album version of 'Just Be Good to Me', a song of rhythmic serpentine grandeur that lasts for just over nine minutes and defies the imperative of sweat and motion in funk; instead the seduction is slow, insistent and confident. And Jackson will fling his right arm in the air, the gesture at once abrupt and poised, and his voice will boom as he declares, 'Dear Lord, I love this song.' And he seizes Paul's hand and they all hurry to the dance floor. And I imagine the scene running for the length of time the song plays, and we will see the friends dancing and the dance will be exultant and the dance will be erotic and the dance will be exuberant and the dance will be memory: we must know that these four souls have been locked in this dance before and are united in their love for this song. And one of them, I don't know who it will be and it doesn't matter, slips a small vial of white powder to Paul and he takes it and, still dancing, makes his way to the bathroom, waits for the toilet to be free, still swaying to the dance track, a sheen of perspiration on his brow, his neck, it glistens and his shirt is soaked and clinging to his body, until at long last a young lesbian couple flings open the bathroom door, still lost in their kiss and ignoring Paul, who enters the room and locks the door. He spills the white powder on the enamel basin and arranges it into two wide lines. He looks at himself in the mirror. He looks at himself for a period of time that brings the audience to the verge of discomfort. The light from the bathroom mirror is an unforgiving glare. He makes the decision; he snorts the drugs.

There is a cut. Paul is in his hotel room, naked. There is a body under the sheets next to him. He calls Jenna. He tells her he loves her. And he tells her he has decided to drive up to Sacramento the next day to search for his brother. 'You sure?' she asks. 'Yes,' he answers. 'I'm sure.' He doesn't tell his wife that he has taken drugs. He will never tell her. That secret belongs to America and he knows after this trip he will never see America again.

And just as with ancient cinema, when the leader tape at the end of a reel sputters and tears in the projector's gate, emitting a flash of light and scratches on the screen, the car breaks through the shade of forest, and Los Angeles and Paul flicker, tremble, and they have disappeared. To my left there is a gleaming stretch of sand, almost white from the dazzle of the still-ascending sun; and on my right are the serene waters of the inlet. The car shakes as I cross the old wooden bridge. The narrow gorge is full; the tide is high. I take the next turn-off and for a moment, as I accelerate along the straight road that leads to the bay, the road that cleaves farmland from bush, it is as if the car is flying.

There is no one on the beach, and when I unstrap my sandals the white sand is cool on my feet. Directly above me is the unbroken cobalt sky. Only far to the south is there a hint of a slowly shifting and emerging cirrus, the wisps tentative. I strip to my bathers. With the breeze rushing along the shore, the sun's heat now seems diminished. I inhale, prepare myself, then run into the ocean. The cold water is lacerating, slashing at my legs, and a wave slams against my cock and balls so hard that for a moment I cannot breathe; and then I dive. The world vanishes and I am under the sea. The force of the water is a punch to my chest; and then the chill is surmounted and I am swimming. When I break through the surface of the water, returning to the dominion of the sky to fill my hungry lungs, I don't feel the cold at all.

Ancient volcanic boulders, black and giant, deeply embedded in the ocean floor, form a barrier that isolates the bay from the ocean. Being high tide, only the very tips of the rocks are visible. A flight of cormorants forms a line, their lithe forms perched on the apices, all facing the sun and horizon, like sentinels guarding a citadel. The tearing, desperate waves assault the fortress, the water sluicing and penetrating through the gaps in the towers, but their ferocity is spent as they merge with the calmer waters of the bay. I face the open sea, a lonely auxiliary behind the cormorants, watching the waves crest and break on the horizon visible between the breaches in the stone wall. If Simon were here with me, he would be gently urging me to return to the beach, to lather my skin with sunscreen. Yet the tranquillity of the scene, and my reluctance to face those first few moments of piercing cold as I emerge from the sea, conspire to keep me floating languidly, bobbing in the swell.

On the other side of the camping grounds there is another favourite beach of ours; there are small isolated bays and coves all along this charmed coast. Though it is not readily accessible—it is a nine-hour drive from our home in Melbourne—ever since we first fell in love with this part of the world, we have kept returning summer after summer. I blame my Mediterranean heritage for my inability to enjoy the seas closer to home. Even during the hottest days of summer, the Southern Ocean's water has the burn of ice. I do finally give myself over to it, release myself in the pleasure of the swim, but my enjoyment is always tempered by knowing that I am in stubborn contention with it. The first time I visited the British Isles it was summer, and friends took me swimming at a beach on the Yorkshire Coast. They were excited to show me their beautiful part of the world and I did my best to hide my disdain for the ugly pebbled beach. I ran into the water and the first wave was an axe that hewed into my legs. I thought the cold would cut me in half. I have attempted to swim off the coast in northern Scotland; in the North Sea at the furthest tip of Denmark; in the Atlantic in Brittany. Every time I have entered those northern waters,

I have emerged knowing that my body doesn't belong to Europe. To any of Europe. The warm Aegean is always a pleasure, yet I detest the crowds on its beaches. Those bodies lying on rocks or pebbles or sand, so close together that in my cruellest and most unfair appraisals they look like survivors of some atomic holocaust; the bomb has detonated and all these bodies have been strewn across the length of the beach. Whereas there are times on these southern beaches when Simon and I seem to have possession of the whole of the coastline. Or we share it only with the surfers, tiny dashes of black and indigo in the foam. It is through this enchantment of ocean that I first understood that landscape and place, that land—the earth and its waters—create belonging. In time, all migrants to this continent become covetous of space. If they don't, if they never succumb to that exquisite immense loneliness, they never feel at home here. When I bring visitors from abroad to these waters, they see the beauty in the vastness and the isolation—it is impossible to be blind to it, the immensity of this antipodean sky and the clarity and power of the light; it can't help but overwhelm—yet they want to see people, to drink coffee or wine or beer in a promenade cafe. They want motion and movement: they fear, and are made anxious by, this wondrous remoteness. It affirms that they are indeed outsiders, strangers. Whereas I return here again and again.

Simon and I were here in the summer of fire. We visited again at the end of the summer of pandemic. The fires tore through the bushland all along the east coast; towns burnt out, forests erased; it was apocalypse: day became night, for the skies had turned black. The fires were still burning, smouldering deep in the forest, when we came for a fortnight's holiday. Ostensibly, we came to support the businesses that had been crippled economically; really, we wanted to play in the ocean. The devastation had kept tourists away; it was midsummer, the middle of January, yet the caravan parks were half-empty. There is a small bay we had been told about the third or fourth summer we returned to the inlet. We were in one of the pubs and there was a young woman behind the bar, playing music that ranged from Fleetwood Mac to Antony and the Johnsons, The Israelites to Aretha Franklin. The mix was eclectic but not alienating; clearly these were songs she loved. It was music she had selected herself and placed in an order that had meaning for her—for her it was memory, for anyone listening it was a story. I knew, listening to the sequence of songs, that some affair must have ended. Returning to the bar for another round of drinks I said, 'I really like the music.' She beamed, said, 'Thank you.' Later, coming out to the patio for a cigarette, she sat with us, and she told us her name was Edie. 'Like Edie Sedgwick?' Simon asked, and she laughed and said, 'Yeah, but usually people don't know anything about her.' She told us about the best places to go swimming in the area, describing a bay that was only accessible by crossing a creek and walking along the border of a farm until you found a small path that meandered down a hillside straight to the sea. 'It's perfect there,' she said, stubbing out her cigarette. 'Sand so soft it's like walking on a carpet. And it's pretty safe.' When she returned to the bar, Simon turned to me and said, 'She looks a bit like Edie Sedgwick.' It was true. The alabaster blonde hair, the pale elfin face and deep-set, curious eyes. More at peace, less numbed than any images I have seen of Sedgwick.

It was to this bay, which we now called Edie's Bay, that we returned in the season of fire. We were lying on the beach, sunning ourselves, gloriously alone, almost ashamed of such splendid fortune, when Simon put down his book, raised himself and started sniffing the air. I could smell it too: the sour choking odour of smoke. He said calmly, 'The fires must have started again.'

Some ten or fifteen minutes later I returned to the water; it was almost silken as it swept across my body, the water so clear that I could see the silver glint of tiny fishes darting beneath the oncoming waves. I dived, returned to the surface, and the blue of the sky had vanished; first it was rose, like diluted wine, then it was crimson and then finally it was a fiery red. A fine film of what seemed like chalk dust covered my skin. It was raining ash.

I heard my name being called. Simon was on the shore, his smile encouraging, but even at this distance I could tell he was anxious. We packed up our belongings and returned to the apartment we were renting.

The owners had shoved a letter under the door, instructing us where to go and what to do if the inferno reached the inlet. Later that afternoon, walking to the supermarket, we saw a group of weary uniformed men stepping out of a fire-truck. The exterior of the vehicle seemed charred, with streaks and smudges of black smoke and cinders. The men's faces were coated in grime and dirt and ash, and their orange and yellow uniforms were filthy. Yet they laughed and teased one another and called each other by nicknames, and I wondered how many days, if not weeks, they had spent in the middle of the conflagration, where the distinctions between day and night vanish, where the breath of the firestorm uproots centuries-old trees and sends them plunging across the forest, where the sound is a maelstrom of flame and wind and the abominable, desperate screams of the birds and the beasts being burnt alive. Could they ever wash themselves free of such witness? Yet they were deep in the enjoyment of their friendship.

Suddenly there was the sound of applause. It came from the cars lined up outside the bottle shop; from the youth returning the shopping trolleys back to their bays; from a young mother with her infant strapped across her chest; from a group of teenagers smoking in an alcove. And Simon and I too began to clap, and then the applause became a thunderous cheering. The men's masks of grime and ash could not obscure their shyness and their diffidence and their embarrassment and their pride. One of them—it was impossible to tell the colour of his hair beneath the dirt, but something in the sharp planes of his face immediately made me think he was Nordic, fair-haired—was waving his hand, gesturing for us to stop. The applause died away. One of the firefighters called out, 'Thank you.' And an old man standing by the doors of the supermarket called back loudly, 'No, mate, thank *you*! Thank *you*!' And with this the fair firefighter's resolve crumbled and he turned to one of his comrades, was embraced by him. His face was buried in the shoulder of his friend's sweat-soiled, grubby overalls, his shoulders heaved, and we knew he was crying. Respectfully, we all turned away.

Within a day we were notified that it was safe to make our way back to Melbourne. On the drive south we vowed that we would return as soon as we could, and we began planning a holiday for the coming winter. Then a pandemic struck. The world stopped once more. We couldn't return.

It doesn't take long for the sun's rays to warm my body; the fine goose pimples that prickled my skin are gone and as I lie on the towel, one hand behind my head, the other raising my book as a shield against the sun, I catch a whiff of the sly reek of my own scent, the faint sweetness of the perfumed chemicals of the sunscreen, and the warm, fusty emanations of my sweat. The memory of the firefighters blunts and dulls my vanity. With an almost exhilarating objectivity I examine my body. The tendency to flab, there since childhood. I lay down my book, scoop up a handful of sand, squeeze it and then watch the fine grains trickle through the gaps in my clenched fist. Once the dribble is ended, with the remaining grains stuck to my greasy wet palm, I open it wide and examine it. I am wearing my reading glasses, so every indentation and pore on my palm and fingers is clearly visible, further illuminated by the light of the morning sun arriving at its apex. I wipe my hand on my wet bathers, it dislodges the coarse grit of the sand, and I reassess my hand. I come to the same conclusion. It is a soft hand.

Who was it that first accused me of having soft hands? Is there a reason why this specific memory refuses to make itself visible? It has always resisted my attempts to retrieve it. The mirror remains just a mirror: I cannot pass through it. Yet its reverberations have been profound, for those words—*Christo, you have such soft hands*—have been a challenge and a shame I have been wrestling with for most of my life. I sit up, rest my head on my knees and look out to the bay. The heavy boulders are liberating themselves from the overwhelming clasp of the ocean; the tide has begun to recede.

And there is a moment, as I glance out to sea, when the cleaving of the rocks—turquoise water visible between them like a thick dab of oil on canvas—unsettles a disconcerting recollection. I am looking down at my mother, who is lying in her pyjamas on my single bed. I have entered puberty already, yet I am jumping up and down on the bed imitating the play of childhood, and it is making my mother laugh. Have I been ill? Has she been nursing me through my sickness? I stare at the long golden arc of the shore, the patchwork of blues arising from the depth of the sea and reaching to the very zenith of the sky, but simultaneously I am looking down at my mother through a teenager's eyes and she is young and beautiful and laughing, and I recall scent, the sharp and viscous menthol odour of the Vicks with which she rubs down my chest— so I must have been sick. She is laughing uproariously and with relief, and I know this about my mother: that amid the drudgery of work, both in the factory and at home, the time she spends with me is an oasis of calm and peace. Having no siblings or relations in this country where she cannot speak the language, and terrified of the cruelty and shaming of gossip, it is only with me that she can share her secrets; that imparting of mysteries is a rite and a remembrance. And I am leaping on the bed and she is laughing and the top button of her pyjamas is undone and they are of a coarse cotton, a pink-and-white floral pattern, and as she writhes in laughter the second button pops open to reveal her breast, pale and fleshy, and the nipple, maroon in colour and so much larger and more mottled than the little dots schoolboys draw on stick figures. The shocking sight of her breast alarms me. I drop onto the bed and push myself away from her so that my back is flush against the wall.

'Christo, come closer, let me hold you; you shouldn't have your back to the cold wall.'

I answer her rudely. 'No. I want to go to sleep.'

She puts the back of her hand on my forehead, takes my hand and squeezes it. 'That's good: you don't have a temperature.'

She continues to hold my hand and there is a gnawing in my belly, and I intuitively understand that something has come between us with my glimpse of her nakedness: not the breast itself, but with its intimation of sexuality, mine emerging and hers to be increasingly confined; this was the beginning of a rupture between us, not irreconcilable but permanent; that between woman and man, and that between adult and parent. She brings my hand to her lips, kisses it, then splays my fingers open so she can examine it.

'Christo, you have such soft hands. May they never know hard work.'

I have rewritten the moment to imbue it with tenderness. Certainly, the fondness between mother and child is not in doubt. Yet it is not dishonouring of that love to also note the accusation I perceived in my mother's tone. Otherwise, how could those words have dogged me through the decades, so that I distrust those with supple, uncalloused, unscarred hands? It is a misgiving that tarnishes my loyalty to writers. No matter the content of their fiction or memoirs or manifestos, no matter the urgency and eloquence of their writing, I judge them by their hands. And if their hands are soft—and there are very few writers around the world who can claim to have a worker's hands—I have no confidence in them. In this

I am no hypocrite; I too constantly doubt the legitimacy of what I do.

A precipitous upsurge, a stirring and tussling from within the deep, and the cascade of water that slashes and pours through the gap between the rocks erupts forth with a thundering boom.

It is not my mother's scorn and her immediate compunction—that prayer: *May they never know hard work*—that I remember. There is something else. She gleaned by my sullen withdrawal that something had upset me, and she followed the line of my gaze to her naked breast. She quickly covered herself. She too was shamed.

I have misheard and misjudged those words—*Christo, you have such soft hands*—through the decades. I have wondered: was it Nikos who said them? Had Stavros whispered them to me when I sat on his lap as a child? Had my father flung them at me as an insult when I proved an intransigent, ungrateful youth? But no. They had not been spoken by a man. They had marked the moment when the gleeful intimacy of a mother and a son was subtly tainted by a recognition of difference. We were not one body. She was a woman, and I was becoming a man, and from now on we would be keeping secrets from one another. Of course, my mother would have known this already, and over the following years I realised that the revelation of her loneliness and her griefs and her fears was never a comprehensive confession. She already knew I had soft hands and she knew too that there were secrets women had to keep from men. It was my own naivety that was exposed. Daughters and fathers must have a similar moment of dissonance, with the daughter's first menstruation, or the accidental glimpse of the dark thatch of her father's pubic hair or the wrinkled flesh of his penis. The love need not be shattered; nevertheless, there is the beginning of an estrangement.

To be clear, my innocence was not taken in that moment, any more than it was surrendered in my adoration of Stavros or my love for Nikos. To be naive is not to be innocent; that is a distinction the adult makes to tame their experience of childhood. Possibly it is a necessary fiction for a parent. As with Christianity's allegiance to Original Sin, the belief in a child's innocence fortifies the adult against their knowledge that they will inevitably fail in keeping their child safe. It's a lovely mirror, that notion of childhood innocence: such an elaborate and sturdy gilded frame; such an impenetrable and adamantine glass: it only reflects the adult back to herself or himself. The world of childhood is sequestered to the netherworld forever.

I lie back on my towel and dare myself to stare directly into the sun. I have to turn away; the glare is ferocious. Yet there is also a strange comfort in the coddling of nature: the whisps of ocean breeze brushing my limbs, the sun's warmth licking my skin.

Fire and plague; it is ancient lore, even prehistoric: they create a breach in the world. Those men emerging from the furnace, and my acknowledgement of their heroism, all of us cheering their sacrifice, it is that moment which has returned me to the friction between mother and son on the bed and which also allows me to recognise the tenderness that, crucially, I also kept hidden: *May they never know hard work*. The promise she made at the birth of her children, a promise shared with her husband: that the drudgery and labour and effort of the factory and the mill and the field would not be their children's destiny. Sacrifice.

And so, since the fire and the pandemic, reminded again of the meaning of labour—for it was firefighters, nurses, doctors, cleaners who sacrificed—it is any wonder that my notions of how to write and what to write have changed? No more screeds to capital-J Justice and to capital-S Society and to capital-L Love and to capital-E equality and to capital-R Revolution: how can those of us with soft hands even contemplate such forgery? Our literature of the last half-century has been the babblings from the university. There is much I love in that chatter: incisiveness, interrogation, the engagement with reckoning. But not its arrogance, not its moral certitude, not its self-righteousness, not its smugness and not its masochism.

The book I have chosen to read here on the beach is a collection of Machiavelli's writings. Last night, I had been perusing the shelves of the rental property when I spied the slender volume lodged between a recent American memoir and the biography of a cricketer. I had never read Machiavelli and so I pulled it out, left it lying on the ottoman in the lounge room. This morning, hurriedly packing for the beach, I had impulsively crammed it into the bag. I look now at the book lying open on the sand, the spine broken, on the cover a portrait of the writer in which he looks gaunt, ill—yet there is something sprightly in the alertness of his eyes and the mystery of his grin. This mocking grin is a gift to us from the Renaissance. Isn't Machiavelli's grin equal to the secretive smile of la Giaconda? In one of his essays, Machiavelli writes of a noble gentleman of such refinement and good looks, of such vigour, that when he was a youth he stole husbands from wives and when an adult he stole wives from husbands. I laughed out loud when I read this passage, at the precision of its wit, and the acumen of its observation. I am also surprised at the clarity of *The Prince*. It describes the amorality of power, but it certainly isn't wicked. I am discovering that Machiavelli was the last of the European pagans. He did not believe that the world could change; nor did he believe it should. I wonder if he saw his own reflection when he looked upon his children?

I jump to my feet. I have been returned—just for a precious moment—to the vitality of youth, stunning myself at the daring and the risk of that leap. I run to the water and dive in. The waves slam into me, and then lift me, and I am soaring. I am above the world; and then almost immediately I am flung back into the deep. The water rushes and bubbles and strips all grit and sand and sweat and dirt from my skin, and it does more than that: every step, every walk and every swim of this fortnight has cleansed me. It divests me of the cloying grip of words and ideas and thoughts that must be capitalised. I shed Justice, Society, Love, Equality, Liberty and Revolution. The water is revivifying, and so I am grinning.

It rained last night. I was awoken by a light, spirited arpeggio tapping on the corrugated-tin roof. There was a very distant growl of thunder, so far off that the preceding flash of lightning hadn't pierced the darkness of the bedroom. I lay there, my hand groping for the light switch, but when my fingers found it I did not press it. The excitable speed of the rain continued, with the drops becoming larger and louder, the steady beat now definitely percussive; and beneath the rhythm of the downpour there was a further sound emerging, the running and sluicing of the rainwater as it flowed along the grooves of the tin roof, cascaded into the gutters, gushed through the pipes. The whistling of this roiling, scuttling water was a contrary motion to the insistent measure of the rain, a gentler breath in the increasing ferocity of the storm. There was a sudden loud clang on the roof, and the branches of the jacaranda tree began knocking against the window, the sound of a desperate animal clawing and scratching, intent on invasion. The storm was gaining momentum and now the wind too was becoming ferocious. A spark of illumination infiltrated the slight gap between the drawn curtains: a silver abrasion of light, then darkness again, the percussion and whistling of the rain and water, the threatening bellow of the wind, the scratching and biting of the tree's limbs against the window. Then the thunder booming, so loud now that the house itself trembled. I switched on the light.

It had been a long time since I had been frightened and excited by the symphony that is a storm. Is it living in a city that dulls the severity of nature? It was as if the tempest was a god in human form, and the god was gripping the limbs of trees outside and the very frame of the house, desiring to uproot all in its path and hurl it into the chaos of the ocean. I have seen neighbourhoods in my city in flood. I have felt the sear of that intense heat and ruthless dry wind which can ignite fires: three times in my life I have choked on smoke, felt my eyes stinging and burning from its acrid stench, as fires raged on the periphery of Melbourne. Yet each time the city's walls proved unbreachable. Here, though, in this town surrounded only by the natural gods—mountain and forest and water—one cannot rely on the promise of certainty, and of permanency. I wriggled deeper under the sheets, reminded of a child's terror of storms, of thunder and lightning, and as the light lanced the room once more, as the ensuing lambaste of the thunder followed, this admixture returning me to childhood was delicious, comforting. It was awe instead of terror.

I had finished *The Prince* last night and begun Dante's *Inferno* once roused by the storm. I was slipping further into the past, evading and retreating from the influence of the contemporary. I was normally a fast reader, but Dante required patience. I had begun and abandoned *Inferno* countless times. When packing my bags for this retreat, I had once more taken it off the shelf. This night, I began by reading the words aloud. Without Simon next to me, I was not embarrassed. And by the third canto, having grasped the rhythm and metre of the translation, my voice fell to a whisper and I read them silently. However, I paid careful and insistent attention to every word. The storm was waning; the god's rage had abated. The rain continued its dash across earth and water, window and roof, but unaccompanied by the bellowing of gale and thunder, the startling, exposing jolt of lightning. The drumming pattern of its fall was now comforting; it had returned to harmony with the world.

And so, I was able to concentrate on what was equally startling to the authority of nature: the supreme confidence and command of Dante's verse. Here was a poet unafraid of his language, prepared to honour and love his language and not be shamed by it. He therefore could create and reforge and remake the language without needing to violate it, to debase it and deny it. Yet most of all what I was struck by was the lack of shame.

It was the confidence that shook me, disturbing me more than the storm. I read from the third canto to the seventh. On my previous readings, I had stumbled at what seemed the inequity of the fourth canto, where those unbaptised and those born before the Resurrection and those born after but not raised in the Saviour are condemned to Limbo. The ruthlessness made me turn from the book. But last night, cupped in the stillness at the centre of the storm—for that was how I experienced it: being held in the palm of the ancient poet while outside the tempest levelled—I recognised that my earlier reading was immature. My disagreement was with God, not with Dante. This time, I saw the kindness with which Dante furnished hell's antechamber. It doesn't lessen the severity of the punishment, but there is a solemn light there, in the glade where Virgil shares eternity with Averroes and Aristotle. Dante's conviction is not only in his love of his language and his culture and his world. It arises from his Christian faith. It is not exactly envy that I experienced at reading a poetry that knew fidelity to one's language and to one's God. Instead, I would characterise it as a melancholy, from living in a time when the iconoclasts have desecrated all the gods and have made us ashamed of the words we use and demand of us that we spit on our ancestors. Some of the outrage is justified, and only a fool could deny it. Yet Dante was able to travel through the afterlife and remind us in his verse of the beauty of this world. Now, beauty, we are instructed, can only emerge from the world to come. All revolutionary rage is Calvinist.

I descended with Dante and Virgil into the true hell, into the second and third circles. Sleep, that benevolent and charming seducer, was kissing my eyelids. I switched off the light and brought the blanket up to my chin. My last thought, as the rain continued to play its constant legato on the roof, was to wonder whether English could give birth once more to a poet who could write with a robust pride in the language, who could write unashamed and undaunted by her love for the people and the world that made possible that language. Or is English forever doomed to wistfulness and dissembling, and the sheer unctuous sentimentality of apologetic art?

The glorious aubade of the morning is a golden light that pierces the room, each beam of light—some as sheer as gossamer, some broad shafts with particles of dust dancing in them so that I believe I can reach out and touch them—performs a dazzling ricochet around the darkened room. I leap out of the bed, as if I have been granted the gift of a younger man's body, and I pull open the curtains. The light blares, trumpeting its brilliance. I hear it! I am reminded of the words I read just before sleep, when the poets entered the third circle of hell, the province of the gluttonous, where the rain and the cold are unceasing. I slide open the door; the sweet grace of the jacaranda's scent, and just beneath it the warm, moist odour of sated earth. The light bounds, flings, hops from tree to tree, spins and hurtles from every leaf. I am at the dawn of the world, at the initiation of the universe: time has ceased to exist; it has been transcended in the explosion of light. In the space between my breathing in this truth, this infinity, and in my exhaling, time rushes back and reclaims me. I yawn, am conscious of my full bladder. I hurry to the toilet at the end of the corridor and my body returns to its age; with every step, the tendon above my right heel causes a sharp sting to run up the length of my leg. I sigh with relief as I piss.

I lean on the verandah railing, wearing the sweat-soiled T-shirt I have been sleeping in for the last few days. The steam from my coffee cup rises warily and vanishes immediately in the bright glory of the day. My eyes follow the brittle, twisting limbs of the rosebushes below, and I notice that the buds are full, about to rupture and release their burgeoning flowers to the world. To the right of the roses is a rosemary bush, its perfume fulsome after the storm. Next to the rosemary is a hibiscus, its branches gnarled, the leaves flourishing, its buds still nascent. A gleam of black and indigo, of emerald too; the serpent's skin glistens as it coils around the limb of the tree.

'Simon,' I whisper, 'I wish you were here.'

I could go downstairs, find my phone and take a photograph or even a video of the steady majestic ascent of the snake. I don't. I do walk down the verandah steps to the ground, treading quietly, aware that any unexpected vibration might startle it. Even more carefully, I walk along the gravel path; there is a bench along the wall of the downstairs unit, its unstained grain covered by a sheaf of fine dust. I sit and look across to the tree.

The python's body is thicker than my arm and its length is such that for a moment I can't quite discern its head. Then the animal slithers forwards, and I see its forked black tongue dart and search, and in response the muscles in its body quiver and expand, then tighten, and I am awed by both the serpent's beauty and its power. I wonder if it is aware of my observing it. I study the animal with a keen attention but I am also battling an ancient and irrational dread. Olive-green scales glisten among the shining black skin, and at the heart of those bronze tears there are smaller tiles of blazing sunflower yellow; however, the overwhelming colour is that magnificent black, and as the muscles furl and unfurl and bind the creature to the tree, that blackness catches the sun and the reflection is plum, a *purple* befitting an emperor. Awe and fear share the same root—looking at the snake I understand it now: a fear that leads me back to the first Garden and the first intimation of mortality; and an awe that returns me to the primal understanding that there are mysteries and dangers in the world that cannot be borne by oneself, by the merely human, but require the benefaction and intervention of God. The serpent loops in a lazy spiral around a thick branch that is in full sun. There, it comes to rest.

Sometimes I watch through the kitchen window as Simon works in the garden: hoeing the earth, mixing and shifting the compost, digging new furrows into the soil, planting the seeds and seedlings that will become the greens and the bulbs and the beans that I will cook, attacking the weeds. He squats before the garden bed, gently scraping and revealing the roots with one hand, the other swiftly pulling at the invader plant and hoisting it from the soil. And after the weeding, there is the jabbing and prodding and upturning of the compost to reveal the bottom layer, rich and sparkling and black and moist, the stench fetid but also invigorating, a cunning perfume that suggests new life and new promise, like the sweet tang of a newborn infant, where even the filthy egress of the shit in its nappy cannot spoil the augur of that becoming. He spreads this munificence on the garden beds, on the new tunnels and valleys and hilltops he has built in our garden—for that is how I see the result of his labour: the making of a kingdom, of a new world—and then he stands over his creation and waters it and he sees that it is good and there is a small half-smile on his face as he leans against the frame of the kitchen door, takes off one mud-stained boot and then the other, scrapes his socks on the mat, and comes inside the house. And I see that smile, confident and pleased, the pleasure of hard work achieved: Simon's hands are not soft.

I go down the steps to the granny flat and ring my lover. It is Saturday and he doesn't answer. Possibly he is still asleep; and anyway, awake and working in the garden or sleeping in our bed, his phone would not be next to him. The mistrust of technological ubiquity is something we share. I leave him a message describing the python. I tell him that I miss him. I tell him that I love him.

There are more people strolling on the boardwalk this morning. And crossing the road, heading towards the water, I notice that the caravan park is getting full. I am courteous, reply to the tentative 'Good mornings' and robust 'G'days' that I encounter on my walk. But I am conscious of my resent-ment, my wish to reside in my own head, to jealously guard my solitude. At the end of the boardwalk, a group of people is perched at the edge of the slipway, looking down to the shore where three fishermen—two of them white with their necks burnt a fiery red and the other, the eldest, a handsome Yuin man in a loose blue cotton singlet, his silver hair cut razor-short, the skin on his neck and that of his upper arms a darker pitch of black—are assiduously gutting a catch of fish. The men work with rapid and practised ease, slicing open the silver fish, pulling out the innards, the crimson seep of guts, and tossing the refuse into the water, where three seals, two long-flapped stingrays and a screeching colony of cormorants and gulls battle for the feast. On the boat ramp there are three children, two girls and their younger brother, and they are squealing in a delight and volume equal to that of the seagulls, enraptured by the turmoil in the water, the ravenous craving of the animals. Yet I turn away, decide not to walk along the beach but to head back home for the car and drive to the sea.

With that decision, my vexation lessens. I return an old man's curt greeting with a smile, and hail a trio of elderly women promenading along the boardwalk. My gregariousness is a trait I inherited from my mother. In my youth I was open-armed in my affections, and welcoming to life. It is, however, an attribute with limited purchase; to be maintained, it requires trust never to be betrayed and that is not possible in this world. Secular authorities scoff at the notion of Original Sin, but it does have a logic that is consistent and verifiable: we do suffer and we do make others suffer. More derisible, I think, is the ideologues' notion that we are born with an uncorrupted nature and that it is the torments and injustices of the world that stain our purity. It is a tempting romance, but some people are irredeemable. It may be the influence of Dante on me this morning, the ruthless but consistent logic of the morality of his *Inferno*—and, further, I keep returning to his interaction with his teacher, Brunetto Latini, in the fifteenth Canto, where Latini is condemned to the circle and tortures prescribed for the sodomites. Dante makes clear his fondness and respect for his old teacher, and it seems to me that *this* is the clarity and *this* is the confidence we have lost; one does not have to agree with the existence of hell to comprehend the fidelity of Dante's justice—but if anything has turned me away from ascribing the fiefdom of justice to the novel and preferring now to declare for it the pre-eminence of beauty, it has been the exhaustion of being with people in the world. And it is not as if I have been a witness to relentless cruelty, or have been shadowed by evil in my life. It's not even that I have lost my tender affection for the ridiculousness of people; people still make me smile. But the pettiness is exhausting; the selfishness, the narcissism and particularly the vindictiveness; and so my conviviality has been sapped. In the photographs I have of my mother as a young woman she is laughing. Then there are the years of grimness in her smile. It is only with old age, and an acceptance of the divine comedy, that she laughs again.

I am approaching the final length of the boardwalk, where it no longer follows the undulations of the road but stretches across a narrow neck of the inlet so there is water on either side. Here, with no shade from the trees, the sun is bright, abrasive, and I pull my cap from my back pocket and cover my head. A scoop of pelicans is drifting drowsily across the calm, glassy waters. Out of the corner of my eye, I see a crab. Its hard back is the murky russet of the sand and it is only the thin black markings on its legs as it scrambles over the sludge that make it visible. I lean over the railing and my shadow startles the creature. There is a shower of raised sand, the water churns and then subsides, there is a bubble in the mud, a last expulsion of breath, and the creature has disappeared from my sight.

I cross the road, begin to climb the hill, but I am no longer conscious of the warm blues and greens, the celestine waters and the verdant flora of the world around me. I am captured in a hallucination. This is not delusion, I am sober, and yet although I am unaccompanied, I have conjured a guide. It is the recollection of my mother—in particular, a photograph I have of her when she must have been only in her late twenties—that has lured me towards the mirror between the worlds. She is not laughing in this photo. Her face is quizzical as it confronts the camera; whoever has taken the shot is someone she must have trusted, for there is no animosity in her gaze. She is prepared to reveal doubt. The photograph is in black and white, and her eyes are heavily lined with a black tint that accentuates the Levant in her. They are eyes of potency and of fire, nothing of the shimmering paleness of the Occident. No wonder, years later, when I saw Cocteau's *Orphée* for the first time, I bolted upright in my cinema seat when María Casares first appeared. She is the patron of the poet, of Orpheus, but she is also the guardian and keeper of the netherworld. She is the one who brings him to the mirror that will give him access to the worlds beyond reality. The Spanish actress's eyes flashed with the same intensity as the eyes of my mother.

So: a figure walks ahead of me. Her hair is raven, her gait sure, her posture erect. She wears black, oblivious to the sun. I am eager for her to turn and look at me. I am also terrified.

She stops. And she is in shadow. A rising bluff conceals the sun. The other day, at this exact spot, the youth was trying to hold the attention of the girl waiting for the school bus while her brother stood at a diffident distance. The woman stops and I am terrified and desirous of her turning.

She continues walking.

Gregariousness is not possible in a writer. I had to shed some warmness, some fellow feeling, to commit to the isolation, the self-regard of fiction. As with love, where our choices too bind us to solitude. I chose Simon. Love is the apotheosis of beauty. Love is also selfish and it cannot be shared.

The guide striding ahead of me speaks, and her words carry over her shoulder. I hear them clearly, yet I am unsure if they are uttered in English, in my mother's tongue, or in the French of the role she plays in Cocteau's film.

'Is beauty selfish?'

I can hear her heels click on the asphalt pavement that follows the bow of the inlet. It is full tide and the water seeps onto the embankment, almost covers the small island that lies beyond the oyster beds. The still-vital morning light lends the surface of the water a silvern aspect. She seems oblivious to the glory of this world. Her determined pace does not falter. I hear a sly laugh. I know that she is imagination, that the only sounds are the beating of birds' wings over the inlet, the dull roar of the traffic banging over the bridge, the splashing of a cormorant as it lands on the water. Yet I hear her.

'Are you afraid to answer?' the guide asks, and again that canny, sardonic laugh. 'Don't think that you offend me. Beauty is amoral; we who live in the depths below know that truth. An ancient people ascribed beauty to God and

God to light and therefore refused to acknowledge anything of the sublime that accrued to the Devil. That fantasy could not last. War, famine, cruelty made themselves known in all their terrible majesty. Your generation wishes to bind beauty to a new god named Justice. That fantasy too cannot last.'

I gather my nerve. 'I don't think I have abandoned that illusion completely. I think I still want to revere a beauty that is moral.'

The laugh rings out loudly now. It is scathing. We are approaching the steep rise that we must ascend to reach the house, and my breath is shallow. She continues to walk at a steady pace.

'You are not of an epoch that has the consistency for such a morality.'

For a moment I think she is going to turn, look over her shoulder, allow me to glimpse her face. She doesn't.

'Would you place yourself alongside the sodomites in the Inferno's seventh circle?' she asks.

'That's not an ethics I believe in.'

There is savagery in her mocking chuckle now. 'Don't think I haven't noticed that cunning slip of yours, substituting the word *ethics* for morality. As if that will clear you of the suspicion of religion. That too is a symptom of this age. Morality is what you permit for yourself, and immorality is your name for desires you don't share. You judge the other more harshly than you judge yourself.'

Having reached the summit, she is still. I come up behind her, and there is a trembling, a dull pain along the left side of my abdomen. A trickle of sweat runs down the small of my back. I am behind her.

'You all judge the other more harshly than you judge yourself,' she repeats, and this time she sounds weary. 'We are so exhausted with the pettiness and self-justification of your generation's art.'

'What would you have me do?'

I dare to lift my hand: it hovers over her shoulder. Will it slice through empty air if I place it there?

My fingers touch skin. It is icy cold. She doesn't stir.

'Beauty belongs to both God and the Devil. There is beauty in cruelty as much as there is beauty in tenderness. You know that.'

She raises her own hand and places her cold fingers over mine.

'I am not your mother. You can't hurt me. Shit on the censors of the Church and the state, urinate on the puritans of the left and the right. Pursue beauty.'

I lean in to kiss her, with my eyes shut. My lips touch air.

Below, the inlet is a tremulous, shimmering screen. A kooka-burra's laugh peals so loudly that its pride and defiance seem almost indecent. A cacophony of white cockatoos answer it, their screams ferocious. And then abruptly, with the ceasing of that screeching, a fluttering fills the air and their plump white bodies spring from the trees and they take over the sky. They soar across the inlet, and as they do, their voices and then their forms dispel as they fly towards the mountain. The chirping of swallows, the sad call of a bowerbird seeking its mate, the rustle of a creature burrowing in a garden bed; this world never falls into complete silence.

As soon as I enter the house, I take a pen from the kitchen bench, tear a page from my spiral-bound notebook, and I write.

Paul stops at a red light. There is a bus shelter across the road, and schoolkids are waiting for a ride. A tall lean boy with greasy fair hair, trying to impress a girl, is imitating the motions of a surfer. She has her arms crossed, obviously embarrassed by the size of her breasts, too inexperienced, too young to know her beauty. She is looking at him quizzically, not sure if she should be flattered. The other boy is younger, and for some reason—possibly because their hair shares the same dull orange colour—Paul is sure he is the girl's brother. The boy stands aloof, his schoolbag full and high on his back. He keeps looking down the road, waiting for the bus. The sense of deja vu is so overwhelming that Paul shudders. Sweat pours from his armpits, the back of his neck. He exhales, the light turns green and the tremors stop. The car shudders and the tyres squeal, so hard has his foot landed on the accelerator pedal. The younger boy looks up, startled; for a moment he and Paul catch each other's eyes. Then the car speeds away. Paul can't shake the fear kindled by that boy's insistent and curious gaze. I know you. It is almost as if Paul hears the words. I know you. What the fuck are you doing back home?

As soon as I have scribbled those words, I grab my swimmers and my towel. She has led me here, and I know that I will write when I return. First, I want to swim. I need to swim. First, I need to dive into the sensuous, bestial and amoral splendour of this world.

It is the destitution that shocks him. He had thought that he wouldn't recognise the neighbourhoods, the city itself. That after so many years away it would have changed. But so much of it is still here. The Quattros' chicken shop, the Lopez sporting goods place just before the turn-off to the mall. All still standing, though the lettering on the Quattros' shop is no longer a vivid red; it has faded to a dull, ugly beige. And Mrs di Quattro would never have put up with the smudged dirty whorls on the glass. The backboard over the sports store is peeling, and the 'p' in *Lopez* had slipped from its screw, is dangling lopsided. It gives the letter a desperate look, as if it knows that it is just hanging on, and that it is a long way down.

Paul is aware that the driver behind him is annoyed at the slow pace of his driving. When they stop for a red light, she reverses then slides quickly into the empty lane beside his. Paul glances across; she is looking straight ahead, her expression grim, one hand slapping the wheel impatiently.

On the other side of the road, three kids are waiting for a bus. A tall, lean boy, maybe about sixteen, is balancing precariously on the edge of the sidewalk, his arms outstretched. Something about the angle of his arms, the precise bend of his knees, gives the impression he is miming the motions of a surfer. The short sleeves of his T-shirt are rolled up almost to the shoulders. Paul is reminded of himself at that age. Even in winter he preferred sleeveless shirts or the sleeves rolled high and tight, and it could get chilly in Sacramento. The youth's arms are ghostly pale, no colour there at all. His hair is lank, greasy, and flops limply. Paul smiles to himself; that style hasn't changed in decades. There is something rat-like about the boy's thin face, and even from this distance Paul can see that his eyes are clearly too close together, sharpening the rodent aspect.

A girl around the same age is standing looking at the boy, nodding from time to time. She has her arms crossed, slightly pulled away from him. The tightness with which she holds herself is odd; she is too tense, her stance awkward. Paul suddenly gets it: she is embarrassed by the size of her tits. *Oh, honey*, Paul wants to call to her, *you're beautiful; you will never be more beautiful.* But of course he doesn't do it, and of course she is too young to know her allure. And she doesn't know that the young man, seemingly full of bravado, is besotted with her and doesn't know how to tell her.

At a distance from them both, his full schoolbag sitting high on his back, a younger boy is watching the road, impatient for the bus. He has his back deliberately turned away from the other two, as if they are strangers. But something about the burnt orange mop of hair, the same colour as the girl's, convinces Paul that they are siblings. The younger boy looks up at something the older boy has said. And Paul sees it, a wistfulness there, and then a deliberate attempt at a sneer. For a second it makes his young face look mean, ugly. The boy quickly turns back to his scrutiny of the road. That jeering expression has gone and now the kid just seems sad. He looks up, stares across the road at the man in the car watching him. Vertigo bashes through Paul: he feels as if he is slipping, melting into the bucket seat of the car. A hollow whistling in his ears drowns out the world. The air is like quicksand. Then the strident blare of a horn. The light has turned green. Paul slams his foot on the pedal; the car judders, the wheels spin, squeal.

'Get it together, Paul.' He speaks the words aloud.

It isn't dizziness; it is deja vu. It is as if he knows those kids. And once, he is convinced of it, he has been that younger boy.

The streets became narrower and the houses smaller as he approached his grandfather's old house. It was my house too, he tells himself. *Our* home. But he and Andy and their mom always referred to it as grandpa's house. It belonged to *him*. The cunt never let them forget it.

He is shocked at the resurrection of the old hates. And the memory is almost corporeal, so sensual is its intensity. He can smell the sharp odour of his grandfather's dipping tobacco, the old man's stale reek; and he can hear that desperate, racking cough, the bubbling wheezing that used to terrify him. If his grandpa was suffering one of his violent emphysemic seizures, Paul would stand there watching him, terrified that the old man's heaving chest would explode, that he would buckle and die right then and there. How Paul detested the spittle that would rain all over him. And every time, *every time*, he hoped the old bastard would die.

There is a young guy shuffling along the sidewalk, naked except for a pair of ripped black Everlast sweatpants a few sizes too big, querulously screaming out what seem random names. Georgiana! Phylena! Letitia! Jacquelina! Those Cali names that sounded like make-believe in children's play. The man is clearly stoned, out of it, and Paul breaks, scared that the man, lost in his psychosis, will abruptly leap into his path. Impulsively the man stops, drops his pants, and there under the noon sun starts pissing. As he does, his hands reach up to his face, and there is something graceful in the slow stroking of his cheeks and the underneath of his chin. The stream of piss splashes over the man's bare feet.

The sadness overwhelms Paul. Mate, he tells himself firmly, it's the comedown, it's the drugs.

And it stuns him how easily that word *mate*—even though he hasn't spoken it aloud—how easily it has come to him; it is part of him now.

Disorientated, he peers through the windscreen, searching for street names. Most of the signs have been vandalised, bullet holes rendering them indecipherable. The roads are in appalling condition, potholes everywhere and the white lines faded, the paint worn away to bare chalk scratches on the asphalt. The destitution shocks him.

The neighbourhood has always been poor. Now it is poor and black. And the perspiration collects at his pits, drips down his back; he has to wipe it from his brow. As Paul makes a quick left off Broadway, a trio of teenage girls look through the driver's window and their faces are scrunched, unfriendly. One of them purses her lips, hawks a thick wad of phlegm in the direction of the car. It just misses landing on the bonnet. The three of them burst into triumphant laughter.

It isn't only fear making him sweat. He can smell in these rancid secretions the trace of something metallic, something chemical. For what seems the hundredth time that morning he repeats the mantra: *You will never ever do drugs again, never do fucking chemicals when you get back home.* And every time he makes the vow he wishes he had his wife's faith, that he could rely on the strength of God. Not having that, he makes the promise for himself. And he means it. If he slides back into addiction, if he fails himself again, then he will take a sharp blade and he will slide it across his neck, he will sever his own throat. He will not fail Jenna and Neal. The violence of that promise lends him strength. He is alert now, and the codes of behaviour return to him: that constant attentiveness to race that is part of living in America. His whiteness, having to negotiate it. In Australia, he always keeps silent when the subject of race comes up in conversation. He gets it—he knew that every place has its wretched history and its atrocities—but he never proffers an opinion. If he did, he'd just blurt out: 'You guys have no fucking idea!'

He will never ever do drugs again, never do fucking chemicals when he gets back home.

Home? It isn't instinctual, this belief that their house on the green hills above the western Pacific is now *his* place. It doesn't feel like home in his guts. And maybe it never will. Yet these dismal Californian streets are certainly not his place either. Home is Jenna, and home is Neal.

You will never ever do drugs again, never touch chemicals when you get back home.

He recognises the house immediately. It is collapsing, the weatherboards at the front rotting, the foundations sinking so that the narrow house has an absurd cartoonish lean; one of the porch posts has snapped, the remnant dangling like a stalactite from the beam. But it is grandpa's house. The same old metal mailbox; and, absurdly, it seems to be the only part of the house that has been tended to, maintained:

it has recently been painted a bright fire truck red. The grass, urine-yellow and dry, hasn't been mowed for an age. It almost reaches the height of the mailbox.

He knocks on the front door, can hear a dull thud of music, something harsh and rhythmical, coming from the other side. The hard slamming boom of hip-hop. It is impossible that his brother could still be living here. Part of him, and possibly the greater part, hopes he isn't.

There is no response to his knock. He tells himself he'll try one more time, and then walk back to the car, drive back to Los Angeles. And fly home.

To compete with the music inside, he thumps hard on the door. A curtain shifts at the side window of the neighbouring house. When he glances across, the curtain is quickly drawn.

The door swings open. The man standing there is white. His head is shaved, his beard a thin and stringy chestnut wisp across his sharp chin; there are flecks of grey in it. Paul can't see the man's eyes behind the enormous silver-framed reflector shades he is wearing; Paul sees himself, tiny, anxious-looking, in the mirrored lens. The man is thin, terribly thin, every track of his veins and every projection of his bones visible down the length of his pale arms. They look like they belong to the frame of a much older man, but he knows—knows as soon as the door opens—that it is his brother.

'Paul?'

They stand there in silence.

'Paul,' the man repeats, sadly. He lowers his sunglasses. The iridescent black of his pupils seem tiny in the pale blue wash of his eyes. He is hammered.

And then he does something that alarms Paul. The man falls on him, embracing him, holding him so tight and for so long that Paul fears he will never let go. And he is weeping, unashamedly, his body shuddering, his tears wetting Paul's cheeks, his neck, one hand stroking Paul's hair. The man's lips, wet from his sobbing, are kissing Paul, on the cheeks, on the nose, on the brow. He kisses Paul hard, like a lover, on the lips. The danger of that, the strangeness, is what makes the man finally pull away. He snorts into his bare arm, wipes his nose, his eyes.

'Come in, bro,' he says, then peers at the hire car parked outside the house. 'Give us a minute.'

He pats the seat of his jeans, puts his hand in the back pocket and withdraws a piece of dirty checked cloth, the size of a handkerchief but the fabric is thicker, stronger. He walks to the car and ties the cloth to the aerial. Then he turns, smiling, and gives Paul a thumbs-up. One of his front teeth is missing, the lower row decaying, gnarled and black.

'Shouldn't be any problems now.' He jumps back onto the porch and as he does the loose post swings precariously, almost slamming into Paul's shoulders.

'Come inside.' His hand is on the small of Paul's back. 'You want to get high, bro?'

*

259

There is no way Paul is not going to get high. He knows it as soon as he follows his brother into the house. There is no hallway; the front door opens directly into the living room. It is almost in darkness. Old blankets hang from the curtain rods above both narrow windows: cheap acrylic blankets in lurid colours—one a garish orange, the other the blue a child would choose to render the sky—that Paul remembers from his childhood.

'Hang on.'

His brother pulls on a cord that dangles from the ceiling. There is a flicker, a wane pulse of light, then a growling sound; another flicker and a weak fluorescent light fills the room.

The two men stand looking at one another.

Andy looks terrible; and the house stinks. It seems to Paul that these things are connected: the fetid odours coming off the walls and the floor—the mould is pitching through the torn seams of the wallpaper, releasing its damp decaying reek; the synthetic carpet is streaked with muddy shoe prints, and there are bald patches where the fibres have been burnt, exposing the dark green plastic of the underlay—and his brother's pinched aged face, the ferret thinness of it, the scrawniness of his limbs. It's as if the house's poisonous decay and Andy's evident physical deterioration are interdependent. An anguished, ineffectual sadness tears through Paul. Andy has plonked himself down on one of the two sofas in the room. A pipe, the glass bulb blackened by smoke marks, sits on the low coffee table. Andy flicks open a round tobacco tin. Inside is a clutch of tiny grey and white crystals. Andy selects three of the small rocks and places them in the bowl of the pipe. He holds it out to his brother.

'You got a light?'

Paul should say no. But his helplessness is unconquerable. He has been returned to his childhood. He is trapped, he can't escape, he is sinking into this foul carpet. Once, in junior high, Paul had taken acid and when he returned home he had been convinced that demons possessed the house. He remembers entering the house that long ago afternoon—it was early fall, the days just starting to shorten—and how the hair on the back of his neck rose in fearful readiness, recalls the heaviness of malevolence in the house that day. Their grandfather had been dead some six or seven years by then and Paul had wondered if it was the old man's ghost. But in his hallucinatory discernment he knew the demons were much older.

He takes the pipe.

•

I pause and I isolate the word *discernment* within square brackets. I had wanted to use the word *perspicacity*—it seemed closer to describing that uncanny sense of wisdom one experiences when in the midst of an acid trip—but I am doubtful if Paul would use that word.

•

He takes the pipe. The amphetamine crystals bubble, ignite, and melt; the smoke fills the chamber of the pipe and he inhales. The smoke rushes into his lungs.

Paul has limited experience with meth—it was not a drug in common use when he was younger—and he is unsure of what effects to expect from the narcotic. A saliva of liquefied rock is still gurgling in the bowl and Paul inhales once more. Nothing seems to have changed. The room still looks the same and his brother on the armchair opposite is beckoning impatiently for Paul to hand him the pipe. He does so and then sprawls back into the soft springiness of the couch.

The fluorescent light is sputtering; there is a moment when the bulb threatens to shatter, and then the solid wave of light returns. The dull headache he's had all day is gone. There is so much he wants to say to Andy and he doesn't know where to begin. He fumbles in his pockets, finds his cigarettes, brings one to his lips and lights it. That first intake of nicotine, the feel of the cigarette between his fingers, the pleasure of it on his lips. Paul leaps up, slaps his brother's knee, almost shouts, 'Fuck, it's good to see you!' He falls back onto the sofa, grinning. Andy releases a long stream of smoke, places the pipe back on the table. He too is smiling.

There is a shuffling, a series of heavy thuds. Someone is coming down the stairs. Paul looks up. A woman, large—large everywhere, with full plump breasts, a double fold of fat on

her upper arms and the evident balloon bump of pregnancy—
and with a stern broad face framed by black shining hair
knotted in a crown of cornrows is looking him up and down.

'Who's this?'

Paul jumps to his feet. As he does, he is aware of the
lightness of the movement. He hasn't felt this agile in years.

Andy is refilling the pipe. 'This is my brother, Paul. Paul,
meet Cynthia.'

She is looking him up and down. Unimpressed. Before
he can say anything, before he could offer any greeting, she
hisses sharply, 'Your mama left this house to Andy. You'd
run off on them both.' She comes up right next to Paul. 'Your
brother don't owe you shit. You understand me?'

And Paul wants to laugh; and it must be the strange high
of the drug, but he also wants to kiss her. She reminds him of
the girls he'd lusted after at school.

He holds up his hands. 'I don't need anything from my
brother. I've got my life. I just wanted to see him.'

'Yeah,' Andy adds sourly. 'Don't be such a cunt. He's family.'

Yet Paul hears the relief in his brother's tone.

Cynthia holds his gaze for a beat longer, then shrugs,
smiles and reaches for the pipe Andy is holding out to her.

The flame ignites the shards of crystal.

'So, where you been?' she asks, then sucks loudly, thirstily,
on the mouth of the pipe before passing it to Paul.

And the smoke curls and flutters in the dirty glass bowl
and then, just as Paul is about to take it deep into himself, it

solidifies, becomes thick and sinuous, and as he inhales and the drug creeps down his throat, slithering in both nostrils, he wonders if indeed there is a spirit in the meth and whether the deity being called forth is that of a serpent. He isn't frightened. Yet he is wary. Paul watches Andy and Cynthia reverentially pack the crystals tight, watches as his brother's lighter hovers over the rocks, the swift sour stink emitted as the balls ignite. They are not the only ones in this tiny, cramped room: Paul is sure of it. There is another presence.

He vaults from the sofa and begins to pace the room. His brother is talking, his brother can't seem to shut up, and the television is blaring, Cynthia has turned it on, has her legs curled underneath her, is patting her extended belly as if it is a young kitten that she is slowly, tenderly trying to tame. Paul hasn't asked, hasn't dared ask, 'You're pregnant, right?' She is watching some reality show, everyone on it is yelling, screaming; their shrieks remind him of the thunderous din of cockatoos. He understands Jenna's taunts now: 'You Americans are so loud.' And she is right; he can't bear the noise from the television.

He keeps pacing the room. He stops before a photograph of his mother, just before her end. He used to think her pretty, real pretty. And she was, but all traces of that beauty had long been obliterated and desecrated by the time the photograph was taken. He can't reconcile his memories to this decrepit old woman's frightened sallow face. There is a presence here. He is sure of it. It is not his grandpa. The spirit is menacing yet not nasty. Their grandpa was wicked. But it isn't his mother. She's no longer here.

Whatever the spirit is, it is coiled and waiting, it has infinite patience. And that is when Paul, remembering the slink of the smoke filling his throat and his lungs, understands that meth is indeed a serpent: quiet, looped, forbearing. Waiting.

His gaze shifts to a photo of a family, a mother and four children; a selfie, printed and pinned to the wall. The mother, who is holding the phone, is wearing a lime green jumpsuit that emphasises the ebony gleam of her skin. Her free arm is enfolding three daughters and a son. The youngest girl, he is sure of it, is Cynthia. The girl is skinny, still only a child, yet already there is something of the older woman's cynical remoteness in the girl's unsmiling face. And next to that photo, their grandfather's belt buckle is hanging from a nail. He remembers it, the interlinked Celtic loops. The loud jangle when the old man unclasped the belt; and the other sound, the one he hated more, the swishing of the leather strap through the loops on his grandpa's jeans.

Paul lights another cigarette. It calms him; he can't remember why he ever gave up. Fuck those puritan cunts, denying a man his pleasures—he will smoke for the rest of his life.

He moves across the room towards a shelf screwed to the wall. One of the screws in the left bracket has loosened and Paul sticks his thumbnail into the slotted groove, turns it carefully, all his focus on the task. And as the screw tightens, as his breath releases, he senses that the snake is exhaling too. He nudges the wooden plank: the shelf is stable again. A Bible, the New Testament, and a dog-eared, watermarked copy of Michelle Obama's autobiography, the pages crinkled and damp.

On the other end of the shelf is a clutch of DVDs and four old VHS tapes. On one of the wide video spines the face of a handsome young man. At first, for the quickest of moments, Paul wonders: Do I know this guy? Then comprehension floods.

He swings towards his brother and Andy is looking up at him, his smile radiant, as when they were boys and Andy would follow him everywhere. That dogged trust. And Paul's rage vanishes, as do the words he was about to scream: 'Why the fuck have you got these here?' His brother is proud of him. The obsolete DVDs and VHS tapes on the shelf aren't meant as censure. They are a shrine.

He goes over to his brother, he leans over the couch, he kisses him.

•

A screech so blaring and abrasive that it sounds hostile. I look up. A cockatoo is perched on the railing, watching me through spherical black eyes. The white cottony down seems a heavy pelt: hide not feathers. I wonder if its scream is a warning. The afternoon is tumbling to evening but as yet the sky shimmers in a cloudless blue calm. I look at the letters across the laptop screen. In what I am writing I am descending further into Hell. The bird's gaze has not shifted. Should I delete all of it? Should I resist following Paul into the furthest reaches of the netherworld? I whisper the words, 'Beauty belongs to both God and the Devil. There is beauty in cruelty as much as there is beauty in tenderness.' I do know that. I have lived that. Orpheus has to descend to Hades. It is only with the knowledge acquired there that he can return and not look back.

I continue typing. As I do, the bird takes flight, and it is gone.

●

The flare of more crystals igniting, the sulphur release as the rocks burn, the serpent rushing down the chute of the pipe, sliding into their lungs. And he is telling Andy and Cynthia about Australia and the life he has there, and he mentions Jenna and speaks proudly of Neal but he doesn't name the nearby towns and rivers and mountains; he keeps the location vague. The spirit that weighs on this house, the coiled, listening snake, isn't malign; it is counselling prudence. So he speaks of the clearness and vastness of the ocean, the unceasing space, both enticing and frightening, and he keeps smoking as he talks, and very soon his packet is empty and he walks with Andy to the nearest store, its windows covered by iron grills, and Andy introduces the young and alert man behind the counter as Sam and Paul asks, 'What's your Korean name?' which is a mistake, for the man answers wearily, 'Sam, my name is Sam,' and Paul asks for a packet of Luckies and he buys tobacco and smokes for his brother and on opening the wallet to pay he notices the bag of white powder tucked in a corner, a gift from Jackson, and on the way back, excited, he says to Andy, 'Should we do some coke?' and his brother hollers and whoops and slaps him on the back, and as they return to their grandpa's place—is it condemned always to be their grandfather's place?—they pass a tall young man who nods contemptuously at Andy then yawns, stretches, and as his basketball singlet rises Paul is shocked to see peeping from above the waist of his sweatpants the shining black handle of a gun.

The cocaine brings him to normal. Within a minute of snorting the powder, the serpent has gone, the house is emptied of its spirit.

Cynthia is sitting in the little alcove in the kitchen, talking to her mother on the phone. 'Mama, you can't say that, you can't say that!' And then she breaks out into giggles. 'Damn, Mama, you *did* say that!' There is no trace of suspicion in her voice; it pitches and peals warmly.

His brother has snorted his line, is sitting upright on the armchair, silent.

'Why did you leave me?'

Paul has been waiting for this question. He'd been antici-pating it all that long drive from LA. And because he has been considering it for so long, returning to distant choices, to a fate decided long ago, he thinks he has an answer. And the drug—the steely exactitude that must be part of the very molecular structure of cocaine—reinforces his conviction. He could say: I was seventeen, Andy, fucking up at school, and I hated Sacramento, thought if I had to spend one more day here I was going to die, I was going to kill someone or I was going to die, and Mom had a new boyfriend and the thought of attending one more math class, one more sociology class, one more fucking English class, well, brother, it made me think of getting a gun, pointing it at my head and spraying my fucking brains all over these ugly stinking walls, but I knew I didn't want to do that and I had made some money from that shitkicker's job at Trader Joe's and I was making good money off the faggots in the parks and at the truck stops, and one day I took the bus and headed to LA and when I got there I phoned Mom and said, 'I ain't ever coming back, you can't make me come back,' and she cried a little, and she asked, 'Do you want to talk to Andy?' and I said, 'No,' 'cause I didn't know what to say to you, so instead I said I'd call again soon, but the days became weeks and the weeks became months and the months became years and it just got too hard to call and I did what I had to do: I got out of this shithole, Andy. I left and I didn't look back, and I didn't think of you at all.

His brother's silence, the cracked lips, the old man's trembling chin, the greasy thinning hair, the cadaverous frame, every knob and bump and plane of bone visible under that thin greyish skin. Andy can't have long to live. That thought, a bolt, immediate, charged with the alacrity and augury of the drugs, is in his head and he knows it as certainty. This man across from him, so much older than he should be, wheezing like their grandpa did, with his hands that can't stop shaking and his toothless rancid gums, Paul will not hurt him. Andy has known pain enough. There is no fairness in a world that hurts someone so harshly and so much. So Paul doesn't tell the truth. He makes up a story.

'Michael,' he says. 'You remember him?'

Andy looks uncertain, then he asks tentatively, 'You mean Mom's old boyfriend?'

Paul nods.

'What about him?'

'He used to fiddle with me.'

And then it becomes easy to spin it and weave it and make it concrete, and Andy is enraged, shouting so loud that Cynthia rushes into the room, and they do more lines, and then Andy is crying and Paul is holding him, and then they smoke some more crystal and they are laughing until Andy's mood shifts, a sourness at his lips and in his eyes, and at that moment Paul realises that the snake has returned with the glide of the vapours into his lungs, and Andy snarls, 'Did Mom know?' and Paul says, 'No, God no, of course I never told her,' and Andy asks, 'But why didn't the perverted cunt ever touch me?' and Paul answers, ''Cause I told him

I would come back and slit open his fucking pig throat with a knife if he ever touched you, Andy,' and then the hostility vanishes from his brother's face and they are embracing. And Andy says, 'I don't even have your number! Give me your number and we'll never be divided again,' and Paul gives it to him, they exchange numbers, punching their details into each other's phones. Then they hug and they are snorting and smoking and the television is blaring and Cynthia is sitting with them and watching the television and the show is terrible, the light over-flooded and the actors desperate and confused as to their marks and the senseless motion on the screen and the infernal din from the speakers rekindles Andy's fury and he is on his feet again, pacing around the dark dank room, screaming curses and threatening Michael and his wrath is so palpable it terrifies Paul. He knows that outrage, that venom, the fury that can smash a wall, break a face, throttle a soul.

But Cynthia knows how to soothe him. She croons, 'Sit here, baby. Sit down next to me, baby boy.'

Andy pivots, the anger still demonic. Then he hangs his head and sits next to his girlfriend. She cradles him, his face smothered in her enormous bosom, his hand reaching for a breast. Having comprehended the source of his anger, she coos softly, 'That old pervert faggot. Don't you worry, lover, Satan has him now; that old white devil is in Hell.' She laughs with a savage glee. 'He'll burn for eternity, baby. He'll suffer till the end of time.'

Paul draws on the pipe, the drug now inside him but also outside him. The serpent has uncoiled and is tightening itself around him. Paul isn't scared; the meth insulates him from such terror. He takes in the smoke, releases it in one long icy stream.

There is darkness in the gaps between window and the blankets. Day is gone. The TV is still on but muted now. Dense and muddy hip-hop blares, the raps hard and spiteful, the music metallic and battering. Paul reaches for his Luckies and is startled to find the pack half empty. When the fuck did he smoke them all?

His hand is trembling as he lights a cigarette.

The smoke seeps through his body and it merges with the curling flow of the meth, coursing through him as if seeking something and, not finding it, darting across vein and capillary, atom to atom, molecule to molecule, desperate to find this conclusion, and Paul is convinced it will tear his body apart, and he is weary of the snake, of being watched, so he finds the bag in his wallet, a residue of white across the plastic, tips out the last dregs of cocaine, slashes at the crystals with the sharp base of a credit card to turn them into the finest of powders and sweeps up a final long line. He knows his brother and Cynthia are stretching towards him, looking longingly at the line, but he will not share this with them. He snorts, hard and swift, the powder scraping the inside of his nostrils; and then he feels the numbness in his gums, he senses the gathering of metallic phlegm at the back of his throat, and then there is clarity and the snake is gone. He takes the empty bag, turns it inside out and licks it clean of white dust. He exhales, falls back on the couch. The music seems louder, a drill of discord.

'Can we change the fucking music?!'

Cynthia swipes at her phone. The music abruptly ceases.

'What music do you want to hear, baby?'

She holds out her phone and, ashamed of his outburst, Paul stands and goes to sit next to her. He scrolls and scrolls through an endless list of song titles. He can't make sense of the words. All he is conscious of is the woman's warmth next to him, her shallow breaths, the doughy scent of her. Cynthia is patting her belly, stroking it. Paul puts down the phone.

'Can I listen for its heartbeat?'

It is the first time he has dared mention the baby.

Cynthia cackles; she is not offended.

'Sure, honey,' she says, and he puts his ear to her stomach. He hears a gurgle and for a moment he wonders if it is the murmur of a heartbeat but it is only the rise and fall of the woman's breath, and he can feel the weight of her breast on the top of his head and then she is pulling down on her neckline and a breast flops out of her jumpsuit, enormous and brown, hard and soft at once, and she is pushing his face into her flesh with one arm, and with her other guiding his mouth to her nipple, and the rubbery plum knot is in his mouth and it tastes of salt and of sweat, and it also tastes sweet. She clutches at his hair, lifts his head, and they are kissing now, and his hand is on her breast, kneading it, squeezing it, and her hand is at his crotch and he is hard, and she is unzipping him and her fingers are sliding up and down and then firmly binding the shaft of his cock and he can't stop kissing her, they have disappeared into each other, and the drugs are currents of electricity in his spine, in every strand of hair, sliding on the surface of his balls, sashaying across his tongue; all is fire and all is light and so lost is he in her kiss that it is only gradually, as when emerging into awakening from a dream, that he remembers that they are not the only two people in the room. He pulls away from her, looks across at his brother.

Andy attempts a smile that comes out as a grimace. He swallows, sucks the air, chews at his lips, as if it is difficult to breathe. He looks like their grandpa. He sounds like him.

Paul hears Cynthia whimper. He turns to face her and in her eyes he sees that she is young, and fearful. 'Please,' she says softly. 'Please don't take away our house.'

And his brother is nodding, not daring to face Paul, as if he is the one who should be ashamed.

Paul finds that he cannot speak. Finally, with an effort so great that it seems as if he has wrenched the words from the very core of himself, he insists, 'I don't want your house; I promise I'm not taking your house.'

It is clear that neither of them believe him.

The silence, broken only by Cynthia's quiet sobbing, by his brother's ugly wheezing breath, the low piercing scream of a police siren, is unbearable. Paul picks up Cynthia's phone and hands it to her. She taps; booming funk blares. Andy, coughing, reaches for the pipe, packs the bowl, raises the lighter's flame over the blackened rocks. Only the pipe brings them peace.

When it is time to sleep, Paul's brother crushes up a handful of Oxy. The three of them snort it, and as the narcotic somnambulance begins, the only sound in the night, apart from Andy's wheezing, is the canned laughter, the exploding commercials, from the TV. Cynthia is the first to fall asleep.

With the opening of his eyes, a rod slams into the side of Paul's head, as swift and unanticipated as the expert punch of a fighter. The pain of it brings bile to his throat and with an effort that feels superhuman he pulls himself up from the sofa and staggers to the bathroom. His mouth, his throat, reek. He retches, splashing watery bile into the toilet bowl. Then he pisses. The stream is long and the smell putrid, the colour almost orange. He looks at it in distress; he's never seen piss that colour before. There is a small mirror above the basin, the bottom shattered. Paul shuts his eyes, his hands grip the rim of the basin; he opens them again to face himself in the mirror.

The foulness of the old man staring back at him with bleary red eyes appals him. And then it all floods back and he is engulfed by shame, drowning in it, as if a malevolent deity has reached down his throat and is squeezing his lungs: his brother sitting across from him, Andy's forced smile a broken, miserable plea.

And though it has been years—is it decades?—since such feelings have overwhelmed him, it is only the thought of destroying himself that returns him to calmness. He rubs his fist, ready; he will smash it into the mirror then choose the largest, sharpest fragment and slice his own throat. He isn't afraid. His finger probes his neck, finding the artery. He recalls doing this as a child, daring himself, as a youth in this very bathroom—a different mirror then; rectangular, not square. Back then, it was the thought of what it would do to his mother, to Andy, that curbed the exquisite anticipation of suicide. That doesn't matter now. Andy is unredeemable. Paul has seen death in the living before. For such souls, rehabilitation, rebirth, resurrection are impossible.

Paul raises his fist, ready to slam it into the mirror.

His son's eyes, the eyes they share, are looking back at him. Paul drops his arm and begins to weep.

His brother is asleep, splayed across the sofa. Cynthia must have gone upstairs to bed. A large wet patch covers Andy's crotch and has spread down one thigh of his jeans. The stink of the piss. That ugly hoarse wheezing. Even asleep, Andy's body isn't at rest.

Paul kneels, brings his lips close to his brother's cheek, kisses it. And he whispers, 'I'm sorry.'

He looks for Andy's phone, finds it sitting next to the meth pipe on the coffee table. Paul pockets it. He remembers Andy punching in Paul's details. He knows there is no way his brother could ever come to Australia—with what money? With what resolve?—yet he wants to erase any trace of opportunity. He was right all those years ago to leave and never look back. Paul will not betray this promise. He will never return home. Home is death.

Outside, he unties the cloth knotted to the aerial and pushes it through the mailbox slot. He drives until he finds a McDonald's. He eats so much he fears he will be sick. Yet still he continues to eat, to dilute the poisons. He drinks coffee and water, water and coffee. He belches, pats his bloated stomach. Then he goes back to the car and heads for LA. He stops only once, just outside Fresno. He finds a small boulder in the desert scrub and, taking his brother's phone, he smashes it again and again and again and again. The plastic and silicon and metal bleed into the asphalt. He returns to the car and drives straight to the city. Three more nights; just three more nights. He won't leave the hotel in Bel Air. He will not ring Jackson, he will not contact anyone. He will not take drugs. He will swim in the pool and he will order room service for breakfast, lunch and dinner. He will swim and eat, eat and swim, prepare himself for home. All that matters is getting home.

•

A dinkus seems appropriate here, to separate my fiction from my truth. Even as I type that word—*truth*—I know that it is inadequate. I dutifully save my work, and then save it again onto the mustard-coloured USB stick. Once that is done, I stand up: the working day is done. I will not write any more today. I start to lower the lid of the laptop.

When I was young, the primary school I attended was only a short walk from the auto parts factory where, for a period, both my parents worked. There were some days when it was necessary to walk straight to the factory rather than return home after school. Possibly my mother had made an appointment with her doctor after work, and she needed me to interpret for her. Or it could be that my father had organised to see his sister after finishing his shift, to pick lemons from her bounteous tree or to write some words she wished to send to their mother back in Greece; my aunt lived on the eastern border of the neighbourhood and my father's visits offered the opportunity to play with my cousins, whom I adored. Whatever the reason, it was always with a beating heart and a keen rush of anticipation that I approached the factory.

There was a front office, reached by three concrete steps that led to swinging glass doors I cannot recall ever seeing opened; and though I do not think we were ever specifically forbidden, my brother and I knew we should never enter by this way. Instead, we went to the massive roller door around the corner on Burnley Street. Once or twice I remember seeing that door raised, the cranking of the rollers releasing a continuous shrill screech, a truly horrific din; it sounded like a poor beast in its death throes, the screaming only stilled with a final bang, a convulsion, when the metal had rolled to the very top. Through that cavernous open mouth, trucks and vans would come and go. But that was rare. Those days when I was summoned to the factory after school, the roller door would be shut and I would enter the same way as the workers did, through a small door cut into the metal sheet, so low that even as a child the top of my head would scrape the sharp surface if I forgot to duck. Many of the adults would have to drop to a comical squat to enter and leave the building.

As soon as I stepped into the factory, there would be a frenzy of noise. It sounded delicious to me, the clanking and banging and ringing and pealing and thudding of the machines. Yet after a minute or so, the unrelenting volume made my body tremble and I knew what it meant to have your head ringing: if I closed my eyes, I could imagine my brain shuddering inside the casement of my skull. So loud was that world!

The ceiling reached to the heavens and the only source of light were the skylights above, crisscrossed by metal rods and an underlay of wire. The sweat would begin to pour off me as soon as I came through the door. There were lines of blue-overalled workers, the women with their hair covered in blue or white or clear plastic caps, the men often having stripped off their shirts and singlets, the straps of their overalls dangling from their hips, the hair on their head, on their chests, on their arms flattened against their skin, as if they had just emerged from a swim or from a shower. And as the men pulled hard on the steel levers that crunched a hole in the pistons that dropped onto the churning belt of the assembly line, the muscles along their forearms rose and rolled, and it seemed to me as if they would rupture the thin shell of skin, so powerful was that cranking motion; and with each third or fourth drive of the lever they would grab a soiled cloth and wipe it under their armpits, across the back of their necks.

My mother would look up from the dizzying continual procession of pistons that she had to pick up, examine and place back on the endlessly rolling belt, and on seeing me her smile was a dazzle. Or my father, a workmate having pointed out my arrival, would wave from the machines at the back, his face blackened by oil and grease, only the warmth of his eyes indicating that this was indeed my parent. Always I was enthralled. I had stepped into a forbidden world.

'This will never be your future, Christo, nor will it be your brother's.'

And all these memories return, the ruckus and the heat and the dark and the blue overalls and the sweat. My mother or father would come to collect me, and then walk to a rack against the back wall and search among the cream and white cards for the one with their name on it. They would insert it into the slot of a bulky green machine that jingled then released a piercing whistle like a firecracker popping, and the card would spring back up from the slot and my parent would place it back on the rack and then say to me, 'That means I've clocked off. Now we can go.'

Clocked off. I push down the lid of the laptop. With my soft hands. I am clocking off.

The jacaranda scent first tickles then rushes into my lungs, as if the art of rejuvenation is contained in the flower and I am being restored to youth inside out. And indeed, the sweetness of the perfume seems to land as fine powder, as if the usually invisible atoms and their subatomic particles are physically manifest in that alluring, elating scent.

Truth: I know that the word is inadequate. I experienced a certain satisfaction immediately on pressing the keys that would insert the spherical black omen of the dinkus; and reflecting on my use of the symbol, was I not seeking something akin to supernatural protection when I had selected it? The asterisk would not do; I wanted a shape and an intervention suggestive of that ancient, almost primordial mark: the evil eye. One requires such safeguarding when navigating the space between worlds. I place that safekeeping between the story I tell of Paul and the story I tell of myself. The sign also segregates the depraved broken world in which Paul was brought up from the safe haven of my own childhood. And the dinkus does one more thing: it connotes the border regions between consciousness and the netherworld. It is no accident that as soon as I described the shame that almost destroys

Paul—I desired to crash my own fist into that grimy, cracked mirror—I was swathed in memories of childhood. They filled me with a reassuring, placating joy.

My writer's will demands that I return Paul to such delirium; Jenna and Neal are his guides through the darkness, and just as Eurydice led her mortal love up through the circles of Hades, Paul discerns deliverance in the shadow forms of his wife and of his son—and they must be as shadow, because he has been tossed into the furthest abyss of Hell, and that misery is the vision he will never be able to extinguish, that of his brother watching him make love to Cynthia, his brother believing that no love, filial or compassionate, can exist any longer in this world. And in recalling this moment, let us return to Paul and attest that for the rest of his life Paul will never recall that moment without feeling a shame so profound it is a lance that tears him from bowel to throat; and he will one day declare to Jenna that he is thankful he does not believe in her God, for he now understands how a sin, a transgression, can follow one into eternity, and how no punishment can erase such evil. And so his impossible atonement must begin with his faithfulness to those distant figures up ahead, the faint emanation of light that he glimpses even in the most rank and benighted prison of his sorrow, knowing that he must place one foot in front of the other, that it is required of him to follow, to climb, to ascend, and it is not they who cannot turn and look for him, ensure that he has not stumbled over a rock, mistaken the path; no, it is he who must not look back at Hell. He must forsake Andy to the devastation. He does not look back once.

Truth, it is inadequate. For the factories my parents worked in, they were not strange and fantastic worlds, shapeshifting universes. They worked in furnaces, and their bones were destroyed, became atrophied and arthritic from the numbing brutality of their work. I recall their bodies as heroic, stained from the oil that spluttered from the machines, wet from the sweat that poured from their bodies. And yet my memory is not untruth. Creeping through the door cut into the gate, I did see a magic world of sound and ferocious motion emerge. The men and women were Vulcans, the gods of blacksmiths and ironworkers and tillers of land and forgers of metal. But the truth is also that their bodies were being broken.

Like Paul, I too am mindful of my fortune in this world. I am aware of the world's beauty. And like Paul, I will wear my shame till my end: for we know there are worlds without love, neither filial nor compassionate.

The light floods back. Though I have not shut my eyes, for they have been wide open as I have stood here on the deck, it is only now that I see the tremulous wafting of cloud from the south, am aware of the white-hot heart of the sun about to descend behind the forest. It is only a couple of hours till the advent of night. The jacaranda's perfume is once more teasing my nostrils, caressing my skin. I go to take my swimmers off the line.

After the day of work, it would be a sin not to swim.

*

I decide not to drive out to one of the isolated coves on the outer edge of the town; I head straight to the mouth of the inlet, where the long arm of the northern spit divides the inlet beach from tumultuous chunder of the ocean. If one walks the length of the spit, constructed from quarried rock and dolosse, then one is at the head of the ocean. The fingers of the southern spit seem to stretch towards its sibling arc, the northern spit, but the ruthless force of the ocean waves keeps them separate. I have stood there on days when gales whip and strike ferociously, when it seems impossible that the wind will not lift me off my feet, raise me high and hurl me against the rocks. On such days I don't dare creep close to the edge. Even on mild days, the waves roll and plummet in a dizzying clamour through the narrow pass, only a few dozen metres from the point of one spit to the other; and it seems heroic how the sailors and fishers guide their craft through the slim gap, braving the heaving and agitation of the waters beneath them: at such moments one can believe in the ancient gods, in immortal Poseidon. That groundswell under the waves, is it not the roll of his shoulder? That breaker about to roll into the bay, is that not his giant hand smacking the water? And yet, on the inlet side, the bay is tranquil. A shark net is hoisted from the rocks. Beneath the surface, banks of concrete slabs hold the hemp net in place and bright orange buoys tied to the ropes mark the boundaries. At high tide the water is deep, but the net, and the serenity of the bay, make it the safest beach in the region. In high summer, families crowd along the slender curve of the beach. The orange buoys dip and sway in the water. The ocean god has no dominion here.

Plonked in the middle of the beach are five adolescents: three girls and two boys. Music is coming from one of the young women's handbags: the tinny, repetitive call and response of a house beat. The female vocal is shrill, the eccentricity of the pitch amplified by electronic manipulation. I choose to disrobe against the concrete wall of the spit, to keep as much distance as possible between me and the youths. Their forms are slender and their limbs stretch out in preposterous symmetry, as if the panorama of the beach was sculpted by a meticulous artist who has placed the bodies in perfect unity with the undulating curve of the platinum sand; the shore is made more exquisite and more perfect by their addition.

Stripped to my bathers, I glance at my own body with cursory irritation. Whereas the ivory skins of the youth are a complement to the white hot blaze of the sand, my paleness is intermediary, a wasting: my skin calls out, requires the ministering of the sun's rays to return it to its rightful golden olive hue; and there is that flab around my middle, those wisps of grey across my chest. If there is a great artist shaping this creation, this miniature of beach and sand and shore, then their hand should reach down from the heavens and pluck me from their wondrous landscape.

Yet as soon as I dive into the cold, invigorating water, I am released. My body returns me to myself; also shed are shame and timidity, as if they are only surface afflictions, an irksome epidermal reaction that is staunched, conquered, as soon as the bracing salt water scours my skin. I break through the surface and gasp for air. I swim towards the net. As soon as my fingers touch the sodden rope, the feel of it grossly slippery, I tread water and turn around, look towards the shore. The youths are still lying along the beach; only one of them, one of the boys, has risen. He is sitting up, looking in my direction. His form is a glimmering shade.

Held by water, I finally understand why I ascended from the ordeal of Paul's disgrace to heroic memories of sacrifice, of my parents' dedication to arduous labours that promised them the incredible: to raise a child with soft hands. That understanding, as I am kept afloat by this pacific, antipodean sea, comes to me with such zeal that it seems to have the force of an angelic annunciation: it radiates a glow that is scorching, a brilliance akin to that of the sun, the sand, the daub of whiteness on the beach that is the young man's body; all pertain to an originating resplendence.

The English language eschews the physical, a quarantining of the erotic that was unleashed by the austere righteousness of the Protestant's cause. I write in English, but I speak it with a Greek tongue, and therefore I am constantly translating the language, for translation is the art of speaking in tongues. This is not either/or, a demand that one tendency be ascendent over the other; the Greek language has its own borders and heresies that its writers and artists must navigate and traverse and defeat. Yet, raised Greek and Orthodox Christian, I was not forged in the hostile sparks discharged from the blows on the anvil of sensuality by Luther's and Calvin's hammers. The domination of the English language is vast. The Irishwoman linked to the Scotsman with his arm folded tight around the Englishman's arm who is holding the hand of the Welshwoman who is coupled with the New Zealander; or is she Yolngu? Canadian? Australian? Jamaican? South Nigerian? Marathi or South African? Even when we disavow the dominion of that language—wish to resist it, to rebirth it, even to shatter it—we are too often trapped in that puritanical fear of the body. Terrified of the erotic, resenting its allure, we fortify ourselves against it by mocking it; or condemning its wildness, demanding it be tamed.

To write English not as an Englishman or Englishwoman. To not sequester beauty from the body and from sex. To dare enter those paradises and all those hells, all those labyrinths and mazes and maps that lie on the other side of the mirror.

I swim back to the shore and then I stand and look towards the youth. The boy who is sitting up yawns and stretches. First there is the hurried thrust out of his elbows, and then the extending of the length of his arms until his hands form fists. The hair of his armpits is blond; I am tempted to describe it as having the tint of hay, when the sheaves of wheat and grain have been so long assaulted by the summer sun that they are almost, not quite, deracinated of colour; what remains is the most subtle blush of yellow. But the hair of the boy's armpits is so sparse that it almost disappears against the paleness of his skin; only the glimmer of perspiration.

At that moment, he turns towards me, sees me looking at him. What shame can accrue from admiring beauty? One of the activities I most treasure when travelling through the eastern Mediterranean is observing how men and women look at each other with an enthusiastic and yet dispassionate appraisal. And it is not a fascination only with the opposite sex: I will never forget a group of young men in Patras crammed around a small table in a cafe, smoking cigarette after cigarette with their coffees, discussing politics and football and girls, when unexpectedly one of them, broad-shouldered and heavy, embraced his friend, who had the languid poise and slight fey looks of a young Alain Delon, kissed him hard on the lips and exclaimed: 'My God, you are so handsome!' And years later, in Athens, at another cafe, a woman leaning across to tap the shoulder of another young woman who was leaning back in her chair, her eyes closed, enjoying the Attic sun. 'Excuse me,' said the first woman, 'I had to compliment you on your legs—they are beautiful.' Can one imagine this occurring in a cafe in Bristol or Chicago or Wellington? Impossible. The reverence that those Greek boys and that Greek woman had for beauty accrues no shame: that mortification is a sin whose origin is the Occident. However, as the Protestants purloined this continent, I too must turn away from the boy.

I don't want to cause embarrassment and I don't want to arouse suspicion. I pack up my belongings and head back to the car to drive home.

Yet I have not forgotten one part of him. Let me continue sketching him for you. His fair hair is of an impossible thickness, recently cut short, the style perfunctory, the kind of style favoured by country lads who wish to resist fussing and preening; a cut that requires the minimum of attention when returning from the surf or emerging from the morning shower. It frames a long, almost equine face, with a firm chin and a large nose that one immediately guesses causes the boy endless agony and adolescent shame, though in fact the stark plane of it lends his visage a masculine purpose that enhances his youth while also alluding to the promise of a long and consistent handsomeness in his adult life. His green eyes, round and not deep-set, so that they seem one with the graceful plane from brow to nostril lack guile and lack suspicion: the gaze he fixed on me was curious, not distrusting. A long svelte neck sits with proportionate grace on wide shoulders, his pale chest is devoid of any flab or fat, the pink nipples erect from the sea breeze, and his stomach is also flat, sculpted by long morning walks to school, by dawn surfs and afternoon ocean swims. He has fine strong limbs. The hair on his legs is black, a distinct contrast to his fairness. The playful twirls of hair on his belly are not dark; they form a steep triangle of honeyed down that disappears into the waistband of the black football shorts he wears as swimmers. There is a faint ridge visible through the wet synthetic fibres; the outline of his cock.

I am careful to ignore all sensations that arise on the short drive home. My actions are sure, I am conscious of the other cars on the road and I take no unnecessary risks, wait patiently for the northbound cars to cross the bridge. I notice the silvery light that pricks the bay, making the waters glisten and blister as if sparks are dancing across the inlet, the final breath of the receding sun. Yet though the real world is around me and enters me, I do not linger or let myself be transfixed by colour or tone, sound or birdsong. I carry home with me the image of the young man, so that if the car were to careen off the road and plunge into the waters below, if I were to drown or be torn into two by the resulting carnage, then the last image burnt into my retina, the last vision I would take into Hell or Paradise, into eternity, would be the features of that young man.

As soon as I have parked the car, I run into the house, find a pen and scribble my description on paper. The words capture the youth. And I am at rest.

I sleep soundly till morning. I am not ashamed to love the beautiful. I know many shames and humiliations, regrets and mistakes: I do know guilt. But I can't be cowered to sleeplessness and anguish by the admiration of an exquisite youth. This is not an English book.

My awakening this morning is immediate and rousing, the jolt of consciousness teeming within me, a pitching flood that drowns sleep. I prop myself up in bed, eyes wide open and their perception unsullied, so swift has been the eradication of slumber. The heavy curtain is drawn and the light that trickles into the bedroom is weak, callow, for its faint luminescence has the quality of youth; nevertheless, I can discern the definite shape of the wardrobe, the low dresser, the vivid colours of the prints and paintings on the wall. Also, when I get up, walk up the hallway to the toilet, there is no clumsiness to my tread, no arthritic grazing bite at the heel of my foot. My ears discriminate between the caw of a raven, the stuttering warbling of a bower, the belligerent screams of a flock of white cockatoos; and as I piss, the strong yellow flow smacks the bowl. The toilet itself has a faint stink of ammonia sourness that seems to waft off the vinyl matting, as if years of men missing the basin, their piss dripping or splashing on the floor, is a memory impossible to fully eradicate. And also, isn't there among that faintly obnoxious odour the sweet and elating perfume of jasmine? I raise myself onto my toes and peer through the window to see a cluster of fragile white buds, their pearly petals trembling in the gentle breeze. I land back on my heels. I flush the toilet and that sound too is a hoarse sucking, a giant's inhaling, before the water gushes and roars. No impression seems lost to me this morning: sight and smell and hearing the keenest I have experienced them in years; my limbs divested of weariness, the humiliating prods and tickles, lances and piercings of age; no cloudiness, only clarity in my mind. A most blasphemous thought: is this how a god is in the world?

This purposefulness, and this renascence, continues on my walk. The morning is still cold, there are kisses of dew on the leaves of trees, so I make my strides long and fast. As I reach the bottom of the hill, I wonder if, in the alchemy of sleep, some strange science has not been enacted whereby my writing of the boy from the beach has occasioned our exchanging places, so that I am in possession of his youthful body? Of course, such musing is an absurdity: I can look down at my old man's hands, drop the collar of my shirt and expose the grey hair on my chest, stop and stare down at the mangled shape of my flat right foot. I am no changeling; I am in my body. Yet describing the youth, capturing him in words, has an aspect of sorcery.

There was a moment last night, as I was scraping and washing the plates in the sink, when I thought I would make the boy the very image of Andy when he was younger, before drugs and poverty and lassitude poisoned his body. Not that there would be flashbacks, scenes or chapters that returned to Paul's past in *Sweet Thing*. That was clear to me from the very first envisioning of the story, whether it was to be novel or a play or a film. Nevertheless, might not a memory arise from Paul's looking at old photographs, an unsettling disturbance that occurs in the very middle of his methamphetamine daze, the recollection of his brother's youth resulting in an acute perception that for a moment overpowers the sovereignty of the drugs and returns him to sober consciousness? He sees and understands and therefore laments the suffering of his brother; then the siren drug pumps through his veins, kisses his brain, returns him to self-seeking forgetfulness. However, this morning, I know that the youth's body cannot belong to Andy; it must be returned to Paul.

And with the immediate settling of this thought, as when a recalcitrant wire is hooked back and resettled on a fuse, the flooding of light within me seems to have sprung forth and released creation—as if the blasphemy of my earlier thought is now trampling wickedly across the breadth of the earth—and the sun has sternly separated the cumulus that has obscured it since dawn, ripped it open and tossed its innards across the breadth of the sky, obedient fleeces of white strewn across that vault; and I understand what has lent my lungs and limbs and consciousness such a youthful vitality: this understanding must have been guided and prepared in the depths of night when I was asleep. Some shade, some ghost, some spirit has led me here. I have the Paul Carrigan whom I first saw in those pornographic videos and, as Conrad also has done, I have made a fiction of him that I have carried with me for decades. But in writing *Sweet Thing* I have liberated my Paul from the tyranny of video. The high school student on the beach doesn't look like Paul Carrigan, though there is a confidence in that young man, neither arrogant nor self-regarding, that I suspect they both once shared. I am sure, of course it must be so, that the youth on the beach, in his final year of school, possibly in silent love with one of those girls stretched out next to him—or if not with one of the girls, one of his fellows—I am sure that this young man is anxious about the trickle of acne under his lip or the size of his cock, or his biceps are not as large as he would like them to be. Nevertheless, his quiet beauty offers him a reverie of being in the world, as I think it must have once done for Paul, the Paul I am creating and Paul Carrigan the real actor who made porn.

The great injustice of beauty—for beauty invalidates the republics of Plato and Rousseau, devastates utopias—is also what enchants us and astonishes us, and makes us wish to bear witness to it. Beauty allows us to spy on a tranquillity that is rare outside the sweetest, most succoured of dreams. What it must be to only once, for one small second in eternal time, experience a unity of self with what is most sublime, most wondrous in creation. When the young Paul stepped off the bus in Los Angeles, there must have been old queens who saw this virile and confident and untouchable young man, and the young man returned to them a smile that was kind rather than derisive—and this is what was made clear in the netherworld of my slumber: it is the kindness of the youth's smile that anchors and elevates his beauty—so that they wanted to drop to their knees and kiss the asphalt ground. It is not I who am the god.

I am halfway along the boardwalk and I am returned to the world. Two elderly women, deep in conversation, are walking towards me. I dip my head, almost a bow, and greet them. They return the salutation, sincerely, but also some-what offhandedly, and I have a sense that their deliberation is of such fervour and purport that even the observances of everyday civility must seem a hindrance. They were not rude, far from it, yet something in their demeanour has changed the flawless symmetry of the day. For though it is early enough that there are only a few people walking, jogging, I notice now that everyone I pass seems to have an aspect that is grim, almost forbidding. Abruptly, I decide that I will turn back at the end of the boardwalk and forgo a walk along the beach. I *must* call Simon; I apprehend it as an urgency. And with this foreboding—for that is how I experienced the wave of intuition that flooded my body and then finally inundated my consciousness (after all, isn't this precisely why rationalists are suspicious of the word *intuition*; has it not the spoor of faith, of the supernatural?)—the universe of dreams collapses, and so sudden and ferocious is the disintegration that it is a whirlpool that sucks in all the ghosts that reside in the netherworld, drowns whole the youths on the beach and the schoolchildren at the bus stop, and all I have remembered of Nikos, and all I have imagined of Paul and Jenna and Neal: one final swallow and the mirror is sealed. I am in the world and it is ferociously satisfying: the stroke of the sun's rays on my face and the crooning of the inlet's water as they are pulled back with the indomitable strength of the tide to return to open sea; there is the tickle of the wind on the hairs along my arms and that too seems to have a sound, its own song, the most light strumming of keys; and how overpowering the odours: the brackish water on the port side of the boardwalk, the menthol clarity of the eucalyptus that towers above on the bluff road, a perfume that seems to scurry through one's nostrils and descend straight to one's lungs: how fine is the clarity of that scent! I am breathing it all in, every sensation, for the misgiving that overtook me in that exchange with the two women—their fearfulness, the sense that they were attempting to contain and tame some terror—had initiated my own misgivings.

The rising heat of the morning, the calls and songs of the birds, the scents of eucalypt, and of the jasmine and frangipani, all the sweetness and loveliness there is in the world, all this cradles me as I climb the hill and reach home. I rush to the granny flat below: a torrent of texts and a bank of missed calls. I ignore them and phone Simon.

'How are you?'

His response is heavy with glumness. 'There are no words.'

'What's wrong?'

And now he is incredulous. 'You don't know?'

'No—tell me.'

And so, he tells me. Once again, the world has turned, has churned.

My father knew how to remove the evil eye, a knowledge that was gifted to him by his mother. There were some who accused my *yiayia* of being a witch. I think that such a slur arises from the jealousy and suspicion which gives way to that most detrimental and poisonous of devastations in village life: gossip. Gossip is fear and gossip is judgement, and it is also that ruthless banishment from community and honour with which the outsider or the rebel or the dreamer is punished for their transgressions. There was an element of the magical about my father, in his ability to return to an antediluvian world. For indeed, all peasant and village lore and magic is in that sense existing before the Great Flood, in which—we are told in ancient Hebrew apocrypha—not only sinful men and women were drowned in God's wrath but also the titans and goblins and sprites and centaurs and

changelings of all the ancient worlds. A friend or neighbour
would knock on our door, sometimes even in the middle of
the night if their anguish was acute, and my mother would
put the *briki* on the stove, start brewing coffee, while my
father would ask our guest for a piece of cloth they had been
carrying with them all day, maybe a handkerchief, a shawl;
once I saw a man unbutton his shirt, lay it carefully over
the back of the kitchen chair and start removing his singlet,
apologising shyly to my mother as he did so. If the visitor
had no cloth to give, then my father or my mother would
hand over a kitchen towel and the woman or the man or
child would drape the towel over their shoulders and wait;
we would all wait until my father declared that enough time
had passed—an understanding of the temporal nature of
the spirit world comprehensible only to himself—and then
he would take the handkerchief or shawl, singlet or kitchen
towel, lay it across his knee, mark a measure with his thumb
and extended little finger, as if he were a tailor chalking his
fabric, and then he would begin his incantation. I recognised
a few words—the calling to the Panayia, the plea to Her
son—but all the other words were unfathomable to me; and
it is in this way that I perceived, even at a young age, that
they were rooted in a language much more ancient than those
which spoke the stories and words of the Bible. Often, the
guest would thank my father profusely after this incantation,
offer a God Bless to my mother, tousle my hair and leave.
Other times, if the guest's pain was so profound, their mood

so dark and grim that one could sense it in the house—as if by straining my ears I could hear the shallow and unhappy breaths of that spirit; and surely, by the raising of the hairs on my arms and the back of my neck, by the cold flush of the perspiration on my skin, I could detect the physical being of such despair—my mother would announce, 'The viper has entered the house.' And at such times, it would mean that my father would have to repeat his rites one more time or a third time or even a fourth or fifth time, until finally he himself was dripping in sweat and his own breathing was rapid and hoarse, for he was fighting with the beast, wrestling with that serpent, until finally, roaring out the Holy Mother's name one last time, he pronounced that She had conquered. And we all felt it, the furious retreat, the whipping of its tail in its fury, as the snake slithered out of the body of the poor possessed woman or man or child and out of the house. The relief was such that often we would all break out in laughter.

Nostalgia blinds us to grief. I am writing a largely merry recollection of childhood. It was not always so, and certainly not so for the adults who I make characters in my imagination. Yet it was not a blighted childhood, not the misery of some. The peasant world has secret routes and highways across the seven continents, is a form of protection even when one has to wrench oneself from it, flee it to escape the more prosaic and earthbound terrors of gossip and small-mindedness. Those gifts of family and heritage stick to you; and if you do not reject them wholesale in order to enter modernity (for myself the choice was preordained by the force of my desire, and it is why desire is the pivot of all my obsession, of all my revolutions; and even that arising was preternatural, was not necessarily secured to reason: the whiff, the reeking perfume of Stavros's scent as he raised his arm and I smelt his sweat), then they are there to guide you even in the squall of the most unmooring of tempests or the most precipitous of narrow paths along towering cliffs. I did not understand my father's spells, but I memorised phrases and I used them to emerge from the fog of narcotic senselessness, of moments when I came closest to annihilation. They are gifts forgotten in the exodus from the village to the city, and I doubt they can extend past the third generation: the clamour of the urban is too loud, too fast, who can hear within it? In some Scandinavian or Frankish or Saxon past, Paul and his brother Andy, their mother and their grandfather would have had peasant roots such as mine. Paul divined the menace, saw how it possessed and doomed his brother. He had no knowledge to combat it. Such knowledge had long been forsaken, forgotten and condemned as nonsense. And the consequences are lives that are blasted.

My father entered the netherworld through his knowledge, and through his intuition. His ministering for me, his care, allows me to do the same. A different route and possibly a different mirror. But the netherworld, nevertheless.

I need to return home. Simon's trepidation was clear in the measured remoteness I heard in his voice. In the very early days of our falling in love, I had misinterpreted it as emotional reticence, but I had come to understand that it was a necessary protection for himself, a means of guarding against the intensity of emotions, when they come to overwhelm us: his speaking distantly meant that, as if by a supreme effort of will, he was challenging his fears, denying them ground to gain root. And in that strange yet comforting manner by which habits and tics and mannerisms are transmitted in a couple—that prosaic occurrence, say, of finishing each other's sentences or finding oneself gradually imbued with the anxiety of their phobia (Simon now has a trepidation of reptiles he never felt before he met me, and my breath now shortens when I find myself in a crowded lift or in the middle of a dense mob)—I no longer am aggrieved or made defensive by his reserve at such a moment. Instead, I understand that these are precisely the times he requires comfort. 'Mate,' I said, 'I'll come home. I have a few things to finish off tomorrow and then I'll leave first thing Thursday morning.'

His relief now was no longer guarded.

'Thanks, Chris,' he said quietly. 'I miss you. I love you.'

'I love you too.'

As soon as I hung up, I did something which I have not done since I came to this idyll by the ocean: I fired up the laptop and started to scroll through the information feed of the world. For a good hour I was lost in unending images and words, the distraught and outraged and disturbing interpretations and reflections on what had occurred.

At first, this immersion was sobering. The stark and shocking abruptness of the violence; and then, as with the unravelling of a piece of wool from an old jumper, the picking of one strand of yarn that spirals and unthreads and in no time results in a disorderly spool, so that finding the original thread becomes impossible, the misfortune of the carnage is lost in commentary—partisan, threatening and galvanising—that attempts to make sense of what is truly and ultimately insensible: the cruelty that we humans are capable of; such an impossible task, to find the original thread of chaos. And the equally human and therefore understandable, if unattainable, desire to qualify the terror by comparison. Is it worse than the desperate citizens of a besieged city running the gauntlet of sniper fire in order to secure a meal? Is it equal to the apocalypse inaugurated by two planes flying into the centre of the world's tallest buildings? Will it humble us as did the last pandemic?

Lost in the vortex myself, I could imagine Simon at home, or with our friends or families, all watching the screen, shouting over each other, cradling each other in their fear, trying to explain it to the young children, arguments already emerging, online and certainly already between ourselves, arguments of economics and justice and history which, already, even within twenty-four hours of the cataclysm, are hardening into sureties and certainties, are now circulating in a feverish whirl of electronic activity in the hive of the internet, so that already Economics and Justice and History become emboldened, shield and armour, as do Compassion and Equality and Liberty, brandished as weapons, lances held high in the air to make the incomprehensible comprehensible. I click from looking through that mirror that is the computer screen into which one can only look darkly, for there are no guides—no Virgil, no Eurydice, no Heurtebise—and I log on to my email. There are requests, polite but insistent, enquiring if I could immediately, straight away, is it possible to have it filed by tomorrow, wanting my opinion, my perspective, my words on what has just occurred. None of this needs more words. And with that enlightenment, I switch off the computer.

My father did not pass on his ancient knowledge to me; instead, he passed it to my brother, who has sharper instincts than do I. My brother can intuit the danger in this world in a way that I cannot. What I can do, a different gift my father gave to me, arising from my observation of him being still in his garden—for even when hoeing and digging and planting and watering he was quiet and still—is sit in the silence. I light a camphor coil to ward off the mosquitoes. On the deck, I sit and close my eyes and give myself over to the silence.

No, not silence: the world is never mere silence; it is always music and song. The chatter of two lorikeets that have alighted on the deck's railing, their insistent chirping sounding belligerent, as if they are a couple in querulous disagreement; and through the trees, the raucous squawk of a cockatoo, answered by another from somewhere behind the house. The ocean too, with its constant and reassuring pulse, is a faint choral that never ends, never disappears. There are also human sounds: the clunking of the truck wheels as they cross the bridge; the buzzing drone of a lawn mower; the muted electronic percussive beats emitting from the car speakers of maintenance men working on a street below; and the intermittent barks, sharp and quick, of a dog, as if it keeps guard between the borders of the natural and the human-made world, its nature divided between the untamed of the first and the domesticity of the latter. And it is that snapping yelp of the dog that pierces my consciousness and I shake my head, come to, as if I have been awoken from sleep. I had disappeared into the sound. The greens and blues and greys and whites and blacks, the buds of a hydrangea in the garden next door, the flush of yellow on the skins of the fruit hanging on the lemon tree.

Knowing that I must return home, all I want is to plunge into the ocean. And as I kick off my runners, pull off my socks, unbuckle my belt and fling my jeans on the bed, strip off my jocks and put on my bathers, I realise that even within a matter of a week—has it only been eight days since I arrived here?—I have fallen into rituals. This undressing, the careful preparation of the bag I will take with me to the beach; my book, my reading glasses and my sunglasses, the bottle of sunscreen; and then there is the buckling of my sandals, going back out to the deck, pulling the beach towel from the railing and shaking it over the garden below, the fine grit of sand and salt forming an almost translucent vapour that sinks over the rosebushes and shrubs. I fling the towel over my shoulder, lock the back door and head to the car. Only as I turn the key in the ignition do I recall some of the images I had glimpsed on the computer screen, and I wince at the memory. I had forgotten all about the most recent calamity visiting the world in the retreat into nature's song and music. Then, as I turn right at the end of the street, and as the inlet appears at the bottom of the hill, the cloud that has been placidly sitting across the face of the sun chooses at this very moment to divide, to become two formidable forms in the sky, their glacial separation completed precisely as I make the turn so that on either end it is as if their fingers are touching then slipping away from each other: and it is now, through the ensuing chasm, that the sun is victorious, and the inlet glistens and flickers as if it is a lake of diamond, and the sight overwhelms and is rapturous and I release a gasp. The terrible injustice of nature, equal part beauty and equal part cruelty, and so oblivious to tragedy: I am defeated and conquered, and I surrender to its beauty. All I can experience is joy.

Every writer of fiction is selfish. It is one of the first choices we make, when we submit to the claims of our vocation. This time, knowing that I no longer had the luxury of another week to explore the surrounding coast, I head north out of town, thirty or so kilometres, to an idyllic bay Simon and I had discovered on a previous holiday. It is a section of a narrow peninsula bordered on the north by a long rocky expanse of cliffs, desolate, battered by the ferocity of the southern Pacific Ocean, and on the south by silt estuaries where a river rushes down from the mountain and empties into the sea. Almost equidistant between the two ends there is a tiny cove, a hull of soft, dazzling white sand, and when the sun is out, the sapphire waters are clear and safe. We were here in the height of summer one year and for most of the day we were the only people on the beach. Just before we left, a young surfer arrived, waving to us as he passed by. I recall him still, the eagerness with which, his board under his arm, he ran into the waters; the fine dash of him as he lay on the board and paddled beyond the breakers.

I park the car on the side of the road. There is no one else here. I hurry down to the beach and plunge into the water.

After drying myself, I spread out the towel, sit cross-legged on it and look out to sea. The swim was invigorating. The sun is already beginning to warm me up, and as the last drops of water evaporate, there is a slow flush of heat tangible just under my skin. I know I should search in my bag for the sunscreen, yet I resist that obligation, the rebelliousness of that opposition striking me as youthful. And with that realisation—inhaling the bracing salt-crusted air, my lungs expanding and contracting effortlessly and with ferocious appetite, the tautness of the muscles on my arms and along my calves still distended from the efforts of my strokes in challenging the pummelling, advancing tide—for the smallest of infractions of the rationality and laws of space and time, it is not myself who is sitting on the beach, exhausted but elated, intoxicated by his battle with the waves. Rather, I am the young surfer, and mine is his body: his straight back; the square bulk of his chest and torso, tapering to the slim, almost feminine camber of his hips; those neat cups of his buttocks, no fat visible under the tight cling of his swimmers; the long equine length and nimble sprint of his slender legs as he ran to meet the waves. Then I look down. To the cluster of grey thatch on my chest, the rolls of my belly, the solid and pale slab of thigh revealed through the gape of my shorts; and as if my corporeal self chooses to claim victory over my mental self in that brusque awareness—that I am not young, that I am this old man sitting on the beach—all visions of the young surfer disappear, time and space return to their authority and the sun's rays stab my skin. Wearily, I reach into my bag for the sunscreen.

In turning to reach my lower back, a contortion that demands some dexterity and which I accomplish, but with an old fella's embarrassing snort and grunt—and on that beach, alone, I giggle at myself for the outlandishness of the joy in releasing an inelegant sound—I chance to look away from the sea and up the beach to the road where I have parked the car. And I notice what I don't believe pricked my consciousness before: the scorched thin trunks of the she-oaks. Soot clings to the bark, yet that layer is being shed, as if the trees are sloughing off the violent memories of the fires that so recently ravaged these forests, this coast, this land; and instead, emerging in their new skins of mottled brunette and silver bark, they are releasing their first green buds among the sharp bristles of their leaves. By next summer, the last of the burnt epidermis will be gone. The evidence erased. The memory submerged.

Some writers wish to howl. They will demand testimonies and they believe they must uncover the past. Some writers wish to mourn. They will seek justice and they will atone. Some writers want to forget. They will write stories set before the fires, or conjure fantasies occurring in worlds that are existent long after. I no longer have the confidence to apportion blame and I no longer have lust for either punishment or self-flagellation. I offer you this image of the trees, vital and vigorous in their rebirth. I turn back to gaze upon the ocean, force myself to recall the images on the screen, the anxiety in my lover's voice, the truth that the world of humans is again being bedevilled by terror and venality and crisis; yet the reflection doesn't even last half a breath, for the sea dashes and crashes and ripples along the pure white sand of the beach, and there is an eagle soaring up high over the water, hovering, searching the deeps for the silver flash of a fish's scales; and the sun's heart remains beating and this tide has been surging and abating, like the most diligent and disciplined of sculptors, forging and chiselling and forming this coast for an eternity, and it will continue to do so long after the ages of testimony and uncovering, the eras of justice and atonement and even the centuries of forgetting are gone.

It is to this coast that Paul returns. He too has passed through a mirror, and it is both reflection and refraction. For it must be that the sculptor of this coast is also the blacksmith who has hammered and wrought the surfaces where the Pacific Ocean kisses and tumbles into, shatters and sledges the American coast. That is the mirror. The deflection in the image, what he saw in his encounters in that world, was a life lived in shadow and darkness; a life that would have been his if he had remained. If he had not found the succour and grace and understanding of Jenna; if they had not been blessed by the sturdiness and rightness and gentleness of their son, Neal.

•

Drowsily, Paul presses the screen to retrieve the flight map. The continent's eastern contours come into view. And with that glimpse of Australia's outline, he starts to cry. It is not an exaggerated form of grief—no convulsions, nor does he moan—but he is grateful for Conrad's generosity, that he is isolated in the lavish comfort of the reclining business-class seat. Across the aisle a young woman is asleep; she has her blanket pulled up to her chin and is wearing the black cotton eye mask supplied by the airline. Her snores are quiet, of a purring faintness that suggests a feline pliability and grace. Even if she had been awake, the luxuriant distance afforded by the seating would most probably have made her oblivious to Paul's muted anguish: he has the top of his hoodie dropped low over his brow and nose, his body is curled into itself. It is not that he is ashamed of his sorrow; but the long years of circumspection and secrecy over his life and all that he holds dear make him wary, distrustful of broadcasting emotion.

He pushes back the hood from his face, wipes his eyes, looks through the window. In less than two hours they will be arriving in Brisbane. From behind the drawn curtains of the cabin he can hear the clinking of cutlery, the rattle of the food and drink carts as they are stacked with trays.

There is a yawn, long and languid. The young woman across from him is stretching out her arms. She then drops them to her side, nimbly raises the blanket and draws her hands within the folds. Her snores resume.

It was her hands that had broken Paul's heart. They are long, with tapered fingers, her skin that purple black that is defiantly, indisputably African. This young woman is svelte, has nothing of Cynthia's plumpness, and Cynthia's skin is lighter, with the sweetness and shine of maple syrup. And yet, those fingers: he remembers Cynthia's hands holding his face as she was kissing him, the warmth of those fingers, the sharpness of those long nails as they softly prodded his cheeks. It was in this association, made lazily, turning from the panorama of the universe outside the aeroplane's window to glance casually at the passenger across from him, seeing that she had fallen asleep and then noticing her hands, struck by that one and only resemblance to Cynthia, and from that reminder returned to the ugliness and squalor of their grandfather's house—it would only ever be their fucking grandfather's house!—and also then recognising the distance between the sleeping woman, flying business class, a gleaming diamond ring on her finger, that cruel distance of money and advantage that cleaves the world, the sharpest of blades, that he remembered smashing his brother's phone, and he reflected on the quagmire that is addiction and narcosis and how he must never ever return to it; recalled too the desperate longing for companionship that he gleaned looking across to Andy's face, and so of the ruthlessness and rightness of the escapes he had made. And he thought too of the child in Cynthia's womb and how it was coming into the world; and next to him, the beautiful hand of a sleeping young woman as they both flew like birds, like gods, above the peaceful sea: that is how the tears had begun.

He feels blanched, his body tingles with sleeplessness, as he navigates the rituals of disembarkation. He once more gives a silent thanks to Conrad as an immigration official glances at his ticket and politely ushers him into the express lane. Paul turns to look back at the queue of weary economy travellers shuffling along slowly; and indeed in their tiredness and lethargy, the dazed confusion apparent on their faces as the first strokes of jet lag begins to take effect, there is something bovine and desperate in their countenances. He knows that if he were to fly again, it would be a return to that; he also knows that he will never leave Australia again.

He wonders about Conrad: was it worth it? He has no doubt of it for himself and for his family; the money, an amount incredible and transformative, has already been deposited in his and Jenna's bank account: the old man's behaviour has been gentlemanlike throughout; and Paul is not ashamed of the transactional nature of their weekend together. He doesn't believe that either secular shame or religious sin attaches itself to the work of sex. Rather, he wonders how had Conrad reconciled a long fantasy of an idol called Sean with the reality of an ageing man sitting across from him at dinner, sharing whiskies late at night, having sex together, the lovemaking tentative and careful? Paul had assumed it would be Sean's rough and genial persona that Conrad sought. Yet, when Sean had placed his hand on Conrad's crotch in the car, had assumed possession, the old man had recoiled. And before Conrad had turned away from him, Sean had glimpsed the man's disturbed countenance. Was there a word for a combination of anger and disappointment? That was what he had seen on Conrad's old face at that moment. So, when he leant in to kiss him the second time on the patio, as tenderly as possible, he had been Paul, not Sean. That will be his abiding memory of that weekend.

He will tell Jenna this. He will also come clean about his use of cocaine and MDMA at the parties, his smoking and snorting; he will not hide this from her, and he knows she will trust him not to return to the chasm of addiction. He will not tell her that he has been to see Andy. Instead, he will say that he had phoned and his brother had answered, slurring his words. 'Obviously so fucking out of it, Jenna; he was so fucking out of it'. He has already memorised the words he will use. 'I knew on hearing his voice I was right never to go back and I'm never ever gonna.' It is not a lie, the evasion; it is a protection, the *ojo de venado* that Arsenio and his family hung from their wrists, that so fascinated him as boy in Sacramento; and the heavy black-kohled eye in swirls of blue that always hung from the rear-view mirror of Tass's ute in the workshop in Byron Bay. Paul is convinced: a lie is not a lie when it is offered as protection against evil. This is why he will not tell Jenna about Andy, but he will tell her everything that occurred between himself and Conrad, and explain to her that what will remain precious in the core of his recollections are the moments when the veil between himself, Paul, and the stranger, Sean, was lifted. And that there was a reciprocal kindness—certainly diffident, shy, not fully formed, but nevertheless a sympathy—between himself and the man who had flown him to LA, and so there were rare moments, like the old man's embarrassed chuckle when he inadvertently farted on awakening that first morning, or the easy silence between them as they lunched at a marina on the last day, when they had been not john and whore but Conrad and Paul. Not throughout, not even for the majority of their time together, but enough to make Paul thankful. When he went to kiss Conrad that second time, to apologise for the bluster and the swagger that had tainted the first kiss, that bravado he had thought the old man was seeking, he had kissed him tenderly, lips just touching lips. It had been Conrad who kissed him back with force.

'Enjoy your vacation.'

Paul looks up.

The young woman from across the aisle is smiling at him. A customs official, proudly tapping a finger at his straggly, straw-coloured beard, is waving her through. She looks stunning, has deftly applied lipstick, has brushed and released the dense coils of her luxurious hair: the only visible trace of the distress of that long flight on her face is the slightly exaggerated bafflement of her expression.

'This is home,' he explains. 'I'm returning home.'

Her back to him, her arm raised, her long dancing fingers signal a farewell.

That sense of the whole world being bleached, drained of colour and all the illumination too bright—not only from the fluorescent lights of the cavernous arrivals hall but also the morning light pouring through the enormous windows, the refracted shales and shards also seeming unnatural, of an inorganic provenance—continues as Neal leads them through the subterranean maze of the airport car park. He and Jenna had both been there waiting for him when Paul emerged from the baggage claim area, Jenna excitedly calling his name, Neal's smile on seeing his father so immediate and so strong that Paul was struck by the thought: My god, my son is handsome, and when my son smiles, it is with all of his body. And, of course, Paul had been pleased to see them both; yet he felt no excitement, and he found himself exaggerating the effusiveness of the kisses he gave Jenna and the hug he gave his son, as if in the boldness and the franticness of his actions he could forestall any suspicion and temper his own self-doubt. He is happy to be home, to be with them again, of course he is. He must be. And yet, as Neal expertly hauls his father's bags onto the tray of the ute and secures the canvas, as Jenna insists that Paul take the front seat next to their son, as the vehicle slowly chugs along the crowded exiting lane until, with a swift release of the clutch and with his foot pressing confidently on the accelerator, Neal is sliding into the southbound lane of the freeway, Brisbane's city skyline a grey shimmer in the distance, Paul cannot shake the feeling that he is seeing all of the world as though through water; the too-bright lights are almost painful, as if there is at once too little and too much clarity. There had been a moment back there at the airport, the ute idling as they waited for the driver of the car ahead to insert her ticket into the machine's slot and release the boom gate, when he felt his wife's hand on his shoulder and, turning to her, it was as if he could not place Jenna's face. Her nose, her pinched nostrils, the almost translucent blue of her eyes; it all seemed to blur and waver as if it were the beginning of a hallucination, and he was almost repelled by the savage cut of the lines at the ends of both sides of her mouth, the brutal wrinkles and raw red skin on her neck. He wills himself to exude gratitude and ardour. He must not betray his confusion; he must not reveal his disenchantment. He turns back to stare out the window. *Disenchantment.* A word that contains both anger and disappointment.

Paul reminds himself that surely it is the wretched tiredness from the trans-Pacific flight that is responsible for his fragile emotions. A relief arises from that naming and he settles back in his seat, watches the world arrive and disappear in the continuous smooth motion of the drive. Brisbane, from this distance, seems small, inconsequential, still struggling to declare itself a city. He knows that Aussies like to compare their cities to American cities, and he too has found himself coming to believe that Californian cities and Australian cities had much in common. Well, he knows now that it is not true, that his long time away has made him forget the sharp differences on either side of the ocean. Los Angeles and Sacramento have more vitality to them, they aren't as antiseptic. Everything here is so damn clean. No life in any of it: the straightness of the asphalt highway, the functional and uninspired lines and shapes of the buildings being constructed across the widening sprawl of the city. No diversity, no individuality in the shape and style of windows, in the roofs and fencing: just like the population, everyone and everything looked the same.

Paul doesn't realise it, but he is frowning as he looks out the window.

'You alright, Dad?'

He knows one thing: he must conceal this disappointment—this disenchantment—from Jenna and Neal. A tearing in his heart: not an agony that is physical; rather, the pain arising from disgrace. Has his debauchery—not the days with Conrad, which had been clean, but the drugs and the unbearable sadness and malevolence of his brother's house—destroyed peace forever?

'I'm okay, son. It's just the jet lag.'

He closes his eyes, pretends to have nodded off to sleep.

And it is indeed somewhat restorative, the shutting off of the world, the amelioration of that stabbing artillery of light. He is conscious of the uncomfortable jam of his sunglasses on the base of his nose, between his eyebrows, but he makes no attempt to shift them, to take them off; they afford Paul a discreet vantage from which he occasionally opens his eyes, glimpses through the window at the edge of Brisbane's metropolitan limits the vista of prefabricated villas and cold, squat identikit apartments and office towers, the outlandish colours and luridly designed billboards of franchises and chain stores and supermarkets, all unchanging as the limits of the city glance the approaching extremities of Surfers Paradise.

So, yes, better to keep his eyes closed, to ignore that baroque commercial world outside, to instead sink into the trance of sombre colours and pulsing emanations that form and re-form, expand and contract, under the heavy lids of his eyes. While lost in those kaleidoscope visions, he hears fragments of conversation between Jenna and Neal. His son's hushed whisper: 'Is he asleep?' And his wife's soft answer: 'Poor love, that flight is so exhausting.' And throughout, the hushed music, falling in and out of Paul's reveries: the snaking arrogant riff introducing the Stone's 'Miss You', the percussive jubilation of Aretha Franklin's version of 'Spanish Harlem'.

The shifting patterns beneath his eyelids form their own musical accompaniment, as if the beat and course of his blood through veins and capillaries is the bash of a snare, the roll of a drumstick, resulting in spills and torrents and waves. The strain in his stomach, the sensation of nausea kept at bay has abated. He dares open his eyes, and, even with the filtering layer of the sunglasses, the world is stunningly and shockingly green, the supine hills and smooth valleys of the coast blazing with the verdant richness of the coming summer. The blanching void has gone, as has the endless suburban rotoscope of estates and car yards and office towers. The world is again full of colour.

His child and his wife are singing along with Aretha Franklin: Neal's voice just hanging on to the note; Jenna's voice loud and clear.

Paul removes his sunglasses, blinks and re-enters the world.

Neal turns down the volume.

'Good morning, Dad. We're in New South Wales. We're nearly home.'

And this time, Jenna's hand on his shoulder doesn't feel an imposition, there is no discomfort there at all, and Paul can't conceive how he could even have contemplated being disenchanted. *Disenchanted*? What a callous, inappropriate word for what he has and what he holds!

The serene ocean dips in and out of view as the car glides along the vacillating road, this vast expanse of green and blue. Are they the only car on the highway this morning? He is returning home to the house he and Jenna have built, and he has a son who is hardworking and kind and roughly handsome and who is aware of the shadows and netherworlds within which his parents both have lived and is at peace with such knowledge and who does not accuse because he has no cruelty in him, and who is faithful to family and to love, that which Paul never knew as a child and a youth. And Jenna's hand is on his shoulder and he clutches it, suddenly afraid. The day is warm but he is cold, for fortune can destroy as easily and swiftly as it can bless, and he won't let go of her hand, this woman, so beautiful and now so aged, so courageous and now so gentle, so broken and now so serene.

And Paul can hear the lilt, the joyous pluck and striking of the guitar's strings, and he can hear the voice, placating and slowly rising to rapture, and Neal turns the volume high and Van Morrison's voice and Van Morrison's song floods the car and is of union with the grace and sumptuous beauty of the world outside and Paul is crying, a weeping that is joy, for now his wife's grip is firm, consoling, on his shoulder, and his son is patting his father's knee and whispering, 'It's alright, Dad, all of it is right,' and it is also a sobbing that is grief for the vicissitudes and unfairness of fate, for the hardness, the fear and the shadows that are his brother's life, and finding himself in the middle of the song—for the song has now entered Paul—as Van Morrison sings 'Sweet Thing', the music and the lyrics evoking ancient and lost worlds, Paul silently calls on gods or God, wishing he had Jenna's faith, that he could believe, and whispers a prayer for his brother and Cynthia and their coming child: *Oh please, Lord, within those moments of darkness please let there be moments of silence and peace and love and grace.* And so, Paul is sobbing, for what could not be altered and what could not be returned *and I will drink the clear clean water to quench my thirst*, and he is crying for all that he has, and the song becomes a prayer and a lament and a jubilation, and it can be all those things at once, for that is the miracle of the song. And from that point on, when people will ask Paul, Do you believe in God? he will answer, No, but the miraculous is possible, *and I shall drive my chariot down your streets and cry*, because in this moment he does believe himself to be saved, to have been one of the fortunate ones, blessed and provident, and he owes it to this woman whose hand he cannot let go of and he owes it to this son who is faithful. *We shall walk and talk in gardens all misty and wet with rain.* The music rises to a crescendo, the car is enveloped in the song, but then so is the whole of the world: the earth outside, the unfurling ocean, the impossible antipodean sky, all of it is praising and all of it is singing and even their bodies, Paul's and Jenna's and Neal's, are as much song as they are flesh, as much praise as they are bone and as much gratitude as they are blood. Paul is sobbing. It is a miracle for a man to be blessed in life, it is a miracle to have a home. Paul is home.

•

For a moment it is as if I can hear the Morrison song; but no, it is the swelling rhythm of the ocean tide, the rough thunder as the waves crash upon the shore and the sibilate gasp as they retreat back into the deep. The last four pages of the Machiavelli are blank and it is over these four pages that I have given an ending to *Sweet Thing*, making my handwriting deliberately small so I can fit the outpouring of words onto the pages. As I write the last three words—*Paul is home*—I find myself experiencing a contradictory, perplexing emotion. On the one hand, I am certain of the integrity of the ending, for the question of home not only dominates my age and my time in history, but its enquiry and its pursuit has been my own personal work: what is home? In writing, in language, if one is fortunate and finds the right story, then words can refute opacity and offer precision. *Paul is home.* Yet, it was film that first offered me this idea and it was in film that I first imagined its trajectory. I understand that VHS—a technology that appears more makeshift and erosive over time, diluting colour, shredding the image and weakening light—is not film; but as moving image it shares in the magic of cinema. And it was magical, that first time I put a pornographic tape into the VCR machine, pressed play and immediately was overwhelmed by the youthful and awkward beauty of a young man sitting before a fire. The pugnacious yet unthreatening visage of Paul Carrigan. I swooned. Cinema is an art that can make one swoon. And so, inevitably, I have imagined the ending of *Sweet Thing* as film. An interior shot. Paul is in the passenger seat next to his son, asleep. We hear Van Morrison's 'Sweet Thing' playing on the stereo. Paul jolts awake and the audience is now sharing his point of view. The liquid ferocious colours of the northern New South Wales coast: the cobalt Pacific and the green of the forests, those trees that shoot as straight as needles up to the sky. In the car, the man starts sobbing, a weeping that is long and seemingly inexhaustible. His wife's hand is on his shoulder, his son patting his knee, simple gestures of love. And the man is weeping. Jenna is singing along to the song, and so is Neal, the one voice sweet and confident, the other shy, even grace-less, but affirming, nevertheless. Paul is weeping and Paul is home. The moving image itself can never be as precise in its intent as can writing. The camera can offer documentary veracity, claim the real, but it can never fix meaning; there can be voiceover, for sure, directing the audience, but that isn't the moving image; that is a reliance on words and thus writing: cinema, film, the motion of images always leaves interpretation open to chance.

The tide is rushing in and it is streaming out. Film was not to be my vocation. I massage the ache and numbness at the protruding bone of my wrist. These words scrawled on the back pages of a book, these etchings and markings and scratchings in blue ink, are my craft.

I pick a section at random, quickly read it through to make sure that I can decipher the tiny and messy prose. I fall across a word: *baroque*. I used it to describe what Paul sees as Neal drives out of Brisbane and into the hinterland of Surfers Paradise; he uses it to describe the elaborate and exaggerated commercialism of the architecture of that region. It captures what I experience when I make that drive. However, it is my word, not Paul's. I circle it and place a minute question mark within its boundaries. I close the book, stash it and the pen deep into my bag.

A man has come onto the beach. I had been so lost in my scribbling that I hadn't heard the rumble of his van as he parked. He is standing some ten or so metres away, and he is tearing off his T-shirt. His arms are sinewy, a dark tan roughened then smoothed by the coast's endless sun. He is about thirty, the slight flop of belly on an otherwise svelte form. Dropping his shirt onto the sand, he turns towards me, flicks his chin to the water and asks, 'How is it out there?'

'It's bloody beautiful, mate.'

The man smiles and stretches his arms out wide. 'This is beautiful country.' He brings his hands together, rubs them, starts jogging on the spot. 'Time to brave the cold, cuz.'

I watch him run into the waves, dive into the water, to emerge a few metres further, his strokes so sure and rapid that he seems to be belting the frothing sea.

It is dazzling country, his country. I am sure this is his country. The Yuin have a languorous beauty, a gift granted to all people who know the consolation of life on a temperate coast. His is a hardened, toughened body; the insignia on the chest of his shirt advertises a plumbing business. Yet there is also a delectable softness, evocative of a warm sun and an equivalent sea. His is a striking handsomeness that owes both to his ancestry on this land and that of forebears from lands on the other side of the world. The harsh, angular but potent Glaswegian mien, and the genial and round Yuin face, they have cojoined; I know that it has been a long and exhausting and ugly battle, and yet I can't help having an heretical thought: it was all worth it to have produced such singular beauty.

I watch the man dive again and swim further into the ocean. He knows this land and he knows this water, and with expert knowledge and keen intuition, he avoids the ever-present treachery of the currents and the rips.

The man is returning to shore. His breath hard, long, he collapses on the sand.

'How was it?' I venture.

His laugh is first a gurgle, then a rupture, a buoyant release.

'Fucking wonderful, mate.'

With a supple and youthful adeptness, he turns onto his back and stretches out his legs so that his feet slide over the edge of the towel onto the sand; and in seconds, a sprinkle of what seems like fine concrete dust has coated his heels and ankles, all the length of his calves. The angle of his left arm, splayed the length of his side, is such that the first thing I notice is the bracelet over his wrist, chunky pebble squares painted in an alternating rhythm of black and yellow and red, the sky and the sun and the land, threaded through a thick black twine. On his forearm is a tattoo, a black-outlined crucifix with a cyan shadow of the cross underneath it, giving the design the impression of a third dimension as well as evoking something medieval, even ancient, as if the tattoo is the ancestral insignia of a lost heroic age. My eyes move to the damp black hairs spread delicately across the man's dark belly, which rises and falls in a slow and steady movement, as if he has fallen asleep. I turn away from him, conscious of the lechery implied in the intensity of my gaze; a misinterpretation, for I am simply observing and marvelling at the man's unforced and captivating male beauty.

I look to the sea.

The panorama has altered sharply, as if while I was contemplating the man's form a Creator God has seen fit to mix Her paints in dark and sombre tinctures and slash Her brush across the sky. An igniting cumulus is descending in haste from the eastern horizon; where it casts its shadow over the ocean the water is night; the speed of the cloud's rampage is discernible by how fast the shadows fly across the sea's surface. And yet, with the sun behind us, where the sea is unhindered by the cloud's shade, the water seems as a sparkling bejewelled lake, the waves breaking the shallows as alternate surges of emerald and sapphire. It is as if the world has been torn in two, a cosmic diptych of light and dark, each dimension—one wild and turbulent, one serene and luminescent—of an equal astonishment.

There is a rustle in the sand.

The young man has sat up, is staring out to the sky and ocean.

'Storm coming,' he pronounces; and then adds, 'Won't last long.'

And indeed, in a hurried swoop, the temperature drops, and the wind now nips and bites as it rushes over my face, my neck and shoulders. I grab my shirt, shake off the sand and put it on.

'You a writer?'

For a moment there is vanity: has he recognised me? Then I realise that, as he parked his van and walked down to the cove, he must have seen me scribbling that first draft of the novel's ending.

His question, as always, gives me pause. That sense of the word—*writer*—as pertaining to a world and caste that is not mine, how it ruthlessly banishes me from my childhood and adolescence and class, and yet always leaves me outside the gates of the aristocrat's castle.

The man is slapping one hand against the other to dislodge the sand. They are strong hands, gnarled hands, with the small bruises and tiny scars and raw blisters of work. His are not soft hands.

'Yes,' I answer. 'I'm a writer.'

There are times when that answer can be met with a diffidence or with the defensiveness of contempt, even with the stirring of belligerence, as if the word suggests segregation and arrogance, an elite condescension. But the man is smiling and in that expansive cheer of his grin there is nothing of reserve, nothing of aggression.

'It's kind of cool to see someone actually writing by hand. Don't see that much anymore. My nan used to write. I always remember her hunched over the kitchen table at her place in Bega, scribbling away.'

'So, she was a writer as well?'

'Not books, though I reckon she'd have had some deadly stories. She was a great storyteller.' He shrugs his shoulder.

'Letters. She was from a large family, eleven brothers and sisters.' And as he says this, he slowly moves his hands away from one another until his arms are outstretched as if the physical gesture can better communicate the enormity of family than mere words.

He smacks his hands back onto the sand.

'I think my youngest has her gift; she was a reader from the get-go. That's the only present she wants at Christmastime or on her birthday. "Can I have a book, Dad?"'

The pride in his voice is resonant, as bold and as clear as the holler of the sea.

There is so much I want to say. That in the crucible of his love and his pride for his daughter he has already accomplished the first labour she will need to be a writer: he has taught her that she need not be ashamed of her story. I think of my own father's gifts to me. Every Thursday afternoon, payday, he would line up with his fellow workers to collect his little yellow envelope from the paymaster, whose office was above the factory floor—and indeed, I recall my father taking me there once and how as soon as my father pushed open the solid wooden door with the word *Paymaster* and then the gentleman's name etched in heavy white letters across the glazed glass, and that door shut behind us, the raucous ceaseless din of the thundering machinery disappeared, and there was only the glory of silence. On the way home, he would stop at a little newsagent on Bridge Road, look at the books scattered across the bargain table and, unable to decipher the English language, he would choose one book or another because of a bright cover or because of the seriousness or humour he interpreted in the inks. And so he bought literature for me, and science fiction, and crime fiction, and novels way too dense and too adult for me; and I read them all, because I did love reading—that does indeed come first, the disappearing into the worlds. Without that hunger for reading, one cannot be a writer. However, I was buoyed by his and my mother's joy in and gratitude for reading. I want to tell all this to the young father, but the rain starts to fall. The drops are heavy and land with a smack on our heads and shoulders. We each scramble for our towels, I grab my sandals and bag, and we are both running to our cars as the sky growls and the rain descends in a torrent. He is younger, faster, and is at his van first. He turns around, lifts one hand in a thumbs-up salute and I wave my farewell.

His van is already thundering up the narrow dirt road as I start the engine.

He was right: the lashing shower doesn't last long. By the time I approach town the writhing python fury of the cumulus has crossed the ocean and the coast and is vanishing behind the mountain; only its tail whips the summit, obscuring the apex in a haze of rain and mist. The sun, too, is dropping westwards; liberated from the choking embrace of the clouds, it shimmers with a final ferocious force. The inlet comes into view and it is as if the waters are silver. The gleam has a metallic sharpness and the intensity from the sun annihilates all colour: the sparks that fling off the water are resplendent.

My first stop is the greengrocers. I select a red onion, a handful of green beans, a cucumber and a tomato for a salad. Conscious that I will be leaving at first light tomorrow, my intention is to buy fish fillets from the shop under the north side of the bridge to cook myself the simplest of coastal meals this evening.

Heading back to the car, I quickly check my phone. A bank of messages and missed calls. I throw the vegetables onto the passenger seat and impatiently tap my passcode; the screen bursts into colour and I scroll through my messages. A journalist from *The Age* wants to know if I can contribute a thousand-word essay on the unfolding global crisis, and there is a missed call from the editor of *The Guardian*. I press the mail icon and there is a flood of emails. Veronica from the Wheeler Centre wants to know if I can participate in a hastily organised panel. A similar request from Chris at Readings bookshop. I close my mail. There is text from Simon: *I miss you, baby. Are you sure you want to drive straight through? Text me xxS*

The phone is in my hand. I have the car window wound down and I rest my arm on the frame, look out along the main street. A group of four old men, all bearded, one of them with his grey hair pulled back in a long ponytail, are laughing together outside the tackle shop. There is a young woman, a Jehovah's Witness, outside the supermarket with copies of *The Watchtower*. A boy, still in his school uniform, the bottom of his white shirt untucked, is helping a frail elderly woman down the steps outside the butcher shop. A portly old man, in stained red football shorts, so old that the colour has faded to a dull crimson, is whistling as he crosses the street from the caravan park. His belly is enormous, rotund and perfectly spherical; it appears hard as steel. I recognise the man from the beach earlier; he is holding the hand of his young daughter, who is tentatively licking at her ice cream, her eyes squished shut in apparent joy with every lick, followed immediately by a look of concern, as if worried about how long she can make her pleasure last. His son, younger than the daughter, is skipping ahead of them; he is biting chunks from his cone, as if impatient to feed his appetite: spools and splashes of chocolate ice cream stain his chin and are dripping down the front of his oversized Sydney Swans footy singlet. The boy, lost in the pleasure of his treat, is about to step off the footpath when his father calls out in stern warning, 'Che!' The boy spins around, startled, then nods and waits. The father takes both his children by the hand and they walk across the road.

I return to my phone. It is a long drive home along the Princes Highway, close to nine hours. Simon is anxious about me making the drive in one day, suggesting that I stop overnight in Cann River or Bairnsdale. I understand his concern, and in truth I too would have similar reservations about him undertaking such a drive, but I stubbornly insist on driving all the way home in a day. I relish the in-betweenness of long drives, those canny hours between departure and arrival, in which the whole of the world suddenly drops away. Of course, I can turn on the radio, the world can flood back in, but there are long stretches of highway where radio waves struggle to penetrate, so that there is only the crackle and spitting of the depleted and vanquished signals. In such moments I am an astronaut in my car, and the drive along the straight empty roads is a flinging into space. I avoid driving in the city, and when I have to, I fill the silence in the vehicle with sound: music, radio, interviews, podcasts. Yet on these open roads—the shooting majesty of the eucalypt forests on either side, or the dense lush tunnel of effervescent temperate forest; the parched endless plains and scrublands, the titan inland seas of red or yellow or gold desert; or skirting the serene infinity of the ocean—I find myself shrugging off my frustrations and disappointments with my nation; it is on these open roads that I rediscover it as country and as land, as vista and as panorama, as earth and sky, and I fall in wild love with it again. The open road, vast, seemingly without end.

I text Simon. *I promise to drink lots of coffee and I will make sure I stop every time I yawn. I can't wait to be with you, I love you, xxC.*

I know I can wait till I am back at the house, sit out on the deck and reply to my messages and emails then. There is a knot forming; it is as though with every breath and thus with each churn of blood through my body there is an awakening within my belly. It is not a soreness exactly, and I could not call it pain; it is an aggrievement, an apprehension of something sinister that is oddly alien and yet organic. I know the nub, that locus of unease, grows from within me and belongs to me; yet I am unsettled by the unease of some exterior malign weight bearing down on me. I examine the emails again. My breath is short; there is a cold touch at the back of my neck.

A sharp blast of horn. I look up from the phone, return to the world. There has been no accident. A driver has tooted in greeting to another. A trio of schoolgirls, arms locked together, are sprinting across the road, the last in the line clutching a parcel of fish and chips under her arm. Their laughter is a peal of joy as they run to the park at the edge of the caravan park. I shield my eyes from the luminescent glare of the afternoon sun. The tide is high, and the genteel waves lap at the shore of the gardens.

I write to the editor of *The Age*: *Thank you for the offer but I am not a journalist, I am a poet; I suspect you are confusing the purposes of each of those professions. There are times to speak and there are times to be silent. I am choosing to be silent. My best wishes, Christos Tsiolkas.* I send the same reply to *The Guardian*. In this way, I answer all my emails and then I can delete them. I switch off the phone. The intrusion in my belly has gone.

I sit a moment before starting the car. The faint odour of salt water on my skin, the brine sharp in my nostrils. The strong and not distasteful reek of my sweat. For an instant, I am pulled back into the past and I see with the eyes of a little boy a tall handsome man, his black hair slicked back with Brylcreem, the white cotton of his singlet hugging his wide chest and slender torso, his arm raised, so I stare fascinated at the flutter of moist hair underneath, trace the trail it forms on the underside of his arm, which disappears under the strap of the singlet until it erupts again on the other side to meet the dense thatch of black hairs on his chest. And his pong, Stavros's scent, for a moment it floods the car and I utter a short prayer, the praise not even in the forms of words; thanking Stavros for the simplicity of ritual introduced into my life so very young, watching him wash the factory off himself and then dress and emerge a man. Why not say a prayer to Stavros? He was once a god to me.

I turn the key and start the car.

It is as if the decision made itself, and I played no part in it. Instead of making a U-turn and heading back across the bridge, I find that I am heading south. At one of the highest points in town, where a ridge forms a gradual elevation alongside the main street, there is an old church, with a humble wooden steeple. An enormous water tank sits in squat dominance next to the church, its metallic girth seemingly mocking the Protestant austerity of its neighbour. As I take the turn off the road around the ridge, I notice a For Sale sign planted into the earth before the water tower. A crudely outlined hand and extended finger at the bottom of the sign is pointing to one of the side streets that lead to the sea off the main highway. I check the rear-view mirror; there is no one behind me. I swerve left and into that side street.

The house is perched halfway up the sheer ascent, the street's extreme gradient giving it an air of precariousness, as if it might at any moment—buffeted by wind, lashed by storm—be unmoored and set adrift. It is a small, utilitarian cottage; the mustard-coloured weatherboards have been recently repainted, but the paint is already beginning to peel from the assault of the ocean air. The land is of a decent size: smaller than a quarter-acre, which is not unsurprising in a house situated so close to town. I can imagine unlatching the industrial metal gate, the rusted wire threads spooled on diagonals to form a plane of diamond outlines, and then strolling the few hundred metres up the street to town to purchase the morning papers and a coffee. And as I have that thought, my fingers are releasing the latch, swinging open the gate, and I enter the front garden.

The house looks to have lain empty for some time. However, the lawn is being maintained—the grass so short and neat it must have been mown in the last week—and there is a trio of white rosebushes in the bed along the side of the front yard. These are untended, the branches overgrown, brittle and gnarled, and there are outcrops of weeds circling the bases of the plants. The cracked wooden boards creak and groan as I climb the three short steps to the front porch. The imposing front door is painted a deep military green. There is a double-hung window on either side of the door, the grilles and sashes painted white, the heads, casings and aprons painted a similar green to the door. An old armchair, battered by the elements, sits in one corner of the porch. Bird droppings, splotches of white and grey, have soiled its headrest and arms. On the other side of the porch there is an abandoned kennel. A veil of silken cobweb shields the entrance.

I stand on the porch and look out.

Light is volleying and refracting across the surface of the inlet. Pelicans are gliding effortlessly towards the nearest shore, where two fishermen have waded into the still water. Leaning over the railing, I can see the far reach of the south head and the azure and emerald waves that crash against it. Beyond that tumult, the body of the ocean seems at rest, a straight blue mirror reflecting the sky.

The rapid incline of the slope is such that the gardens and house seem protected from the scrutiny of the near neighbours. I peep through the first window. The room is bare, the wooden floorboards scratched and unpolished, scarred and marked by fallen drops of white and yellow paint. My breath forms a cloud on the surface of the dusty window.

I am shocked at the sight that confronts me at the second window: the room in there is blackened, the wainscot boards and plaster of the walls charred by fire and smoke. A fine dust of ash and cinder still covers the floor.

Fire, lethal and terrible and ferocious, bore down on this town. Simon and I watched the footage on television: the townspeople evacuated to the shore as the fires blazed closer to the town, the sky a pulsating red fire until the debris of the exploding forest, consumed by the apocalypse of flame, cast a black shadow along the length of the coast. A reminder of the elemental gods who can make day night.

And a reminder that the elemental gods hold faith with fate. The wind changed and the fire forged another path. The town was saved.

I bring my face closer to the window, indeed so close that I feel the moist heat of my breath caper off the glass and touch my face. This fire was internal, caused by one man or one woman, and therefore not of the elements and not an indictment of a whole population or a whole civilisation. Mere accident. When we cannot abide the terror of accident in our individual lives, we respond with faith. And when we resist the idea of accident in history, we counter with politics. I am so close to the glass that in the resultant mirror formed by the blackened walls and floor I see my reflection approaching, and it is myself that kisses the image of myself: and for a moment we are one.

The seared walls and floor, the singed ceiling, all have vanished. A very old man is lying on a tartan sofa. A book, Sōseki's *Kusamakura*, lies open on the man's chest; the small mound of his belly rises and falls as he sleeps. At one end of the sofa, snuggled within the valley formed between the old man's legs, a small black-and-white terrier is also sleeping. In the middle of the deep green wall there is a painting of a long-limbed spindly pine resisting a fierce wind sluicing across a small hilltop; the artist has depicted the thin struggling branches so vividly, with a realist's verisimilitude but also an expressionist's passion, that they suggest human hands grasping for rescue. To the left of the painting is a mounted A1 poster of a book cover, the bold and stirring colours, the play of light and shadow that is Caravaggio's magnificent *Conversion on the Way to Damascus*, where Saul of Tarsus is rendered in the image of a youthful and supple late-medieval soldier, with cuirass and tunic, his long, sinewy arms outstretched in astonishment at his bizarre vision. On the other side of the painting of the straining pine is another framed print, this one Manet's sublime *The House at Rueil*. The placid watery colours, the softness of its greens and whites and blues, offer a calm that balances the passionate dramas of the painting and mounted poster.

Another man walks into the room. He too is aged, his near-white hair cropped close to his skull. He is portly and there is a suggestion of a slight shuffle as he steps softly over to the sleeping man. Under his arm there is a folded laptop computer and in the other hand there is a notebook. The terrier awakes, sniffs the air and begins to thump its tail joyfully. The man places his computer and notebook on the coffee table. Pasted across the notebook's cover is a black-and-white image—a scan or a photocopy—of a group of young men seated on benches, the martial crop of their hair and their identical black uniforms suggesting that they are sailors of some mid-twentieth-century navy. At the centre of the photograph, a boxer, young and sturdy, dressed only in his nylon wrestling shorts, a white towel across his shoulders, is showing a piece of paper to a mate, a ticket stub or some receipt. The boys' closeness, their unashamed and virile intimacy, suggests great affection. And love. As does the gentle action that the standing man now performs as, with a motion that is in part a caress and in part a shaking of the sleeping man's shoulder, he whispers softly, 'Wake up, Simon, I've got some dinner on.'

I step back from the mirror and there is the return of the scorched room. And, made more vivid, more alive and more molten by the dark shadows beneath the glass, the reflection of the inlet and the descending twilight.

The next morning, I am up before light, and it is only when I turn off the water in the shower that I hear the first trilling and call of the birds. I brew a coffee, drink it on the deck, watching the faint line of silver, the initial foaming and then seeping and then eruption of the blood reds and fire yellows of dawn. One moment the smooth inlet waters are in shadow and then, with the first glare of the sun, they are blaze. The alto timbres of the bowerbirds and honeyeaters, the soprano shrillness of the lorikeets and magpies, the bass booming of the cockatoos and the unique baritone chuckling of the kookaburras: the whole world in song. I wash my cup, the breakfast plates, leave a note to the owners to thank them for the stay, switch on my phone. The green illumination of a text from Simon: *I cannae wait for you to be home x*

It is early, not yet seven, when I set off. The sun's light is mellow grace; all is illuminated but without harshness: this is not the fire of terror and calumny but a soft and tender incandescence. As I accelerate on the open highway, the eucalypt forest thickens on both sides of the road and creates a canopy so dark and imposing that I shiver from the sudden cold. Just as I am about to turn on the car's heater, there is an approaching white light, the flare of warm sun, and the forest to the left of me drops away and an immense stretch of yellow sand and sapphire sea is visible. The chill is gone.

At one point on the drive I switch on the radio, but at the first intimations of the news from the world I turn it off and return to silence. I drink coffee at every stop and I drive carefully, slowly. I know that I am returning to the city, to clamour and fury, to passion and zeal. But for the moment I am in the splendid in-betweenness. Yet in the midst of this enjoyment, this quiet exalting, there is also impatience. For his touch, for his kiss. I remind myself that it isn't necessarily to the World I am returning. None of us can live in that capitalised world for it is an abstraction; it isn't brick or weatherboard, not steel, not cement, it is neither plaster nor stone. It cannot offer succour. One cannot shelter there.

This understanding is calming. I drive in silence. I am not returning to the world. I am simply coming home.

Acknowledgements

Thank you to Andrew Bovell, Jennifer Hewson, Spiro Economomopoulos, Angela Savage and Victoria Triantafyllou for your generous reading and criticism.

Thank you to Fiona Inglis and all the staff at Curtis Brown for your advocacy and for your trust.

Thank you to everyone at Allen & Unwin for your loyalty and for your generosity. Thank you to Aziza Kuypers for your patience and care. And I want to express my enormous gratitude to Christa Munns. Thank you for your untiring diligence, for your wisdom and support.

Thank you to Ali Lavau for being a munificent editor and for never disregarding the importance of the sceptical eye. I am so very appreciative.

None of my books would be possible without the inspiration of George and Georgina Tsiolkas, who first pointed me towards the magic mirrors of story and film. Ευχαριστώ.

I have been fortunate to have two exceptional guides in the writing of this novel. They are Jane Palfreyman and Wayne van der Stelt. Thank you for reading and rereading, for pushing and challenging. With your love and friendship and honesty, I am the most fortunate person on earth.

And Wayne, how can I thank you for guiding me to home? I love you. This book is for you, a small thanksgiving.